the
COLONY

A. J. COLUCCI

THOMAS DUNNE BOOKS
ST. MARTIN'S PRESS
NEW YORK

This is a work of fiction. All of the characters, organizations, and events portrayed in this novel
are either products of the author's imagination or are used fictitiously.

THOMAS DUNNE BOOKS.
An imprint of St. Martin's Press.

www.thomasdunnebooks.com
www.stmartins.com

ISBN 978-1-250-00129-0 (hardcover)
ISBN 978-1-250-01731-4 (e-book)

First Edition: November 2012

10 9 8 7 6 5 4 3 2 1

To Al, Rachel and Julia

Go to the ant, thou sluggard; consider her ways and be wise! Having no commander, overseer or ruler, provideth her meat in the summer and gathereth her food in the harvest.

—Proverbs 6: 6–8

the
COLONY

PROLOGUE

New York City

PIONEER GENETICIST DR. PHILLIP LAREDO leaned into an early morning breeze that skidded off the choppy whitecaps of the Hudson River. It was spring and sunny, but the biting wind cut creases around his eyes, blew long strands of his thinning gray hair and gave the doctor a chill. He was dressed only in a nightshirt. The rest of his clothes were stuffed inside a garbage can on 125th Street, along with his wallet, three gold fillings and a few other personal items.

Laredo knelt in a sandy patch of grass and looked down at the busy anthill. Specks of black scurried around, clutching tiny white crumbs sprinkled from his pocket. It was the beginning of the end. Panic caught the doctor off guard and his body went rigid. Tremendous heat flushed his face. He fought off a surge of adrenaline by breathing deep into the cold and exhaling warm vapor until his heart rate became steady.

You know what must be done, now do it.

Laredo's murky blue eyes scanned the park for spectators. The field was deserted. The only sounds came from an occasional passing car on the Henry Hudson Parkway. On hands and knees he reached into a cloth sack lying in the dirt and retrieved a brown metal canister, a revolutionary marvel of storage technology that appeared old and worn like an ancient artifact, engraved with curls of English ivy. The lid retracted with a suction of air.

Laredo dropped a single ant from the canister into the colony. Just one; but he knew it would be enough.

The enormous ant named Cleopatra was brown and slender and about the length of a mouse. She darted skillfully over the anthill, pressing abdomen to earth and depositing a heady scent in calculated patterns along the soil. She stirred up quite a commotion among the others, but as expected, they didn't attack.

The doctor observed the last ant in his possession with pride and remorse, as he rubbed the tips of his fingers together and felt the sting of having just removed his own fingerprints with Drano and an X-Acto knife. Unexpectedly, Laredo's thumb drew the sign of the cross above his brow, a gesture he had long ago renounced. There was simply no other way; of this he was certain. He considered the chain of events just released on the world by his own hands and lamented that while God might forgive him, the human race most surely would not.

When Cleopatra disappeared down the hole and the doctor was satisfied that the process had begun, he pulled a revolver from his satchel and blew his brains across the grassy lawn of Riverside Park.

Cleopatra pushed through the outer passageway, touching antennae with wary workers. Instinctually she knew from the heavily marked path that she was headed for a nesting site. The others knew from her scent that she was prepared to give birth. On a steady spiral downward, through tunnels that barely fit her body mass, she marked her trail with a sense of urgency.

She reached the pupae nursery, where thousands of translucent yellow eggs had been carried that morning to higher, warmer ground.

Cleopatra knew her first task. Her huge jaws opened sideways, digging into the membrane of the egg and pinching closed with stalwart force. Behind the outer jaws, a second mouth chewed apart the soft innards of the egg.

The clarity and intensity of her pheromones were unlike any the colony had ever detected, and their response was swift and unconditional. Conforming to the signals of the strongest chemical secretions was their most fundamental tenet to one hundred million years of evolutionary survival. Immediately the ants began to eat their young. As directives spread from tunnels to chambers to adjoining colonies, the last of the common black field ants fed on their final generation.

It was now time for Cleopatra to take her place. She moved quickly to the site.

The queen's chamber was bustling with nurser ants, small young workers tending to the field ant queen. They scattered as Cleopatra entered. In the center, the swollen monarch lay in a soft bed of silt continuously pumping out eggs in a rhythmic motion. Dim-witted and feeble, she turned her obtuse head slightly towards Cleopatra, barely regarding her more potent, intelligent cousin.

With thick pincers, Cleopatra decapitated the queen.

TWO YEARS LATER . . .

CHAPTER I

New York City

WINTER, KISS MY ASS, Jerrol Thomas cheerfully mused as he strolled out of the Harlem bodega and the late afternoon sun hit his face. It had been a frigid March and now the air was balmy and sweet. He smiled and counted his lottery tickets. April was his lucky month, so he was surprised to find a boy banging a rock against the lock of his new racing bike, denting the derailleur and chipping the paint.

"Shiiee, Malcolm! Who taught you how to gank a bike?" Jerrol was tall and broad-shouldered with a goatee and striking black eyes, and he towered over the twelve-year-old. "Ever hear of a hacksaw, you stupid ass? Get the hell away from my wheels!"

"I didn't know it was yours, sir," Malcolm said, and quickly sprinted down the sidewalk.

"It's no wonder you're failing my math class," Jerrol yelled after him, but then walked away smiling. He crossed Amsterdam Avenue and opened the garden gate to the back of his building. His apartment was small but surrounded by the community garden. No one messed with the garden. The white picket fence was like a fortress in the neighborhood, which had its share of gangsters and social misfits who went around shoplifting, mugging and shooting each other, but no one would even think about picking a tomato. Jerrol liked that his front door faced the hydrangea, which were still standing brown and dry since the fall.

He strolled over to the patio and fiddled with his keys. There was a noise behind him and, without turning around, Jerrol knew it was a rat. Lately there had been a lot of rats, and they seemed to be acting strangely. Not lazily eating the foliage as they normally did, but zipping in frantic circles and rolling in the weeds. This rat seemed to be dancing on its hind legs. Its tiny arms waved as it swayed from side to side. Then it fell to the ground beneath the fence. Jerrol strained his neck to see that part of the animal's back was gone. In place of fur were patches of bloody flesh, as if it had been skinned.

"Coming in?" a voice said from inside.

Jerrol looked at his wife standing in the doorway.

"Postpartum checkup, remember?"

Jerrol didn't want her to see the bloody creature so he kissed her hard on the lips and pushed his way inside. "You be sure to ask the doctor when we can get back to business."

"Now you're talking." She grabbed her purse and headed out. "I'll be home late. Check on the baby. It's almost suppertime." As soon as the door shut, there was a shrill cry from the nursery. Jerrol went to the kitchenette, heated up a bottle in the microwave and headed down the hallway.

A few hours later, Jerrol was reading a book on the sofa in cut-off shorts and a Lakers T-shirt when he remembered the rat. He laid the book on the coffee table and went to the front door, flicked on the outside light and stepped into the chilly night air.

The patio light cast a shimmer on the concrete terrace and metal chairs. A few yards away, the garden was still visible under a three-quarter moon that shone down on rows of freshly tilled soil. Poppy plants swayed in a gentle breeze. There was nothing between the stakes of dried tomato vines, where the rat had expired. It was gone.

An orange-striped cat sprang to the top of the fence and Jerrol flinched, but then he smiled as the feral beast dropped to the other side with a dead thing in its mouth.

"Good going, Garfield," he said.

Hanging from a leafless elm tree was a string of bamboo chimes that made a clattering sound. They fell silent as the wind died down. Jerrol noticed that the poppy plants continued to move. Dried stalks rustled and quivered in a peculiar way. Then, out of their shadows, a wide puddle emerged. It seeped across the ground like an oil leak, into the whiteness of moonlight. Immediately it was clear that this was not one entity but countless tiny forms.

Ants.

Jerrol had seen a cluster of them scurrying through the garden last spring, moving as a unit just like these but in a much smaller group. The dense pool spread out and broke off into ravines, forming perfect rows twelve inches across. These ants were the biggest he'd ever seen, nearly an inch long. Jerrol observed their pageantry, curiously amused, but at the same time his nerve wrenched at the way they marched in formation like platoons of soldiers. It was a hauntingly familiar image.

Driver ants.

They had been featured on a Discovery Channel special in one of the school classrooms—*Killer Ants of the Congo*, it was called. They were known to hunt in groups, attacking anything that breathed. But this was Harlem; you had to keep out the drugs, not the bugs.

The yard suddenly grew darker and Jerrol turned around,

squinting at the patio fixture. Black splotches encased the glass ball, moving and blending together until the lamp disappeared and only the moon was left shining. In the shadows, millions of tiny agile bodies were forming bridges and ropes ten feet long, connecting bushes, flowerpots and lawn chairs.

Ants don't do this, he thought and a shiver of impending doom ran up his spine. He blinked hard and refocused on the garden. Threads of black were linked like chains between gutters and trellises. They blanketed the ground and spilled over rocks and brush and newly sprouted greenery. They covered the barbecue grill, the lawnmower, a soccer ball, a wooden bench, the toolshed and every other surface on the property.

One exceedingly large ant lay motionless on a tree limb, watching Jerrol from the back of the yard. Her compound eyes lacked the sharp focus of human vision, but with thousands of tiny lenses she perceived movement and the slightest change in light more acutely, which allowed her to observe the man below whose form, shape and erratic movements all signaled prey. His scent, drifting in the wind, was detected between her antennae and made a clear confirmation.

Like cutting sheers, the sharp mandibles of the queen opened and closed with anxious clicks. Her brain was not capable of understanding the concept of time, but she had a keen sense of duty and purpose. As she watched the other ants move toward the target, her snaps became hurried like the fighting claws of a crab. On long, wiry legs she rose and the ants around her began to react with extreme agitation. The queen opened her large mandibles in a roar, but what she emitted from her mouth was far more powerful than any sound of alarm.

The ants rushed toward Jerrol from every direction.

"Sh-shit!" he cried out in panic, and braced for the on-slaught, crouching with arms to his face in defense.

But the ants didn't attack. The front lines reached a few inches from his sneakers and turned at a forty-five-degree angle in unison, circling him in a ring that was nearly the size of the yard itself. Alone in a four-foot patch of grass, the terrified man was completely surrounded by a colony of 22 million insects.

Jerrol began trembling feverishly. Cold sweat ran down his back and his shirt clung to his skin. He spun quickly in circles. There was no way out of the yard and no path back to the house. A sudden, unearthly sound resonated like waves of radio static, growing louder across the yard. With a whimper, he danced on his feet and stared eagerly at the door, where he could see the comforting blue pile carpet and the open book on the coffee table. More than anything, he wanted to be back in his living room.

Instinctively, he pulled a stake from the ground and swept it like a sword across the sea of insects, hoping to create a clear path to his door. Instead, fervor broke out among the ranks. The largest soldier ants surged toward him, flanking the lines with the speed of a creature ten thousand times their size, while the smaller ones ran center like chemically guided missiles.

As the swarm reached his sneakers he stomped down hard. The insects sprang upon his legs like splatters from a mud puddle, piercing skin and clamping tight. The pain of their stingers was fierce. Jerrol's knees buckled and he collapsed to the ground as the army attacked full force.

A hundred collective stings sent him diving headfirst into

the house, where he skidded across the rug and rolled on the carpet as if on fire. He slammed the door, shrieking and hugging his ragged shins that were covered in ant bites and erupting white pustules. He bit through his lip and crawled to the bathroom, leaving a thin red trail along the blue rug.

Cries of agony were muted behind the clear plastic shower curtain as Jerrol sat slumped at the bottom of the tub, groaning, in wet clothes and sneakers, as heavy steam engulfed the room. The insects held tight to his legs from toe to knee. Their three-hook claws pierced his shins, stinging again and again. The venom felt like razors through his veins and carried the toxin from limbs to torso, to every muscle and organ.

The pain of mandibles biting and filling their jaws with meat was excruciating. Jerrol hunched over his knees, digging fingernails deep and scratching away layers of flesh. A few ants spun down the drain in a river of bloody water, but most were burrowing farther into the wounds. Small knobby bumps moved under the skin of his kneecap where black tunnels of ants were visible as they fed and crawled freely about.

A searing heat pulsed from the side of his left foot where a tremendous amount of blood poured into the tub. He peeled back the top flap of his sock with frantic, shaking fingers. Underneath were the tattered remains of flesh and sinew, and a hole the size of a quarter where white ankle bone protruded from the center.

He was overcome with dizziness and nausea, his face sickly and swollen like a rubber Halloween mask. Jerrol fell back into an inch of vivid red water. Shock took over, the pain began to subside and a soothing numbness came to his body.

Jerrol curled up on his side and let the hot spray rain down on him. He thought he would pass out, *wanted* to pass out—when the cry of a baby cut through the steam.

Panic roused him with a burst of energy as he imagined ants crawling over his child. He clumsily flung himself out of the tub and stumbled like a rag doll down the hallway, bouncing off walls in a crooked path to the dark nursery.

He slapped on the light switch. The baby was alone. Not even a moth. She lay screaming on a Winnie the Pooh crib sheet. Her tiny body snuggled warmly in a green blanket surrounded by two blue bunnies, an orange whale, and spit-up from breakfast.

Jerrol was relieved but his heart was failing. He could barely suck in a breath. Dark footprints followed his path from the doorway to the crib, where he stood over the child, looking like a monster splattered with blood from head to foot. He turned to the window and parted the lacy curtains with trembling fingers that left streaks of red.

Below, the entire floor of the garden moved like a graceful undulating sea. Black armor gleamed in the moonlight. Then all at once, the armies began breaking up into geometric shapes that seemed to shrivel in size. Jerrol held his breath with a last bit of emotion as the puddles seeped into the ground. Then the remaining invaders crawled off his own body and fled toward the door. The ants were leaving.

The baby wailed as her father slowly twisted to face the door. He took two wobbly steps, sweating profusely from a 110 degree temperature. Then his eyes swelled shut, his head snapped back and he coughed up a spray of blood.

Jerrol fell to his knees, and then to the floor.

CHAPTER 2

THE LAW OFFICES OF Dugan, Weiss and Kellogg were in an old Gothic-style building a block from Wall and Broadway, right behind Trinity Church, where Alexander Hamilton is buried. The whole area smelled of money. At four o'clock in the morning the head paralegal was still poring over black folders marked *Confidential*.

The firm was preparing for a big case. A drug company had recently disclosed that its fat-eating pill was also a pancreas-eating pill. She pressed her palms to her eyes in quiet meditation, when a low wolf whistle startled her nerves. In the doorway stood the most attractive and most despised lawyer in the firm.

"Still here? Lucille, you're a goddamned paralegal," he quipped.

"With any luck, I'll be your boss in three years."

"I could get you there sooner, sweetheart."

"Don't make me sue your ass."

"You'd lose."

Lucille leaned back as the lawyer sat down on the desk, trying to catch a better view down her blouse. It made her skin crawl, the way his lips pursed, a gesture he obviously thought sexy but she found effeminate.

"I heard the Central Park couple died last night."

"The ant people?" she scoffed. "Next time don't get naked in the middle of Sheep Meadow."

"You know a better place?" His hands pressed against the sturdy Formica. "I'm a desk man myself."

"Is that why they call you pencil prick?"

"First the couple in Soho, and now these two in the park. That makes four dead bodies." He leaned in close, smelling like green Tic Tacs. "Lonely walk to the bus, babe. Bet you could use a ride home."

"I'll take my chances with the bugs."

He shrugged and straightened his tie. Then he left her office with a childish grin, humming "The Ants Go Marching."

Lucille closed the last folder and reworked her hands across her heavy lids.

Four dead bodies . . . Four dead bodies . . . Four dead—

If she hurried, she could still catch the 4:15 A.M. bus to Brooklyn. She grabbed her vinyl briefcase and walked down the hall to the elevator, rode it twenty flights to the lobby, where the security guard was immersed in a crossword puzzle. She took the usual exit, through a side door into an alleyway, an eerie precolonial road paved in original cobblestone that narrowed under the shadows of looming black buildings.

The predawn cool air revived her senses but not her nerve; the alley was silent except for her spiky heels, which struck against the glistening black pavers.

Click, click, click.

Lucille began walking faster and a damp chill spread across her skin. The sound of her own panting quickened her pace, and she clutched the briefcase like a shield.

Four dead bodies . . . Four dead bodies . . . Four dead—

Her heel caught the edge of a stone and she stumbled onto her hands and knees. That's when her thumb touched something wet and furry. A rat. It was nearly devoid of flesh but its round eyes glowed pink and its tiny paw twitched. Lucille stared in terror at the carcass on the shiny black pavers that seemed to come alive with fluttery movements.

She sprang to her feet, grabbing her briefcase and flailing her arms with a guttural cry. Halfway down the alley, she broke into a frantic run, heading toward the hazy light at the end of the lane.

Broadway opened up wide and bright and Lucille stopped, spilling over herself. A few early commuters emerged from the subway, men and women in dark suits toting briefcases. The lights flickered on in the Starbucks across the street and the illuminated banks on Wall Street loomed with noble grace.

Lucille dropped her shoulders with relief and continued down Broadway. The glass shelter at the bus stop was empty and her watch read 4:17, but she stood beside the bench and waited, hoping the bus was running late.

A sanitation truck was parked with its engines still running, the front doors open wide. The dome light revealed an empty cabin. Lucille stepped along the curb and gave the truck a sideways glance. A sound made her turn around, where trash was piled high against a building. Slabs of drywall leaned against the brick and garbage was scattered oddly across the sidewalk.

A faint and unfamiliar noise emanated from the heap, like the crackling of a wood fire. Lucille pulled out a canister of Mace from her briefcase, rolling it nervously in her palm. She moved under the soft yellow glow of a streetlight and in her peripheral vision, something moved.

It was a hand; large and pallid and sticking out behind a board of drywall. The hand twitched. Lucille's heart caught in her throat.

"Hello? Are you all right?" she asked in a meek voice, and

continued in measured steps until the hand was close enough to grab her ankle. There was a slight tremble to her fingers as they extended toward the drywall and gingerly touched the jagged edge.

Whooosh. The drywell fell solidly to the ground and the woman sprang from its reach as shards of ice ripped through her veins. She muffled a cry with her fist.

Two sanitation men lay at her feet, covered head to waist with crawling ants. As light swept their bodies, the insects scurried into the collars and sleeves of their uniforms and vanished under debris. Parts of the men were eaten away, their faces swollen and pale like rising dough. Globs of co-agulated blood protruded from their eyes, ears, mouths, nostrils and long jagged cracks in their skin, as if something inside their head had burst into pieces.

Lucille screamed as the number 12 bus pulled to the curb.

CHAPTER 3

IN THE BASEMENT LEVEL of the American Museum of Natural History, a couple hundred of the world's most brilliant minds studied biology, geology, anthropology, paleontology and every other "ology" in natural science. Along with cutting-edge equipment were mummified bodies, primitive tools, Jurassic-age insects trapped in amber, fossilized bacteria and six-ton pallets stacked to the ceiling with the oldest artifacts known to mankind.

The largest corner office was a relic itself. Under murky light, strained wooden bookshelves were packed with dusty back issues of *Entomology Today* and *Naturalist* magazines, faded reference books and journals. A mammoth desk against the back wall was littered with travel brochures of South America, old anatomy reports, draft copies of speeches and uncashed checks totaling ninety thousand dollars in speaking fees.

The office belonged to Dr. Paul O'Keefe, a tall and elegantly handsome scientist in an Armani suit, who had spent the last thirty-six hours tirelessly peering into a microscope. He had a bookish quality, thoughtful and serious, with quick brown eyes that brightened whenever they hit upon something he'd never seen before, which lately seemed to be every few minutes. Paul wiped the back of his wrist over his damp brow and peered through the lens at the absurdly oversized ant with a degree of respect that was turning into something more like terror each day. He adjusted the steel knob and his fingers shook the image.

The ant appeared to be a precise replica of the others. The head was unusually skull-shaped and twice as large as that of any other ant species, its copper face tilted up in a roar. The claws were enormous, and what the hell was this—a thumb? Paul used a dropper from a vial to dab the ant with nitric acid. Normally the body would dissolve; this insect showed zero reaction. He slid the ant around in the liquid with the tip of the scalpel. Not even the joints broke apart.

Impossible.

No matter how many times he examined them, dissected them and tested them, the impossible factor wasn't going away. He rubbed his closely trimmed beard and wondered how the greatest moment of his career had so rapidly dissolved into the bleakest.

Two weeks ago, Mayor John Russo had come to the museum claiming ants had eaten a couple of New Yorkers. The insects delivered to Paul's office resembled no ant species ever discovered. They were enormous and had no recognizable DNA. Their morphology wasn't linked to any genus of Hymenoptera. The ants acted viciously in the field, yet were docile in the hand. They displayed abnormal behavior and died within hours.

Then colonies of ants started popping up all over the city, seemingly overnight.

For any entomologist, it was a dream come true.

Paul believed he was the perfect scientist for the job. Known throughout the bug world as Professor Ant, he had just come off a lecture series for his controversial book, *Insect Altruism: How an Ant Colony Can Save the Human Race.* For that he'd been awarded a Pulitzer Prize and the National Medal of Science, and there was talk of a Nobel. He'd hosted multiple nature specials on PBS, BBC and Discovery and been quoted in *National Geographic* no fewer than twenty times.

Paul's studies were based on the social aspect of ants. Their ability to survive since 50 million years before the dinosaurs was due to congenital cooperation, not the pursuit of individual needs. Ants performed tasks solely for the benefit of the colony, never for themselves. They possessed an incredible sense of duty; all worker ants had two stomachs, one for themselves and one to feed the rest of the colony. Certain worker ants might be in charge of cleaning out the tunnels, but if they noticed food stacking up at the entrance of an anthill, they would switch tasks and begin food storage. It was called collective decision making.

Paul compared the sociology of ants to certain altruistic human societies, like the Aborigines in Australia, the Siberian Inuit, the bushmen of Africa, monks of Tibet and Buddhists in Malaysia. Based on his study of Hymenoptera, Paul had developed a theory: societies that act in cooperation survive, whereas those motivated by personal gain will eventually become extinct.

There wasn't a scientist on earth who possessed his knowledge or experience in the taxonomy of ants. But Paul had to admit, for the first time in his life, he was stumped. He flung the contaminated specimen and dissecting tools into a utility sink, went back to his desk and collapsed in the leather chair. He leaned forward and rubbed his bloodshot eyes, then gazed around the room. On the walls were photos of Paul with Jane Goodall in Africa, David Attenborough in Madagascar and Edward O. Wilson back at Harvard. Without a doubt, Paul had reached the pinnacle of his career.

That was before the mutant ants.

Paul cringed at his arrogance. Hadn't he promised the mayor he could single-handedly contain the colony? Hadn't he done everything possible to keep out his rivals? Now he was locked in a deadly race against time, anxiously awaiting DNA reports from universities like Cornell, Texas A&M, North Carolina State and Purdue as well as entomology institutes in England, Kenya, Japan, Germany, Australia and every other ant shop he knew. He walked back to the lab, heavy in thought.

Jason, a spirited young assistant, entered the office. He was tall, boyishly handsome, with intelligent eyes and a biting smirk on his face; a younger version of Paul. He carried a thick stack of folders in one hand and held out a cell phone with the other.

"Mayor's office is calling *me* now." He raised an accusing brow at Paul. "Turned yours off, didn't you?"

Paul didn't answer, but grabbed the stack from his assistant.

"Latest batch," Jason said. "They all say the same thing."

Paul slammed the reports on the counter.

Enough paperwork. Falling back on his early training, when all the answers could be found in the physical world, he plucked up a fresh ant specimen from a slide, held it between his fingers and sliced the thorax down the middle with a diamond-blade scalpel.

A clear bubble of liquid oozed from the exoskeleton and leaked onto Paul's thumb. The venom set off a fierce sting and Paul reflexively dropped the ant, snapping his wrist back with a gasp of pain. He shook his hand and frantically scanned the room.

"Looking for this?" Jason nonchalantly picked up a coffee can of sodium bicarbonate.

Paul plunged his fingers into the can.

Jason laughed.

"Thanks a lot." Paul rolled out a length of paper towel, tearing off a piece to wrap around his thumb.

"Geez, you're bleeding." Jason clicked his tongue several times with mock empathy. "That was truly the act of a desperate man. This won't go over well with the Nobel folks, no sireee."

"Perhaps you'd like to go back to assembling Eskimo dioramas."

"I'm just saying . . ." The sarcasm in the room evaporated. "So what the hell are you waiting for? Go to the press."

Paul shook his head. "Not until we figure the damn things out."

"Is that you talking, or city hall?"

Paul felt flushed. He wasn't sure if it was from the toxic hit he'd taken from the ant or from his assistant. A Blackberry lying on the counter rang out Beethoven's Fifth and Paul stiffened. His thumb was still bleeding through the paper towel. He added another layer and answered the phone.

"O'Keefe." A wave of nausea swept over Paul as he listened to the mayor's voice on the other end. It was worse than he expected.

Jason handed him a medical bag as Paul headed out. "Another body?"

Paul shook his head. "Two."

CHAPTER 4

NEON LIGHTS SWIRLED FROM the tops of a dozen police cars, blocking off a chunk of Broadway, where the bodies of the sanitation workers lay under white sheets in the same position they were found. NYPD officers stood stoically over the crime scene while commuters pressed against the yellow tape, straining their necks to get a look.

Police Chief Scotty Harris walked away from the bodies in disgust. The medical examiner, handpicked by the mayor himself, still hadn't arrived and Harris cursed him through gritted teeth. He yelled out to one of his men, "Sergeant! Where the hell is Wang? I got two dozen detectives, FBI, CIA and no fucking medical examiner. I want these bodies gone."

"He's up in Harlem," the sergeant scowled. "Got another one. That makes what—seven?"

"Who's counting?"

A white van topped with a satellite dish screeched up to the scene, FOX FIVE NEWS emblazoned on the side in red, white and blue. The door blew open and a willowy blonde sprang out with a cameraman in tow, ready to roll. She elbowed through the crowd to the first cop that didn't flee from her like the plague, thrust a microphone in his face and fired off questions just as *NBC News* pulled up to the scene.

The rookie cop, caught in the spotlight, raised a helpless brow to the chief.

"Go tell Debrowski to keep his mouth shut," Harris told the sergeant. "Anyone asks, it's a regular, run-of-the-mill New York City double homicide."

"Right."

The chief backhanded the sergeant's shoulder. "Who's that?"

Poking around the bodies was a man in a lab coat and latex gloves. The sergeant shrugged. "Some ant guy the mayor sent over. Probably another one of his cronies who won't give us a goddamn thing."

The chief sighed and stepped off the curb. The stranger squatted over the bodies with a pair of tweezers. He raised a dead ant to the sun and dropped it into a bag, just as the cop reached the corpses' shoes.

"Chief Scotty Harris. Can I help you?"

Paul peered up with affable brown eyes and offered a business card. "Paul O'Keefe."

"Mayor sent you?"

"Just getting some samples."

The chief glanced at the card and read, *American Museum of Natural History*. "You gonna put these things in a display case?"

"I'm purely research."

He stooped down next to Paul. "So what, are these some kind of fire ant? That's what the last guy told us, when they killed that couple in the park."

Paul didn't answer. "Mind if I open the guy's mouth?"

"Forensics hasn't arrived." Harris motioned to a cop standing guard over the bodies and asked, "They take photos yet?"

"Half hour ago," the cop replied.

"What the hell," Harris said, disgusted. "Mayor's running this show."

He pulled the sheet back slightly from the victim's head and Paul winced. The skin of the dead man was shiny white and swollen to the point of resembling whale blubber, the features hardly discernible as human. Thickened blood protruded from orifices and deep cracks in his flesh. The eye sockets were empty and the one remaining eyeball hung like a wet strawberry from fibrous membranes.

Paul opened the mouth with a tongue depressor. The cavity was crammed with ants, mostly dead, but three crawled across the lips.

Harris stumbled back, nearly losing his balance. "Damn. They're alive."

Paul ripped off a glove with a snapping sound and scooped the ants with the tongue depressor, then sprinkled them onto his naked palm.

Harris was startled by the risky move but had a feeling this had become routine for Paul. The ants were unperturbed and seemed to be cleaning their antennas with nimble legs. The cop strained to get a look. "Huh. Not a bite. Guess they must be stuffed from eating this guy."

"Maybe."

From his breast pocket, Paul retrieved a Genetic Barcode Reader; a shiny silver device with a touch screen and small square hole at the base. It worked on the same principal as a barcode scanner at the supermarket but instead of recognizing line patterns on vegetable cans and packs of poultry, the scanner sequenced strands of DNA and could identify any plant or animal on earth from a database of 10 million species.

Paul retracted a stylus from the side and used it to crush one of the ants into the hole. The screen lit up and numbers and letters streamed by like ticker tape. When it stopped, he peered down at the screen and frowned. *SPECIES: NEGATIVE.*

"Thank you." He stood up, a head taller than the chief, and extended his hand.

Harris shook it, but then held on firmly, his expression pleading for mercy. "C'mon, guy. You gotta give me something."

Paul could hear the heavy weight of desperation in the cop's voice. His ruddy face was pinched with lines of worry that stretched from his receding hairline to the bridge of his bulbous nose. Paul looked past the police badge to the early dawn creeping over the skyscrapers and wondered what new horror the day would bring.

"I'm sorry." His eyes showed he truly was. Paul headed toward the uptown subway.

The chief eyed the cadaverous mass on the sidewalk and watched a few ants crawl out from beneath the sheet. A couple stragglers drifted toward his shoe and he backed off, kicking up gravel.

"Hey!" he called out. "Just tell me one thing. Is there anyone out there who can kill these sons of bitches?"

Paul was already gone.

CHAPTER 5

Las Cruces, New Mexico

THE CHIHUAHUAN DESERT WAS alive with early morning sounds of coyotes, ravens and warblers. It was already hot—maybe 82 degrees—but a slight wind blew west off the Rio Grande.

A Quonset hut stood in the sand, lonesome in the middle of nowhere, its oblong solar panels reaching up to the sky. Inside it was still quiet and dark, but a sleek gecko, camouflaged with brown and yellow blotches, scampered lightning quick across the gray cement floor like a paratrooper in fatigues. It raced up the side of a bed to a pillow, across a sweaty cheek, and came to rest on a full, sensual pair of lips.

"Feh! Feh! Oh, guck!" Professor Kendra Hart sat up spitting, with sharp blue eyes focused and alert. She wiped the feeling of slime from her mouth and lifted the lizard to eye level. "That was a dirty trick, Darwin."

Kendra glanced at a retro Atom Ant alarm clock on a side table.

It was five-fifteen. Late again.

"Okay, pal, you're off the hook this time. But if that's your way of coming on to me, I've got to tell you, I'm partial to the warm-blooded type."

She threw off the linen sheet and froze. Slithering across the floor was a six-foot king snake; a sleek pattern of gold diamonds glowed as bright as its milk-white eyes. Kendra kept utterly still as the serpent side-winded out of the shadows toward the bed.

She narrowed her eyes. There was something odd about this snake. A lump the size of a baseball swelled above its midsection. Kendra whipped around to a stack of metal cages. Through the bars she could see the plodding movements of a fat Sonoran toad, the silhouettes of a screech owl, iguana and chuckwalla. The smallest cage—home to a desert rat—was upside down on the floor, open and empty.

"Chomps!" she yelled, flashing back to the snake. "You ate Socrates!"

The unperturbed reptile slithered past her, as the suspicious lump moved farther down its gut.

Kendra sighed, letting her bare feet touch the cool floor. She would have to consider finding a better circle of friends. And it wasn't just the eating-each-other thing. Lately, she'd been talking to herself, having casual conversations and even arguments. Perhaps the solitary life of the desert was becoming a little *too* solitary.

"That's insane," she said aloud. "You've never been happier."

Kendra lifted her body with a yoga stretch, expecting long cascades of hair to fall down her back as they did each morning, but her head felt light and bare. The night before, she'd chopped off her blond locks in a declaration of independence or, more accurately, liberation from her past. She picked up a mirror on her nightstand and stared at her short mop of hair, which was wispy and uneven.

Punky, she thought, pleased with her new look. Although there was nothing punk about her. The plaid nightgown she wore could easily be categorized as granny-style and it was a perfect match for her round metal glasses. She slid them onto the bridge of her nose, which was always slightly runny in the morning, and took a double hit of nasal spray, as she was allergic to dust, pollen, mold, peanuts and a variety of other allergens.

Still, no amount of frumpiness or sniffles could hide her natural beauty. Kendra had been an exceedingly pretty child who grew into a striking young woman, but she cringed when anyone commented on her looks. She attributed one's appearance to simple genetics. Her perfectly shaped face, creamy complexion and sapphire eyes were merely genes passed down from her mother. Her toned, athletic body was the result of having a physically strenuous job.

Slipping into a pair of fuzzy slippers, Kendra stepped across the Quonset hut. Like a faithful dog, Darwin followed her to the lab, flicking his tongue to catch the crickets she tossed from a box before they could hop under the computer equipment resting on the floor. Kendra sprinkled flakes into a small tank that held a dozen crawling insects.

Queen fire ants.

"Hey there, girlfriends," she said, tapping on the glass. Startled, the large red ants paused for a moment and then darted side to side with frantic feelers, tracking each morsel.

"Ready for your morning workout?" she asked. The tank was resting on a metal plate and when Kendra flipped a switch, the plate began to vibrate. The ants, sensing a sudden earthquake, reacted with extreme agitation. The first queen rose on her hind legs, mandibles wide open and antennae working like a couple of whips. Kendra placed a thin syringe into the tank, which contained an absorbent fiber inside the barrel. She aligned the tip of the needle just below the queen's head, catching precious airborne chemicals known as pheromones, secreted by the queen. She did the same with eleven other queens.

Kendra flipped off the gyrator and the rumbling tank fell silent. It would take at least fifteen minutes for the insects to calm down. Kendra switched on a computer and prepared the collected secretions for analysis by a gas chromatograph–mass spectrometer, a device used to identify unknown compounds by separating and breaking them down into characteristic fragment ion patterns, just like fingerprints.

This particular unit was fitted with an extension designed by the university's engineering department specifically for Kendra's unique method of ant study. The structure, made of metal castings and plastic tubes, looked like a homemade distillery. Kendra checked the slow drip from the day before. In the collection flask was about four ounces of yellow liquid, a synthesized version of the queens' pheromones, and she poured the liquid into a brown glass vial that was nearly filled to the top. She was pleased to discover that there was enough chemical to finish off the bottle, so she capped it and placed it in her backpack.

Kendra hit the stereo and Bob Marley blasted through the steel hut louder than most morning ears could tolerate, but Kendra liked her reggae loud. She found the soothing vocals and steady rhythm of the snare drum hypnotic. She stripped off her nightgown, grabbed a towel and kicked open the battered aluminum door.

Music poured like liquid across the silent desert plains and dissolved into the vastness. The sun was a fiery dome of orange just above the horizon and it bathed the sand in the same brilliant hues. In the outdoor shower, Kendra tugged a metal chain and cold water washed the dust and sweat from her skin, revealing a bronze tone across her face and graceful neck, her lithe arms and legs, while the rest of her body was ice cream white. Under the loud spray of water, Kendra was completely unaware of the young college student driving up to the shower stall.

Marshall swiveled his motorcycle up to the hut, never taking his eyes off the shapely calves below the shower door. He slowly dismounted, nervously biting the corner of his student union card.

With a last tug and rinse, Kendra draped herself in a loose towel, tiptoed hastily across the scorched sand and found the boy standing gape-jawed by her door, his hair sticking up flat on one side and T-shirt half untucked.

"Marshall."

"Professor H-Hart."

"What are you doing here?"

"The d-d-dean sent me. He wants to t-t-talk to you right away."

Kendra breezed by the stuttering boy with a flick of her hand and opened the door. "Tell him the check's in the mail."

The music was deafening. Marshall pressed his fingers to his ears and followed her inside, leaping to avoid the swinging door. "He said you haven't answered your phone in weeks." He squinted, trying to adjust to the darkness of the room. "Do you want a ride to campus?" he shouted over a bass guitar.

"No. I don't have time for his whine festival. I have field work to do." Behind a thin screen, Kendra dropped her towel and put on a robe.

Marshall spun around, cheeks flushed, eyes shut and shouted, "What should I tell the dean?"

Kendra snapped off Bob Marley and the room fell silent. "I'll call the university tomorrow."

"I don't think he'll be happy about that!" The young man's eyes were still pinched tight.

"Marshall?"

He looked at her.

"Don't you have a class or something?"

Marshall walked out the door, dazed. His ears were still ringing from the music and he was worried about the dean, but he had to smile at the blissful image of his teacher's lovely silhouette forever embedded in his brain.

Kendra poured breakfast into a bowl, a handful of M&Ms mixed with Cocoa Puffs and granola. Chocolate was the only weakness she indulged and her eyes half closed as she munched the concoction down with warm bottled water.

She rolled up the sleeve of her robe and gave herself an injection of antivenom. It was common for entomologists in the field to treat themselves with venom immunotherapy, especially if they had insect allergies, and Kendra was allergic to fire ants. It stung for just a moment, and she quickly dressed for the worksite.

She couldn't wait to get started. There was a time she remembered all the complexities of a past life, a mosaic of people and places and belongings. A frustrating marriage to an arrogant scientist. A stifling career in the corporate world. The hectic lifestyle in a bustling metropolis. That was years ago and now all the faces, connections and minutiae had begun to fade into the sand.

There was only her research, the desert and the ants.

CHAPTER 6

KENDRA'S OLD YELLOW JEEP Wrangler blasted down the dusty road to the pulsating rhythms of Bunny Wailer. On the back of the vehicle, two bright red bumper stickers proclaimed to the world, WOMEN WHO SEEK EQUALITY TO MEN LACK AMBITION, and, I GOT THIS CAR FOR MY HUSBAND—IT WAS A GOOD TRADE.

The morning drive was Kendra's favorite time of the day. Hot wind licked her face and blew her untamed hair. Tall mountains rose off the horizon, purple and majestic, and the white sand seemed as vast and uninhabitable as the surface of Mars, billions of life-forms silently camouflaged. It took less than a half hour to reach the university's student housing complex, a cluster of shabby trailers roasting in the desert heat and jokingly referred to by its young residents as Death Valley.

Kendra beeped her horn and a student emerged from a boxy building. Kate, a perky redhead with too many freckles, sprinted to the Jeep under a cloudless blue sky.

"Hurry up, we're late," Kendra said.

"Sorry. I was trying to get through to civilization," she said, vaulting into the seat.

"Civilization?" Kendra smirked and threw the Jeep into gear. "Who needs civilization?" She took off down the road, turned a sharp left and headed straight up a sand dune, blasting the music and belting out the tune in the wind. The women laughed and sang and headed straight into nowhere, leaving a contrail of dust in their wake.

The study site was nine hundred acres of parkland; endless flat terrain dotted with yuccas and lilac and flaming red blooms of ocotillo. Kendra drove up to a small metal trunk baking in the sun and took a rough count of the white flags scattered like those of a miniature golf course, marking each anthill.

She spied two other students, Jane and Derek, under the shade of a Joshua tree playing hacky sack with the meticulously rolled excrement of a dung beetle.

"Was I right?" Kendra quipped. "Fooling around like usual."

"Well, this *is* their spring break."

"Uh-huh." Kendra was all too familiar with goofball interns. Most students willing to spend their last big vacation counting ants in the desert were stoners and partyers, desperate for extra credit by the end of the school term.

Kendra leaped out of the Jeep and geared up. She wiped globs of sunscreen on her face and arms. Fire ants had a fierce sting so she wore billowy coveralls with a high collar and stuffed her pant legs into thick socks. To complete the look, she slipped on a black Oilers baseball cap and dark shades that were large enough to fit over her prescription glasses.

Jane and Derek ambled over to the worksite.

Derek stood six feet tall with a long blond ponytail, scuba pants, no shirt and a flawless tan that smelled of coconut; a surfer dude even in the desert. "Hey, Professor Hart," he said with a sleepy drawl, squinting at her enlarged sunglasses. "You're starting to look like a bug."

"Ha-ha," replied Kendra. "Did you get a corpse count?"

"Bloody well did," quipped Jane, an exchange student from England. "Fifty-seven queens." She held out a Styrofoam cup full of ants.

For Kendra, the exhilaration of finding so many dead queens was overshadowed by the insects piled inside a cheap coffin that appeared to have orange juice stains.

"You dumped them in a cup?" Kendra asked.

Jane shrugged. "Sorry. Should we say a few words then?"

"Back to business," Kendra said brusquely.

Ants were already busy at work. It was well past five-thirty reveille when the first workers emerged from holes like children at recess. They were called foragers, small reddish ants that were marking trails and heading back to the nest with news of crackers that Derek had sprinkled before sunrise.

"Man, I don't get it." Derek scratched his head. "Why are they so hard to kill?"

"Ants have been around for a hundred million years," replied Kendra. "They're not going anywhere."

"Hundred million years?" Derek asked. "That's like— almost as long as people."

Kendra frowned at her student's paltry knowledge of basic evolution.

"So what's the secret to their success?" Kate asked.

"No males," Kendra answered.

"Huh?" Derek scratched his head again.

"Ant colonies. They're all female," she told him. "The male lives a couple weeks, does his thing . . . dead."

Derek squinted for a moment and then chuckled. "Yeah, right."

Jane slapped sand from her hands. "I still say we poison them all. Throw some god-awful pesticide on the whole bloody lot."

Kendra seized a black spray can. "You mean like this stuff?"

"Perfect."

A white mist erupted as Kendra sprayed a cloud of ant repellant toward her students and they scattered like bugs.

37

"Unless you directly target every queen, they'll react the same as you. A million fleeing ants, carrying their eggs and larvae through a hundred miles of tunnel." She threw them each a bottle of water and grinned, like a mother teaching her children the hard way not to stick fingers into electrical sockets. "Either that or they'll split into multiple colonies."

"You could have just said that," Jane said, spitting bitter particles from her lips.

"Haven't you been paying attention? Pesticides don't work. The entire world has been hypnotized by a handful of billion-dollar companies that have made nature one big science experiment and human beings their guinea pigs." Kendra's voice rose like a Baptist preacher's. "The same people selling the world's precious seed supply are conveniently selling all the pesticides as well and genetically mutating our plants into toxic, allergenic pseudo-food in an attempt to make them bug resistant. We're busting our asses out here trying to break the cycle of a chemical dependency."

"Is that gonna be on the test?" Derek asked.

Kendra sighed heavily. "I've spent years trying to wipe these suckers out. Best team of entomologists ever assembled. Guess how many colonies we killed?" She didn't wait for an answer. "*Zero.*"

"We've wiped out eleven in four months," beamed Kate.

"Exactly. We might have finally found the answer to a hundred-year-old problem." She threw Kate a bottle of yellow liquid. "So let's move it."

Kendra watched her students get back to business with little enthusiasm and she sighed. They could never understand the magnitude of what had been accomplished. There had never been a chemical to stop the spread of fire ants or any other ant species. Theoretically, if her formula succeeded in wiping out ants, it could potentially control other insect populations as well. Over time that could mean millions of dollars to her company, Invicta, as well as the university that supported her studies. Not that the money mattered to Kendra. Each year fire ants damaged millions of crops and caused thousands of injuries and even deaths to people and farm animals. Since the 1940s, fire ants had spread across the United States as far north as Virginia and, due to their rapid adaptation and global warming, it was estimated they would reach as high as New England by 2020. Wiping out their population was her only motivation. Early tests were positive but not definitive. There were too many variables, but still, Kendra felt more optimistic than at any other time in her life.

She sat down in the sand and observed her students. Kate stood over the fire ant mound and removed the stopper from the pheromone solution. Derek handed her two long cotton swabs and she dipped them into the bottle. Together they began dabbing the liquid onto the thoraxes of ants headed back to the nest. Then Kate used the top of a dropper bottle to suck up six grams of solution, squirt the contents into an ant hole and set off to treat the other mounds.

Kendra threw a nod to Jane. "I see you left the shorts home. How many bites total?"

"Eighteen. All the way up to me bum."

She stirred up a newly erupted anthill. "You have to admit, aside from being a nuisance they're utterly amazing."

"I guess."

"Their social networking system makes Twitter and Facebook look like a joke."

Jane chuckled.

"The perfect society, really." Kendra picked up a single ant with a pencil tip and watched it crawl across the wood. "They work for the good of the colony, never for themselves. So affable and serene—at the same time, dogged and terrifying."

"Terrifying?"

"Formica sanguinea?" Kendra blurted, as if it were obvious.

"Oh, yes," Jane nodded. "I do so love the really nasty ones."

Kendra tried to impress upon her students that ants were not the helpless creatures they appeared underfoot. They acted purely on instinct to secure the survival of the colony—and often in heinous ways. Formica Sanguinea, the slave maker ant, was a favorite example. After the queen mates, she plays dead and is dragged to another colony by her own soldiers. She kills the enemy queen and rolls around in her scent to confuse the colony. After this deadly act of assassination and impersonation, she takes the workers as slaves and begins laying her eggs. As her own brood matures, they emerge to attack other colonies, tearing their enemies apart limb by limb and scurrying off with thousands of eggs to be made into new slaves.

"That's why we're so fortunate," said Kendra, holding the pencil at eye level as the ant crawled across the horizon. "We can study them up close. Understand their uniqueness. Most people *think* an ant is an ant."

Jane raised a brow. "I *think* you need to get out more, Professor."

The two women laughed together.

"Hey!" Kate shouted to the others. "Take a look."

Kendra sprang to her feet, dusting off sand, and headed to the anthill beside Kate. A few of the worker ants were tearing one another apart. She grinned and let out a breath of relief.

Another positive test.

In a few hours, she predicted, the colony would be dead.

* * *

By 9:00 A.M. the scorching heat had sent most of the colony into their tunnels. Blotches of sweat covered the front of Kendra's jumpsuit like a Rorschach test. Kate was counting ants, while Derek and Jane were sprawled out in the shade.

The hum of an engine in the distance perked up their ears. It grew louder, and then a black all-terrain vehicle flew over a sand dune, straight for the worksite. Dust spun in its wheels as it swiveled to a stop by the yellow Jeep.

Derek moved protectively over to Kendra and she held up a finger to her students. "Just hang back. It's probably one of the new park rangers with nothing better to do than hassle hardworking scientists."

A tall, blond, clean-cut man in a black suit and sunglasses got out of the driver's seat and walked toward Kendra. He had a clenched jaw, razor-sharp lips and a seriously determined stride that made her smirk as he approached.

"What are you, FBI?"

"Yes, ma'am. Agent Dan Cameron."

"You're kidding, right?"

"No, I'm not, Professor Hart."

Kendra pulled off her sunglasses and he did the same. The dry desert heat made Kendra feel like bread toasting too close to the coils, but this guy didn't break a sweat. She looked into his blue eyes, light as crystals, and went back to counting ants. "Could you move back? Your shadow is throwing my little friends here off course."

"You're going to have to come with me," he told her. "The fact is, you're needed as a consultant for the U.S. government."

Consultant? Kendra had served as a consultant before, in Texas and Florida. She figured this could mean only one thing: someone important was having problems with insects. She

imagined the president of the United States waking up in a bed full of fire ants, before realizing the scenario was ridiculous.

"A consultant for what?"

"Can't say. I'm only assigned to pick you up."

She choked back a laugh. "I thought you guys only did this in bad movies."

Cameron flipped open his agency identification. "I've already cleared things with the dean."

"I'm going to have to call him myself."

"Fine," he replied and handed her a satellite phone.

Kendra knew she was beat. She lowered her gaze to the rippling landscape that the desert winds had sculpted overnight. All the ants on the surface were dead, except a dozen stragglers fighting on top of the mound. With a grunt, she kicked a spray of sand and they scattered toward the hole.

"Hey," Kate said, flicking sand off her clipboard. The other two students looked uneasily at the FBI agent.

"Just wrap it up, Kate. You'll have to catch a ride with Derek. Looks like I've got somewhere to go." Kendra pulled back her shoulders and asked, "So where exactly are we headed?"

"New York."

"*Really.*" She nodded with a smirk of curiosity.

Forty minutes later, Kendra was standing on the tarmac of Las Cruces International Airport, wearing a fresh pair of jeans, a crisp white cotton shirt and Doc Marten boots. The depressing sight of her pets scampering boundlessly across the desert was still clear in her mind.

The loud engine of a Cessna jet thwotted overhead. Kendra wiped her eyes, which stung from the swirling dust and contact lenses she rarely ever wore. Her hands were shaking.

All the way to the airport she had pleaded her case of claustrophobia, but never had she expected such a small aircraft.

Agent Cameron tossed her duffel bag to the pilot and reached for Kendra's hand.

She pressed her palms to her chest in a dramatic gesture. "Seriously," she yelled over the engine, "I'll have a panic attack! I might even be dangerous."

"It's all right," he replied loudly, pushing her toward the doorway. "I've got a gun."

CHAPTER 7

CARLOS GONZALES HAD WORKED nights in the New York subways for twenty-three years and there was no place he felt more at home than the dark, winding tunnels of the number 6 Lexington line. He knew every track bed, swing signal, wire and bulb.

The trains were fully automated and operated by a computerized guidance system out of Transit Authority Traffic Control, but when there was a problem that none of the electronic wizards could diagnose, Carlos would do a manual check. He didn't mind; it was the part of the job he most enjoyed.

But the call came in on his night off, just minutes before his grandson's birthday party. He grumbled to his wife, "Signal's down, same as yesterday. I supposed to check the whole Six line. Ees going to take all night, Rosa."

"*No quejarse.* The boys will save you some cake. *Mira,* Carvel Cookie Puss."

Carlos entered the tunnels with his toolbox in one hand and flashlight in the other. It was the end of rush hour when he checked the first switches, tightened the circuits and flipped the override buttons, then rode a train to the next stop. By 11:00 P.M. there were few commuters and fewer trains to worry about. The last station was Seventy-seventh Street and he jumped onto the track bed and followed the tunnel to the hotbox.

Carlos knew he had seven minutes until the next train passed so he worked swiftly down his checklist. The job was nearly done when something odd caught his eye and he moved his flashlight to the wall. A huge chunk of concrete was missing and the surrounding tile was pocked full of holes and chinks.

"*Qué es este?*" Carlos whispered. He slid his hand along the wall and flakes fell to the ground. He checked his watch. Three minutes left.

With both hands, he pressed hard against the concrete. This time a mammoth section of wall crumbled to the ground and Carlos doubled back just in time. The flashlight illuminated a storm of dust, and when the debris settled, the light hit a cavity the size of a Volkswagen.

Carlos sucked in a breath of terror. Hundreds of rat skeletons lay across the rubble, skulls and bones glaring white and picked clean.

"*Mal espíritu,*" Carlos rasped and stepped back again, nearly tripping over himself as a shiver of fright raced up the back of his neck. He felt as though he were witnessing something supernatural. Carlos shined the light into the hole and could see an endless carpet of bones. There was a crackling sound and he aimed the beam down the track bed, checked his watch. Two minutes. He was shaking and wanted to get out of there, so he grabbed his toolbox, but a flicker of movement spun him around.

The flashlight fell upon the white tile wall covered in thin lines. Shiny black glass like the bobby pins Rosa wore—only, they seemed to be in motion. He followed the shimmering trails to the steel beams overhead and the concrete ceiling. There was a whistle of a train in the far-off distance. Carlos knew he had seconds to get out of there and he turned to run.

All at once, clumps of insects dropped silently down on him, like the muted patter of moss, falling onto his head and shoulders. He dropped his toolbox and flashlight, bending over and shaking his head wildly as legions of soldiers dropped from the rafters onto his back. Carlos felt the sting of a thousand needles stabbing in the dark. Venom shot into his eyes and burned through his corneas. He screamed and stumbled backward, swatting at his face and falling over the second rail. He gagged as they began to fill his mouth and swollen airways. Then the stings turned into bites, jaws hungry to devour meat.

Carlos heaved out a lungful of air and insects with a croaking sound deep within his throat. He staggered down the tunnel, half blind. Fire ripped through his swollen arteries and his body became a furnace, torched from the inside out. The pain grew unbearable, an agony no human could endure. Frantic for the torment to end, he rammed his head into the concrete wall. There was a whistle above the hammering in his brain and he turned his bloodied face into the bright white headlight.

Carlos tipped his head back in relief as the train struck, nearly cutting his torso in half.

CHAPTER 8

IT WAS TWO WEEKS since New York mayor John Russo had read about the first attack in the *Daily News*. The headline screamed, THEM!

Now he had fifty news stories and computer printouts strewn across his mahogany desk. With raging black eyes, he stared down at the sensational photos. Russo had the temper of a pit bull and the body to match, broad at the chest and rounded at the shoulders, with a long torso that tapered down to a pair of short, sinewy legs. He puffed on a cigar and ran his thick fingers through a comb-over, dyed an unnatural black.

The latest post was from an MSNBC website minutes ago. Last night a subway worker covered in ants had to be practically scraped off the face of the number 6 motor car.

Russo winced.

"The White House confirmed your call for nine-thirty," said his secretary, Olivia, standing outside his office. "And the exterminators just arrived so you better start packing." She went back to her desk. Russo smiled. Things were going better than he expected. Already he had spoken to the president three times and the head of Homeland Security twice. He knew the road to glory was paved with small victories. Like union strikes, terrorism and three-alarm fires, this ant thing was a blessing in disguise.

Olivia buzzed. "Sir, it's the governor on line three."

He grumbled again and picked up the phone. "Hey, Bob."

"John, I asked you to get me those reports first thing this morning. Why offer to handle the paperwork if you're just going to sit on it? Is that what you're doing, John, sitting on it?"

"Look, all we've got is a few deaths, couple of stings, and specimens as harmless as fucking butterflies. This is local. We're doing just fine on our own."

"That's not what I'm hearing. You've got Washington involved and that's where I step in. The deadline is noon, got it?"

"Sure, sure. Noon."

"I'm not kidding. Elections are six months away and you'll need my support."

Russo hung up the phone and laughed. He had won the mayoral race in a landslide without a single endorsement. He didn't need any politician in Albany to get his votes. He was a fierce competitor and devoutly regarded the city as his own. Politics was his calling, like the priesthood to his brother Salvatore. But while Sal had only to satisfy God, Russo had to please a million civil servants who never agreed on anything and 8 million New Yorkers who agreed on even less. He had been tough on crime and tougher on terrorism. The White House practically gave him sole credit for preventing two of the worst terrorist attacks on the city, in which he bypassed federal law enforcement and sniffed out multiple al-Qaeda cells using his own police force and street snitches. With the dismal state of world affairs growing more dangerous every day, citizens felt safe with John Russo at the helm.

Yet he had higher aspirations. A large audience of zealous Republicans clapping wildly on the right, covetous Democrats tapping palms on the left. *Mr. Speaker, the president of the United States—*

It was practically guaranteed.

Russo packed his briefcase. He would be heading to the secret location, the most secure place in Manhattan. Even the press didn't know about it.

He glanced at the clock and grimaced. Paul O'Keefe was supposed to join him for the ride. The mayor wondered if it was a mistake, putting the notable entomologist in charge of solving the ant crisis. Russo had a habit of appointing a single person to manage every disaster. The main criteria for the job was expertise in the field, a deep understanding of public relations, knowing how to balance a budget—and doing exactly what the mayor advised. Paul seemed well qualified.

Olivia buzzed again. "Sir, it's the president. Line one."

Russo grinned and picked up the phone. "Mr. President. Glad to hear from you."

The mayor listened intently, and his face turned grave.

Paul found himself lost in Gracie Mansion. He had declined an escort and took one wrong turn after another. By the time he remembered the mayor's study was in an upstairs parlor, he was out of breath and twenty minutes late.

Russo was hunched over the phone with an expression of disbelief. Paul recognized the look quite well; more news about the ants. He cleared his throat and the mayor looked up, gestured to a chair.

Paul didn't feel like sitting. Instead, he walked quietly to a window and watched the crowd of press photographers crawling all over the grounds. Reporters had been camped out on the porch since dawn, undeterred by a cop at the entrance who kept insisting that the mayor was out of town.

An exterminator strolled casually into the office, whistling through a handlebar mustache, snapping gum, and spraying chemicals along the floorboards. He was wearing a gray jump-suit labeled DEPARTMENT OF HEALTH AND HYGIENE and he carried a tank of poison on his back.

Paul sighed. The man's attempts to kill the ants seemed comical.

Russo hung up the phone and Paul was ready with the same excuses. "I don't have anything new," he told the mayor. "The samples taken from the two victims this morning—"

Russo raised an impatient hand. "Never mind all that. I've got some news, straight from the White House. This is big, Paul. *Really* big." He threw on his suit jacket and stopped at the window. "Those damn reporters still out there?"

"They're just trying to find out what's going on, John . . . sir . . . Mr. Mayor." Paul was still unsure how to address Russo. They'd been "close friends" for less than two weeks, since the first ant attack. "We can't keep telling the press these are normal ants. Letting them believe the victims died of allergies."

"Well, we're not ready to talk yet." The mayor grabbed a cigar smoldering in an ashtray and started for the door. "Follow me. This is a critical meeting."

"Where are we going?" Paul asked.

"The one place *they* don't know about."

Paul passed the exterminator and said, "You know, that's a total waste of time."

Russo laughed and headed for his limo in the underground parking garage.

CHAPTER 9

THE CABIN OF THE Cessna was exceedingly small. The luxurious interior couldn't hide the fact that there was zero headroom, half a dozen seats and an aisle as wide as a squirrel. For three hours Kendra was in a sweat, trapped in a coffin two-thousand feet in the air.

She hated flying. *Really* hated it.

On her tray was a Thai chicken wrap, which definitely trumped the granola she'd been living on for months. But she felt nauseous from the flight—and besides, it almost certainly contained peanut oil. Despite the EpiPens packed in her duffel bag, it wasn't worth taking a chance. That left ginger ale and a tiny bag of pretzels. She took tiny bites and little sips.

Agent Cameron was busy at a laptop across from Kendra. He didn't seem to mind the cramped quarters, even though his legs protruded halfway down the aisle and the top of his head grazed the ceiling.

As soon as they boarded, the agent had given Kendra a stack of forms, nondiscloser statements and questionnaires, having to do with top-secret clearance. Reluctantly, she signed a document that stated, "Failure to comply with this agreement may result in criminal prosecution and up to 25 years in federal prison."

The agent paid no attention to Kendra's barrage of questions, offering only a silencing finger as he continued typing. It was infuriating being ignored.

She strained her neck, trying to read the folder by his side. It was labeled *Kendra Hart*. She let out a huff and slumped in her seat, unable to shake the feeling of being kidnapped, hunted down like a criminal. She turned to the billowing white clouds in the window, a constant reminder that the coffin was flying, and it sent a chill down her spine. Maybe the government wanted her for some kind of secret experiment. If she were to disappear, who would really notice? The university faculty perhaps, but they could be silenced. There was no family or friends checking in on her whereabouts. She was the perfect specimen.

Kendra tried to reel in her paranoia, attempting to focus on something positive, like her work, but even that made her fidgety and restless.

"How much gas does this thing hold?" she grumbled. "Maybe we should stop for a fill-up."

Cameron's eyes didn't wander from the screen.

"Hey," she shouted. "They teach you how to ignore people at the Bureau? Some kind of course—FBI'm a Dickhead 101?"

"Pretty trashy mouth for a dainty desert flower," he said.

Kendra was encouraged that at least he'd finally spoken. "I'm more of a cactus," she replied sharply.

The agent chuckled.

"What's your problem? You have something against entomologists?"

Cameron shrugged. "It's hard to believe there are that many *adults* looking at bugs all day. How can you possibly make a living?"

"Amazingly, the world of insects is quite profitable. Pesticides, royal jelly, silks, soaps."

"That's right. You owned some big company. What's it called? Invicta." He furrowed his brow, thinking. "That's a species of ant. Latin for 'invincible.'"

"You're smarter than you look," she muttered.

"So what's your racket?"

"Pheromone manipulation."

"Oh yeah. Insect birth control—what will they think of next?"

Kendra rolled her eyes, fairly used to snide comments. The work she was conducting in the desert stemmed from a relatively newer branch of entomology. Integrated pest management, or IPM, involved more sophisticated, biologically based methods of controlling insect populations in agriculture. Often this included the manipulation of insect pheromones. By saturating crops with a synthetic version of a female insect's mating odor, scientists could jam the mating communication system of males so they could never locate a female. They would eventually die, single and confused.

Despite studies showing that pheromone manipulation was ecofriendly, highly effective and could potentially yield up to a 1,000 percent return on its investment in one year, it remained grossly underutilized, a tiny fraction of pest management. Not only was the process of isolating, identifying and synthesizing pheromones extremely difficult and expensive, the biggest problem by far was the world's pesticide-dependent mentality. The six agrochemical giants were multibillion-dollar gods of the farming industry that were only too happy to unveil the next generation of toxic chemicals, as insects became resistant to the old ones. Poison was the solution of choice, despite the fact that only 2 percent of pesticides usually hit the intended targets, and 98 percent ended up in the air, soil and drinking water, while killing off beneficial, indigenous insects. IPM was meant to break the cycle of chemical dependence and Kendra was slowly making a name for herself in the small circle of IPM researchers.

"You people like to complain about bug spray," Cameron said, "but God forbid there's a worm in your apple." He laughed at himself.

Kendra turned up her lip. "There are some creatures in the world more annoying than insects."

Cameron nodded, seeming to have missed the joke, and then asked, "You mean like members of COP?"

Kendra knew he was referring to Citizens Overseeing Pesticides, a somewhat radical group of entomology students at Harvard. Kendra had been a member in graduate school and written a number of journal articles for the organization. COP had become notorious by uncovering secret memos and documents inside the EPA and various chemical companies, finding links between pesticides and such phenomena as colony collapse in honeybees, the rise of ADHD in children, and elevated hormones in girls. They made national headlines with claims that the average American is exposed to more than ten different pesticide residues on their food each day, and the fact that more than 50 percent of the insecticides used in poor countries was neither monitored nor approved.

"Bunch of communists," the agent said under his breath.

Kendra's ears popped as the plane seemed to drop, and she threw her attention toward the window. They had reached the coast. New York Harbor was shimmering gold in the late afternoon sun. The Statue of Liberty looked smaller than she remembered, with a melancholy face.

Kendra blew out a disgruntled breath. "So what's in New York?"

"Christ, where've you been for two weeks?"

"Why don't you check your folder?"

"All right," Cameron said with a leer that rattled her. He settled back comfortably in the seat and leafed through the folder. "Parents were both entomologists. That explains a lot . . . died when you were seven years old . . . murdered in South America." He looked at Kendra straight-faced. "How very sad."

Kendra stiffened.

"Well, well. The cactus has a brain. Six years at Harvard . . . married your professor . . . Dr. Paul O'Keefe." He flipped the last page. "Then the promising star of the bug world disappeared into the desert."

For a moment, all she could manage was a cold stare, but then the muscles of her jaw relaxed into a grin. "You're funny, you know? Clean-cut. Slick suit. Probably specialize in water-boarding, right?" Kendra didn't flinch when the agent scowled. "Know what? I didn't break any laws. I'm not your prisoner. The second we land—I'm gone."

Cameron turned away with a slow nod and appeared calm. Kendra felt victorious but then he stood up tall, casually brushing away crumbs from his suit, and sidestepped across the aisle. A chill hit Kendra in the marrow of her bones when he fell into the seat next to her, smelling of fresh linen and testosterone and fixing his pale blue eyes upon her. He lifted an arm over her chair and pulled back his jacket to reveal a gun holstered to his chest. For some reason Kendra found it alarming that this particular federal agent was carrying a weapon.

In his most sarcastic tone he said, "You know, Professor,

that's really brave of you, standing up to the government like that. I really admire that kind of *spunk*."

She turned toward the window.

"Just one thing," he whispered. "Now look at me, dear." His thumb reached out and drew her face back toward him. Kendra was jolted by his touch. "This is a very serious matter of national security," he explained softly. "You could call it a matter of life and death."

Kendra tried to be cool, forced a sarcastic chuckle.

"Yes, I know it sounds cliché," he continued. "But I want to make sure you understand the gravity of the situation and possible consequences of your actions. I *am* authorized to use force to get you to New York." His fingers casually rubbed the edge of his lapel so that his jacket opened wider and the gun was completely exposed. "Do you understand what I'm saying? Nod your head so I know that you do."

Kendra stayed perfectly still, except for a slight tremble of her bottom lip.

Cameron searched her face and found what he expected. "Good. Now we understand each other."

Kendra didn't move until Cameron returned to his seat, and then she shut her eyes and exhaled.

The agent closed his laptop and straightened his tie. "Better fasten your seat belt."

The Cessna seemed to take a dive and Kendra grabbed the armrests to steady herself. They were descending somewhere over Long Island. The plane eased down on the runway at La-Guardia, then taxied to a restricted area for government aircraft. The pilot parked next to a row of matching Cessnas and when the engine fell silent, he released the door and it unfolded into a staircase.

Agent Cameron put away his folders and laptop and motioned Kendra toward the exit. She stopped at the doorway, staring up at the blue sky over Queens and a hazy, far-off view of the Manhattan skyline. She breathed in air that wasn't anything like that of the desert and wiped her watery eyes.

The pilot took Kendra's hand as she came down the stairs. LT. COLONEL DALE HASKIN was printed on the gold wings pinned to the lapel of his uniform. He hadn't said a word during the flight but now he was friendly, smiling, and picked up her duffel bag.

"Trip okay?"

"Terrific."

A black-windowed sedan was idling on the tarmac. Cameron waited by the open door and slipped into the backseat after Kendra, but this time she wasn't afraid. Anger blunted fear. And besides, her curiosity was piqued. She found it intriguing to be back in this particular city and wondered if it had anything to do with the one person she knew in New York: her ex-husband.

CHAPTER 10

KENDRA GAZED AT THE overlapping skyscrapers through
the tinted windows of the car. She had grown accustomed to
the vastness of the desert landscape, layered in earth tones and
unbroken sky. New York City seemed like another planet with
its gray sooty streets and towering granite buildings, throngs
of pedestrians, steaming metal carts of food, vendors hawking
knockoff designer watches and handbags. Angular women in
bright-colored suits and white sneakers walked briskly by and
swarthy men in hard hats relaxed along a chain-link fence.

It was close to rush hour and the car moved slowly. Kendra
tried to figure out which direction they were headed. The
street numbers were getting smaller, so it was definitely down-
town, away from the Museum of Natural History and Paul.
That was some relief. Besides, she thought, with all the travel-
ing Paul did it was unlikely he was even in New York. He was
probably in some exotic country or lecture hall or picking up
an award for being so damn perfect. It was Kendra, after all,
being summoned by the FBI as a scientist for her expertise and
knowledge. Something her former husband never seemed to
notice.

Still, she could almost *feel* Paul somewhere in the city and
suddenly found herself reeling back in time, to the first moment she'd set eyes on him. It was her junior year at Harvard.
Paul was teaching insect ecology and Kendra fell head over

heels on the first day of class. His velvety brown eyes seemed to look into her soul and he had the hands of an artist, long and graceful with large bony knuckles. They moved slowly and sensually. She remembered one particular day when Paul was tracing the exoskeleton of an enlarged plastic termite, his fingers gliding across its body, his soothing voice in a whisper that transfixed her. A delicious feeling of excitement was building inside her and when he placed his hand down on the figurine, cupping its enormous petiole, she actually moaned out loud. Fortunately, hers blended in with a dozen other moans. Unbeknownst to him, there was a fairly large consensus among the female student body that Dr. Paul O'Keefe had some kind of mystical power over women's libidos and they began to refer to his lectures as "quickies."

Kendra grew warm in the back of the sedan, thinking about their sizzling romance in the early years, but her skin cooled as she recalled five trying years of marriage. Paul insisted she play the part of the doting wife. She moved to New York and gave up her research while he flew around the world. Paul was on retainer for a chemical company and they had endless fights over everything from pesticide use to corporate control of the world's food supply. Finally, she had enough and started a research company in California. They excelled in their careers but on opposite coasts, and while their passion for each other never waned, work seemed to overtake their lives, especially for Paul, whose visits and phone calls became more infrequent.

In the end, though, it was Kendra who had an affair and severed their marriage. It was stupid; she'd been angry and she never told Paul about the other man.

Kendra gazed out the window, to the United Nations complex and its majestic array of colorful flags slapping against the wind. The car slowed as it approached the General Assembly building. They rounded a corner to a massive windowless fortress of concrete and steel. A metal bar was raised and they parked in a garage with ten other black sedans.

Agent Cameron led Kendra to the back of the garage, checked his watch and muttered that they were running late. He traveled through a series of hallways and doors that required the swipe of an ID tag, a thumbprint match or iris scan. A rather odd-looking elevator was waiting at the end of the journey. It was circular and made of polycarbonate glass. Cameron touched the small of Kendra's back to hurry her inside. There were no buttons on the wall but the curved transparent doors shut quietly. As they descended, a burst of air shot down from the ceiling as if from an exhausted locomotive, startling Kendra.

"You'll wear this while you're here," Cameron said, patting his jacket and retrieving an ID tag that displayed a photo of Kendra.

She eyed it hesitantly, rubbing a thumb over the photo and wondering when it was taken. In the snapshot she was wearing a bright yellow blouse. She didn't remember ever owning a yellow blouse. She clipped the card to her breast pocket.

Through the clear walls of the elevator Kendra could see that they were dropping swiftly through a narrow tunnel that seemed to be cut right out of the earth.

"How far down are we going?" she asked.

"About three hundred feet."

Kendra felt her throat tighten. "To where?"

Cameron didn't answer but rattled off another warning about restricted space, an oath of secrecy and then repeated the threat of twenty-five years in federal prison. "You're not to tell anyone about this place. *Ever,*" he concluded. As the elevator made a smooth but abrupt landing, he added, "It's an underground bunker, the largest in the world."

Kendra felt her stomach drop. The doors slid open and her mind flashed to Dorothy, opening the door to Oz.

They were at the entrance to an enormous cavern, fifty feet high and the size of a gymnasium. Kendra couldn't imagine what sort of monstrous drill could have sculpted such a colossal space. The bedrock walls were rough and jagged with flecks that glittered like diamonds, but the technology inside looked like something out of a futuristic movie. Scattered about the room were aerodynamic workstations; curved black oval chairs under floating touch-screen monitors that displayed 3-D images of places in New York City: crowded intersections, famous streets and buildings. The floor was covered in shiny metal, and thick steel plates climbed one wall. A network of pipes floated overhead like a silver spiderweb, along with panels of black grating, backlit with colorful luminescent patterns. Three identical elevators sat inside clear tubes that vanished into the rock ceiling.

You're not in Kansas anymore. Kendra stepped out of the elevator. The industrial floor was covered with tiny holes and she felt cold air flow against her shoes, as another burst of wind shot out from somewhere above.

"Radiation checkpoint," Cameron said, "but it detects anything chemical, biological. Real high-tech stuff. The whole place is surrounded by a ground-penetrating radar system that can spot a mole tunneling through the dirt. We can tell if anyone tries to get in," he said, "or out."

She followed him to a procession of crazy-shaped golf carts. Titanium potato chips on wheels, Kendra thought as she eased into the seat next to him. There was no steering wheel or controls, but Cameron muttered, "B-Seventeen," and the driver-less cart took off.

It was a smooth, fantastic journey through white hexagon-shaped hallways that were narrow enough to kick Kendra's claustrophobia into overdrive. The cart followed a pattern of diamonds on the ceiling, backlit in bright shades of red, blue and green, as a mechanical voice repeated several times, "Please keep hands inside . . . This vehicle stops for pedestrians . . ." The cart traversed down straight paths, and other times it would turn or spiral downward and take a new direction. After several sharp turns Kendra felt dizzy.

"So where's the oxygen come from?" she asked

"Vents. It's highly pressurized. You'll get used to it."

Kendra had to admit the bunker air seemed to be doing wonders for her sinuses, but it dried up her contact lenses. She pulled out the bottle of saline from her pocket and squirted a few drops in her eyes.

The cart came to a gentle pause and the voice said, "State Room B-Seventeen."

They were in front of a door marked with the same number. Cameron picked up her duffel bag and stretched his legs. He swiped his ID tag through a keypad and the door slid open noiselessly. He entered the dark room and Kendra followed, her eyes adjusting to the rough bedrock walls and tiny space that allowed only a small cot and dresser.

The room was a cave. Kendra hated caves. When she was six years old, her parents had brought her to Texas to save the very rare cave-dwelling arthropod *Texella reddelli*. It had recently been added to the U.S. endangered species list and was quickly becoming extinct due to an invasion of red fire ants. In a cavern of 100 percent humidity, Kendra's nose had run like mad, but the arthropods preferred moisture and the darkest part of the cave, and therefore so did their predators. Kendra remembered walking toward the ant nest, squeezing her mother's hand, as her father held up the lantern to the glistening rock wall. The red ants were everywhere, moving like rivers of blood through living veins. Six-year old Kendra had screamed.

"We'll drop your things off here," Cameron said and placed the bag on the cot.

Kendra left the room wondering how on earth she would ever sleep in such a confined space. She settled in the cart and it took off once again. There was a familiar tightening in her chest that squeezed her heart. The halls seemed to narrow. She closed her eyes and imagined a vast ocean—a meditation technique she'd learned from her mother—but the ocean waves kept pulling her under.

"Miss Hart?"

Kendra opened her eyes. They had stopped.

"You all right?" Cameron asked, with an amused smile.

Kendra nodded. They were facing a set of doors marked CONTROL CENTER.

"Is this another one of those tiny rooms?" she asked.

"Actually," Cameron whispered in a throaty voice, "it's enormous."

CHAPTER II

KENDRA BLEW OUT AN astonished breath. The control center was another quarried cavern but the size of Grand Central Station. More fantastic than its scope was its shape. The four gargantuan walls were triangular and came to a point twenty stories above her head, as if she were inside the Great Pyramid.

It was a strange dichotomy of archaic and ultramodern. Despite its primitive walls, most of the room looked like a futuristic NASA control center. A sea of holographic computers, gleaming silver and bathed in ghostly blue light, stretched across the floor to a main command unit: a forty-foot tactical workstation packed with enough silicone to run the entire city of Manhattan. Overhead were circular offices clear as glass that seemed to be floating on air. At one end of the pyramid, long tables faced the gold seal of the United Nations and red velvet carpet flowed over the steps to the podium and stretched along a formal dais.

Kendra decided this was one of those secret locations the government hides from the public. Places like Roswell and Area-51 and Mount Weather. This was where all the *important* New Yorkers would flee in the event of a nuclear attack.

Only now the place was nearly empty, about a dozen men and women sitting quietly at a table off to the side. Kendra froze when she recognized two of them: New York mayor John Russo and Dr. Paul O'Keefe.

"You must be Professor Hart," Russo said, squinting over his glasses. He extended a hand toward an empty seat near Paul. "Please, join us."

Kendra struggled to recover. Six hours ago, she was counting ants in the Southwestern desert and now she was standing in an underground bomb shelter with the mayor of New York City and her ex-husband.

She feigned a smile, walked to the seat next to Paul and sat down. He didn't look at her but leaned back casually in his chair, his eyes fixed on the mayor. He was wearing a lab coat with an ID tag clipped to his pocket. It was the same familiar etching in her dreams: the dark hair, graceful manner and the liquid chestnut eyes that sent shock waves through her body. The beard was new, and made him only more attractive. His left hand, masculine with long, gentle fingers, was wrapped around the back of his neck and Kendra noticed he still wore his wedding ring.

Paul was obviously avoiding her gaze, but she could tell he was beginning to crack and finally, without moving a muscle, his eyes shifted to her face.

She shot him a look that could freeze hell, but he only smiled.

Agent Cameron sat down in a seat next to Russo.

"Seems we're all present," the mayor began. "So let's get started."

Kendra's mouth had dried to sandpaper. There were small pitchers of water on the table and she filled a glass in front of her.

Russo introduced his eight municipal staff members; Kendra barely caught their names, but she was impressed by those present from Washington, most of whom she vaguely recognized. White House Chief Counsel George Bennington was accompanied by three members of the National Security Council, who were somber and silent during the introductions.

The mayor concluded, "And this is Paul O'Keefe, head of entomology at the Natural History Museum, and his associate, Kendra Hart."

Kendra's fist tightened around the water glass.

"The reason I've called today's meeting in this bunker will become clear momentarily. I expect other colleagues will soon be joining us, but for now we're trying to keep this thing quiet. What you hear today may be shocking, but nothing leaves this room. The last thing we need is a panic on our hands."

There were hesitant looks among the municipal employees, but the Washington group remained stoic. Kendra was having trouble concentrating. She took a long drink of water and tried to focus on the mayor's words.

"According to army intelligence," Russo declared, "a deadly new species of ant has created huge colonies under our streets and may threaten the very survival of New York City."

Kendra snorted, choking on water. Her laughing eyes darted around the table, waiting for someone to say "just kidding."

The mayor wasn't amused.

Pat Dempsey, the burly Irish sanitation director, chuckled too. "Well, you have to admit, John, that sounds a little sci-fi. Why don't we just shoot them all with ray guns?"

"Pat, you saw what they did to your men," Russo said with a scowl. "I want you all to listen to Paul O'Keefe. He knows more about ants than anyone on the planet."

Paul rose from his seat and walked to a podium, as Kendra's eyes followed the full length of him. He hit a few buttons and a theater-sized screen floated down from overhead and began running a silent film clip. Two ants, projected to the size of elephants, were butting heads over a dead grasshopper. The crowd around the table was instantly alert.

"As vital as they are to the environment," Paul said with authority, "certain species of ants have been a threat to the health and safety of our country for nearly a century. The worst of these is the imported red fire ant." Then Paul said something that really took Kendra by surprise. "Professor Hart is really the fire ant expert. I'm sure she'd be glad to give us a brief overview."

Now everyone was staring at Kendra. She cleared her throat and accepted the challenge. Onscreen a queen fire ant was being tended by a battalion of nurser ants. "The fire ant queen," Kendra began. "She lays thousands of eggs a day and reproduces other queens through cloning, making an exact replica of herself. Each year, five million Americans are stung by fire ants, which can cause injuries ranging from a painful rash to anaphylactic shock and even death. For nearly a century, they've been steadily moving north and the infestation count is now six-hundred million acres. The annual cost to this country is over twelve billion dollars in treatment, loss of crops, livestock and damaged machinery. I suppose it's lucky for humans the main diet of the fire ant is insects and small mammals."

A new creature burst onscreen. It had no eyes, just enormous sharp pincers snapping at the camera like an alien in battle. Kendra blinked hard and the word "Siafu" soundlessly left her lips.

"Thank you, *Ms.* Hart," Paul said, and once again took center stage. "In contrast, the deadly Siafu of Africa is a vicious man-eater and the only insect known to attack people for the purpose of food. Siafu, also known as driver ants, sweep the forest floor in colonies of twenty-two million. They typically attack their prey en masse by entering the nose and mouth and asphyxiating them. Siafu are blind and react to movement and carbon dioxide; if anything stirs or breathes, they kill it and eat it." Paul returned to the table. "That's a brief overview of two of the most deadly insects on the planet. Kendra, if you want to add anything . . ."

She answered with a cold stare.

"So what's with the bug lesson, John?" Pat asked the mayor.

Paul replied, "The insects attacking New Yorkers have characteristics of both species, fire ant and Siafu."

"How's that?"

"I'll let our guest explain," Russo said. "Some of you have met General Leonard Dawson." Russo motioned to a domineering-looking figure beside him. "The general is actually quite familiar with these insects and he has come here today with some vital information."

The two-star general sat a head taller than the rest of the group. He had a frame as wide as a doorway; a powerhouse in full uniform. He took command of the table with a booming voice. "Two years ago, the United States military was tipped off about a secluded laboratory in Bolivia. We sent in a surveillance team, which located a sprawling compound—over ninety thousand square feet—camouflaged inside the Amazon jungle. Naturally, we believed it to be a drug operation and immediately organized a raid with the Bolivian government. However, the incursion was a disaster. There was a shootout. A fire erupted, causing major explosions."

The general turned to Agent Cameron. "That's when the FBI showed up. Turned out they had been investigating the lab for several months."

Agent Cameron said, "We had been following a money

trail, millions of dollars from an unidentified source in the United States. Our information pointed not to drugs but to ecoterrorists. A scientist working at that lab, Dr. Phillip Laredo, had strong ties to radical environmental groups. As specialists in ecoterrorism, my team was assigned to the case." Cameron's jaw clenched. "Until the military got wind of the operation and swooped right in."

The general cleared his throat in annoyance. "It was not a successful mission, that's true. Everyone inside the lab was killed. Except for the ants. Millions of them, living in a tank the size of an Olympic swimming pool. The Bolivian government wanted the insects destroyed, the whole place burned to the ground. So the army complied. We gassed the ants in the tank and firebombed the compound. Some of the specimens were collected and brought back to the United States. That's when we discovered something disturbing—outside of the tank, these ants are indestructible. I can tell you without a doubt, the ants we collected are the same species we're facing here in New York."

Paul looked flabbergasted, as if this was all news to him, crucial information he should have been given before anyone else. He said to the colonel, "You gassed the ants?"

"They can be killed in a tank," Dawson replied. "Certainly not in a city."

"So you've been studying the specimens for two years?"

"We analyzed them for several months. But they died off rather quickly."

"Surely you learned *something* about them."

The general motioned to a uniformed officer by his side. "This is Colonel Tom Garrett. He was working with the team of army scientists studying the specimens and following up on leads with the FBI. Anything we learned in two years, he can share with you."

Garrett was a tall man in his sixties, with a pasty complexion and dour expression. His salt-and-pepper hair was stiffly sprayed. Despite his chicken-like neck, the cut of his uniform hinted at an athletic frame. He glanced around the table and his gaze lingered on Kendra for just a moment.

"I'll tell you what I know," he began. "We believe the project was going on since the 1980s, funded by a group known as Earth Avengers, an extraordinarily sophisticated and clandestine sect of ecoterrorists. These people had access to an unprecedented amount of money, resources and highly trained entomologists. From what the FBI uncovered, it seems their goal was to create man's ultimate natural enemy. One which could fight back against human destruction of the planet. The insect they created was a genetic mutation of the Siafu and fire ant, which they named Siafu Moto, Swahili for 'driver ant-fire.' The result of their work was the most deadly, indestructible creature on earth. The ants live underground and have a lethal sting. They multiply by the millions. They feed at night and will attack anything that moves. Their diet consists of rats and human flesh."

"Just rats and people?" Pat Dempsey asked, amused.

"We believe they were developed to be an urban weapon," General Dawson replied. "Kill off people and leave most other creatures alone."

"New York's a long crawl from Bolivia," Pat said. "How did they get under our city?"

"It was Dr. Laredo, the project leader. We believe he escaped the fire and took off with a Siafu Moto queen."

Cameron added, "The FBI has been tracking him since the

raid. We found nothing until a month ago. A photo of a dead man resembling Laredo was taken by NYPD just days after the fire in Bolivia. He was found in Riverside Park. Shot himself in the head."

Kendra grimaced.

Garrett said, "If Laredo released that queen before killing himself, it's possible she has produced millions of ants, as well as her clones, which would have started their own colonies all over the city. There may be a trillion ants under Manhattan."

"That's insane," said Pat.

"Maybe," Garrett replied. "Maybe not."

Paul spoke with a renewed sense of hope. "We'll need every speck of research you recovered from the lab. All the genetic modifications, the tests and findings."

"Didn't you hear the general?" Garrett said. "The facility was destroyed. All the scientists are dead. I can't give you anything."

"You didn't collect any documents?" Paul said tersely. "I find that hard to believe."

"Like he said," the general cut in, "there are no records. Aside from the president of the United States and the faces you see in this room, there are less than fifty individuals in the world who even know about these ants. Let me make this clear; any information regarding the Siafu Moto is proprietary to the United States military. As a matter of national security, there will be no communication beyond this bunker." He glanced around the table. "You cannot speak to anyone about this. Not your families and certainly not the media."

His words were met with nervous stares among the group, except for the White House representatives, who sat rigid.

Then the general turned almost apologetic. "Of course, the

United States Army takes full responsibility for this disaster. Both the raid and destruction of the facility were tactical errors."

Colonel Garrett showed no remorse. "The problem will be contained. There is no doubt about that."

"A trillion ants. I still don't believe it," insisted Pat. "What, are they invisible? We've had just a handful of attacks."

Kendra was pondering the same question. "He's right. And there would be other signs as well. Fire ants create enormous tunnels. A large colony can loosen soil to the point of road collapse. They're attracted to electrical fields, constantly causing power outages and cable damage. In Texas, ants are the leading cause of traffic light failures. A trillion could black out this city."

The room fell silent and everyone stared dumbly at Kendra. The mayor cleared his throat and turned to his staff with an accusing tone. "I guess that would explain our rash of subway outages. Sixteen road cave-ins this year. Con Ed is nearly out of their minds with shortages."

"Not to mention the missing rat population," Pat muttered. Then he added, "Still, there must be some kind of bug spray we could dump on them."

The mayor called attention to three men sitting around the table in identical pinstriped suits. "These gentlemen are representatives from the largest chemical companies in the world."

Kendra scrutinized the men. All three were beaming with pride, as if they were superheroes flown in to save the planet. She recognized the tall one from Cytex, the largest global manufacturer of insecticides. He was an irritating man named Preston something-or-other, who tried to compensate for his baldness by pulling the last fringe of his hair into a slim ponytail. Preston had tried to shut down COP's journal for what he called repeatedly misstating facts. He gave Kendra a sly wink, signaling that he remembered her too.

"The three of you will be working with Dr. O'Keefe," the mayor announced, and smiled at the men with optimism. "Paul tells me you have some effective methods to stop all types of insects."

"Quite effective, yes," Preston assured the mayor, and the other two nodded accordingly.

Flustered, Kendra eyed Paul, and he turned away. Working with pesticide companies had long been a point of disparity between them. Paul reasoned it was easier to work with them than fight them. "There's never been a pesticide that has been able to stop the spread of fire ants," she told the mayor definitively.

The mayor forced a grin. "And what do you propose we do?"

"I'm not sure," she replied. "Did anyone think about evacuating the city?"

Paul stifled a chuckle, covering his mouth with a cough. The mayor's staff seemed to look in six different directions. Kendra had the feeling the subject had been brought up before.

"Eight million people?" Russo cocked his head, ripped off his glasses. "Do you have any idea how much money that kind of undertaking would cost? Police, emergency crews, assistance for the sick and elderly, temporary housing, transit and traffic—"

She raised a defensive hand. "Hey, you're the one claiming these ants—"

"Forty million dollars!" he declared. "Per day. I'm not even taking into account yet another huge collapse of the stock market and worldwide financial loss."

"Financial loss?" she burst out with a biting smirk.

"Look." The mayor held up his hands with the placating smile of a longtime politician. "This isn't something that's going to be solved with a couple of pest strips and a can of Raid. It may take years to get rid of them."

"So what do we do in the meantime?" Pat asked.

"We play offense. The last attack was underground. We'll be shutting down the Lexington subway line, sending in excavation teams. They'll be in full gear, tearing up the walls next week. Paul, we're going to need the most help from the scientific community. Someone has to figure out how to kill these things. I've assembled this team because we've got to keep this city running, and I know you can be trusted not to say a word about this."

"So we're the whole team? Are we supposed to save the city by ourselves?" Pat asked.

"Don't be ridiculous. We've got the army, the FBI, Homeland Security. People are going mad in Washington trying to solve this crisis."

"Great," Pat muttered, glancing at the attorney general. "Washington."

"So how are we supposed to kill them?" Pat nodded to Colonel Garrett. "Didn't you just tell us these ants are indestructible?"

The colonel replied, "Out in the field, they are virtually impossible to destroy." He looked at Kendra. "You are correct that pesticides are probably out of the question. The same is true for conventional warfare, chemical and biological weapons, megabombs and fuel air bombs. So far, we know of only one full-proof method to kill them. When hit with a blast of atomic radiation, they die instantly."

No one said anything. The White House chief counsel looked pale.

"There are other ways to destroy ants," Kendra finally said. "Advanced technologies that won't leave the city a toxic dump or radioactive wasteland."

The mayor raised a brow. "Let's try to remember, these are bugs after all."

"Insects," Kendra corrected out of habit.

"Whatever," the mayor continued. "Paul has been running tests all week and I have no doubt that he can eventually figure out how to kill them."

"I'm sure you're right," Paul said. "Ms. Hart, would you like to review the findings?"

Before she could respond, Russo said, "That's an excellent idea. Tomorrow I expect your lists of problems and solutions—I don't want any more deaths on my watch."

The group rose in quiet murmurs.

Kendra nearly bumped squarely into Agent Cameron. "Smiling Dan," she said with sarcasm.

He handed her a map of the bunker. "You'll need this. It's a diagram of the entire complex."

She stared at the long tunnels and tiny chambers. "Looks like an ant colony."

"You can enter any of these rooms. Cafeteria, laboratory, computer room, laundry, everything you'll need."

"Everything but sky."

"You won't be leaving for a few days. Cell phones don't work but the mayor has an outside line in his office. All the computers have Internet connections, carefully monitored by a security team. I can escort you outside for emergencies only."

"Thanks, Dan." Paul took Kendra by the elbow. "I think she's all right for now."

Agent Cameron smiled through straight white teeth. "Paul O'Keefe, right? Belong to a few radical organizations."

"I guess. If you consider Greenpeace radical."

"Scientists for the Preservation of Earth. Americans for Responsible Government."

"Your point?"

Cameron looked at Paul, his eyes icy and emotionless. "No point, Doctor."

CHAPTER 12

THE SMELL OF FORMALDEHYDE was a comforting memory to Kendra as she checked out the laboratory. The squared walls were painted white and the lab was well stocked. There were bottles of dead ants with their legs to the ceiling and live ones feverishly cleaning antennas. Microscopes, beakers and test tubes lined black lacquer counters. Inside an open closet she could see a stack of boxes containing ant-proof suits labeled BUG OUT, and she wondered if there was a field trip in her future.

And then there was Paul. Despite the underlying rage of being kidnapped, Kendra felt excited to be near him again. There was no denying the fluttering in her stomach. It felt less like butterflies than a flock of seagulls fighting over the last clam. She was disgusted at the way she licked her lips to make them glossier, instead of turning on her heels and walking out.

"Well, well," she said smugly. "Everything we need to save an entire city."

"I stocked the place myself."

"An actual electron microscope," she quipped. "Guess you thought of everything."

"Yes," he answered, eyeing her from head to toe. "I did."

She finally snapped. "Paul, what the hell is going on!"

The spell was broken.

"You heard what they said."

"I heard an utterly preposterous story. The very idea that ants can be trained like—like circus monkeys is ridiculous." She folded her arms and blurted, "I don't know why you chose me of all people to *assist* you, but if you were hoping for a cheery reunion, it's too late. You blew it."

"I blew it? You're the one who ran off to the desert. Besides, it didn't take you long to get over me and move on to the next guy."

"Are you talking about Jeremy?" Her cheeks flushed. "That was a corporate merger."

"It was a merger, all right. The ant community is pretty small, Kendra. You had an affair."

"It's not an affair when your divorce papers are sitting in the mailbox."

Paul was getting mad. "Can you forget about yourself for a moment?" he shot back. "We're having a little problem here with some very scary insects."

Kendra let out a bark of laughter. She had already decided she wanted no part of this charade. It had been her view for quite some time that the world was going to hell and she had no intention of wading into the mess. National politics over oil, taxes and health care had reached the brink of insanity. Global warming. Genocide. Jihad. A neglectful husband. Mutant ants from hell sounded like just another man-made catastrophe.

"I understand you're angry," he said, trying to sound calm.

"*Angry?*" Kendra was fuming. "Why would I be angry!" She snatched up a specimen jar and the tiny ant braced itself. "I'm in the desert counting ants when Agent Double-O Psycho nabs me, only to find out my ex-husband—"

"I didn't think you'd come," he cut in and swiped the jar from her hand.

"You were right!" Kendra picked up a test tube and flung it across the room. It smashed into the wall.

"Oh, that's real mature," Paul said.

There it was. The same patronizing tone she despised. Kendra picked up another test tube and tossed it like a Frisbee. The sound of shattering glass had no calming effect at all.

"*Jesus,* Kendra. You're a *scientist,* for chrissakes."

She answered with a defiant poke to his chest. "I was about to make the greatest breakthrough in modern entomology. Save billions of dollars in lost crops, not to mention a dozen lives a year!"

"What about the lives right here! There are seven people dead already."

Kendra stiffened and the shouting match came to a dizzying halt. The words spun in her mind but could hardly register.

"Listen to me, Kendra!" Paul was all at once reeling. "This species is like nothing we've ever seen. It's a freaking horror show. The mayor wants this thing quiet and *I can't do this without you.*"

Kendra let out a shock of air. *"Can't* do this without me?" Even under the direst circumstances, it wasn't like Paul to call in the cavalry. He had made his mark with the contributions of extremely bright minds in science but he never, ever, asked for volunteers. Kendra picked up the specimen jar and addressed a small fire ant. "What have you done with the real Dr. O'Keefe?"

"Okay," he admitted. "I've been a jerk. Too busy unlocking the secrets of the ant world with my own brilliant thoughts to consider anyone else's." His expression turned earnest. "I've changed, Kendra . . . and yes, I'm asking for help."

She wanted to make a run for it, let him know what it felt like to be abandoned. But there was no denying that a huge crisis was lurking and her professional ethics told her that desertion wasn't an option. "Maybe you have changed," she said with a reluctant shrug. "So, let's see these monsters."

Paul appeared to spring back to life, keenly adjusting the microscope settings, moving with his usual flair. He was in his element and Kendra was slightly amused. "It's really quite fantastic what they did with this crossbreed. They're genetically altered to be bigger, faster, deadlier."

Kendra peered through the lens and her eyes widened in disbelief. "What the hell is this thing?" she gasped. The strange mutant head was tilted up, enormous mandible spread open in a roar.

He threw out his hands. "That's what I'm talking about."

She flipped the microscope to "view" and the ant image lit up on the adjoining monitor. The body was similar to any worker ant's; thin, oblong and segmented with six multi-jointed legs, but it was abnormally long, over an inch. The head was tremendous and skull-shaped. "A face only a mother could love," she said and scanned the entire body at highest resolution. "The exoskeleton has properties I've never seen. That's some suit of armor."

"Indeed it is. I broke down the chemistry and found an enormously active enzyme similar to laccase-two."

She arched a brow. "Interesting."

The laccase-2 gene had been studied by entomologists for decades. Research showed that the enzyme was responsible for hardening the cuticles of newly molted beetles, providing remarkable strength and flexibility. The discovery was leading to a deeper understanding of insect defenses, as well as the development of numerous commercial products, such as football helmets and lightweight shields for aircraft and military armor.

"Laredo must have figured out a way to supercharge the protein. The exoskeletons can be crushed with some effort, but pesticides flow off like water on a duck's back. Therefore, you're correct—toxins are out of the question."

"So what are the Three Stooges doing here?" she said, referring to the men in black.

Paul averted his eyes. "I gave them all contracts—before realizing what we were dealing with." There was an uncomfortable silence. "Pesticide companies have a place in science, Kendra. Why do you always make them out to be the bad guys? You can thank a dozen insecticides for helping to feed half the world's population, which would go hungry—"

She let out a disgruntled breath, annoyed they were still having this same conversation.

"All right," he said, gesturing defeat. "It was wrong."

Kendra looked satisfied enough and returned to the specimen. Even with calculation tools built into the scope, measuring ant parts was exceedingly difficult, but she was a pro and rattled off each astonishing number to the smallest micrometer. However, sheer size was not the only puzzle.

"The gaster—that's a lot of venom."

"You're right, and it's highly concentrated. A couple of hits could blind a person."

"The claws are unusual. Looks like three hooks instead of two, like a thumb or something."

"Better grip," he replied. "Just like Siafu, they build intricate bridges. Millions can link together like cables spanning a hundred feet. Plus, they're fast. Based on their locomotory behavior and morphology, I estimate they can hit speeds of eight miles per hour."

"So they can outrun most humans."

"It's just a theory at the moment. Along with my calculation that they can chew through leather." He tapped a pencil point toward the image of the head. "Take a look at those jaws. They spring shut at two hundred and forty kilometers an hour, which is by far the fastest body limb movement of any creature on earth. We're talking about a bite force of nine hundred times their body weight."

Kendra focused on the mandibles and inner mouth, where two long spikes protruded from each side like black sipping straws. "Are these stylets?"

"Ah. Now we come to the scary part." Paul leafed through autopsy reports until he came to a photo of a dead schoolteacher. He frowned over the image, rubbing his beard. "The ants are depositing some kind of chemical into the body that produces a heinous reaction. It acts like a digestive enzyme but it moves through the bloodstream like a deadly virus. Looks more like Ebola than ant venom. Shuts down the organs, ravages the brain, capillaries disintegrate. Finally the internal system just dissolves."

"So, you're saying these insects liquefy their victims?"

"Just like normal ants—but on a far greater scale. A couple of bites or stings aren't lethal, but a hundred can kill a normal-size adult in seconds."

Kendra stared at the photo. On the floor of a child's nursery, a man lay in a contorted position wearing shorts and a bloody sock. His gray body was bloated and streaked red. A mass of yellow sclera tissue lay on the floor near his face, pushed out of the eye socket by dark coagulated blood, his mouth stretched open in a scream of impending death.

Kendra had seen photos of ant stings, disturbing pictures of farm animals and even human corpses covered in ants, but nothing remotely resembled this victim. She felt a shiver of

cold terror and dropped the photo on the counter, not knowing what to say.

"This is bad," was all she could finally muster.

"Yeah." Paul took her hand and led her across the room.
"Now for the demonstration."

"Demonstration?"

CHAPTER 13

FIVE TEENAGERS IN BLACK descended like bats at dusk. They crossed the wide intersection of Columbus Circle at Fifty-ninth Street into Central Park, under the awakening glow of old gas lamps.

Leading the posse was Tabor Drake, a sixteen-year-old boy who was tall and striking with milky white skin and ebony makeup streaked across his lips and cheekbones. Long hair, dyed boot black, fell loosely over his forehead. His trench coat and pants were militant, oversized and, of course, black. Only the red teardrop tattooed below his eye saved him from a monochromatic fate. Tabor's Goth followers were clad in equally gloomy attire.

Except for Jimmy Porter.

Porter wasn't a true member of the group, not yet anyway, and he lagged behind the others. While they walked swiftly with purpose, he trudged behind hesitantly, adjusting a backpack crammed with wooden shovels. The handles continuously hit him in back of the head. His chubby build and short blond hair set him apart from the others, as much as his yellow Spiderman T-shirt and khaki shorts.

Porter cast a pleading eye toward Sarah, his only ally in the group, but she was struggling to keep up her own cool facade. In truth, Sarah thought that their plan to sneak a jarful of killer ants into the teacher's lounge was *so junior high,* but at fifteen years old she rarely trusted her own opinion. She stared down at her feet clomping around in heavy black boots and ripped fishnet stockings and thought maybe she would join a different group on Monday. Maybe the Granolas. She looked good in tie-dye.

The vast plaza at the park entrance eventually broke into narrow trails. The ground was covered with the first signs of spring, creeping plants, moss and ferns, and the darkening sky was hidden by overhead canopies of sprouting oak branches that dimmed the last bit of evening light. It was dead quiet. Not even the sound of wild birds, so typical for this time of year, was heard from the treetops.

"Didn't you guys see all the signs? They said, 'Warning! Park Closed!'" Porter croaked. "We should go back."

Tabor kept walking. "Shut up, Porker."

"It's *Porter*."

"No. It's *Porker*."

"I just mean, it'll be dark soon."

"Duh. That's the whole point," said Chloe, Tabor's sort-of girlfriend, an even more female version of himself. "They only come out at night, doofus."

Porter puckered his face. "You know they killed, like, seven people already. They're probably gonna kill us too."

"Don't believe what you read in newspapers, doofus. Fire ants only, like, sting and bite. The teachers are gonna freak."

"We're gonna die."

"Sarah, what's the deal with your fat friend?" Chloe snapped. "He won't shut up."

A boy with three nose rings had taken the lead. When he stopped and pointed, the others fell in behind. "That's the spot. Harley said they were crawling all over the place." He was motioning to the Gapstow Bridge, a stone archway over the pond.

Its thick, craggy vines snaked across the bedrock like bony fingers. The ground on both sides of the bridge sloped ten feet to the pond.

Tabor walked toward the bridge, brushing back the tall grass and kicking over small stones. The other joined in, scraping their sneakers across patches of dirt and weeds, pulling back fronds with a light hand. Someone had a can of bug spray and the kids passed it around, misting their boots.

"Here, take these," Tabor said and pulled a handful of rubber bands from his pocket. "Wrap them around your sleeves and pant cuffs to keep out the ants. I know all about these bastards."

Porter looked down hopelessly at his T-shirt and shorts. While the others looped tight rubber bands over their wrists and ankles, he saturated his body with OFF!

"Yo, Porker." Tabor stuck out his hand, fingers snapping. "Give me a shovel."

Porter let the backpack drop from his shoulder and chose a short but heavy spade. He handed it to Tabor and whispered, "They're gonna kill us, man."

"Hey. Shut the fuck up," Nose Ring answered. "There's five of us against—ants."

Tabor noticed a large area of dirt where the grass didn't grow. He marched straight back to Porter and handed him the shovel. "You. Over there—dig."

"No way."

Tabor turned to Sarah. "You are *so* out."

She seemed to deflate. "Jimmy, just dig."

Porter reluctantly dragged his feet to the designated spot. He raked the shovel gently over the soil as if it were a minefield, but found the dirt was soft and loose and balled into pellets light as sawdust. So he dug with more gusto, taking a scoopful here and another there. Porter speared the ground one last time and the spade flew from his hand, plunged into nothingness.

The earth had gobbled up half his shovel.

Porter blinked hard. "I think we hit some kind—"

Suddenly, the ground caved in like a sinkhole around him. The boy screamed and flung his hands in the air, falling into clouds of dirt, buried up to his chest in soil. Porter was invisible, just a coughing sound as the dust settled. Somehow, he managed to hoist his trapped arms free and wiped the grit from his mouth with his dirty fingers.

"Shit," he cried.

The others just stared, mouths gaping.

"Hey, you assholes, get me outta here!"

Tabor took the first wary step, while the other kids fell back. He shuffled closer and paused a good three feet from Porter's head, then dropped onto one knee, staring right into the face of the filthy boy.

Tabor burst out laughing.

"It's not funny," Porter wheezed.

The fearless leader thought it was hysterical, but found himself laughing alone. "He's fine," he yelled over his shoulder to the others. "I always wondered how long the surface of the earth could hold your fat ass, Porker."

Tabor held out a hand to the boy, bracing for a ton of weight. But as their fingers touched, Porter jerked back violently—and screamed. Tabor scurried away in horror as the boy continued howling cries of excruciating pain.

Beneath the soil, millions of ants were blasting tunnels to the boy's body like desperate prospectors to a gold mine. They reached the torso and thighs in no time. Claws broke through supple skin effortlessly, foraged through muscle and ravaged their way inside the body.

High-pitched barks of agony echoed to the edges of the park as Porter screamed and dug his fingernails into the dirt, staring in wide-eyed hysteria. His hands came up soaked in blood.

Tabor once again reached out for Jimmy's hand, but the trapped boy flew into convulsions, arms thrashing about wildly as the red stain seeped up his T-shirt to his neck.

The ground was shifting below the teenagers and they backed away, slowly at first, and then they took off in a run. They shrieked with fright and cries of warning. They ran toward the park entrance and left the boy dying.

All except Sarah.

Instinctively, she dropped to her knees and began to dig Jimmy Porter out. Her fingers were stained with Jimmy's blood as she clawed through the dirt, but it was useless. His arms disappeared. He sank to his chin. There was a gurgling in his throat right before it swelled shut. When he looked at Sarah, a peaceful expression settled over his face, blood pooled in his eyes and a trickle of pink foam dripped from his nose.

Then Jimmy Porter sank into the earth. Gone.

Sarah rose as the ground vibrated under her feet. She staggered down the steep embankment to the pond, arms turning like windmills to keep her balance. The sky turned dark and the air was suddenly cold. Standing on a rock at the water's edge, she hugged her waist and clenched her chattering teeth, too terrified to even cry. Behind her, every plant and blade of grass seemed to quiver with life.

They're coming. They're going to kill me.

Sarah waded into the freezing water.

Ants can't swim, they can't swim.

She continued down a steep decline, taking long strides in the water, boots sloshing through the mud like suction cups.

Panic gripped Sarah as the water reached her chest. Imaginary monsters nipped at her hands and elbows.

A thick blob swelled along the shoreline like molten lava, dark and unformed. The creature stretched across the bank under Sarah's gaze, driving her farther into the pond and filling the air with a strange song.

Kerka kerkosh ker kerkosh kerka kerkosh ker kerkosh.

The sound grew louder, from every direction, and she spun around, unsure where to go. The *thing* that blanketed the shore was now in the water, cast out wide like a fishing net. It floated across the surface, straight toward her, tiny forms linked together.

Sarah swam under the bridge, taking erratic strokes. The icy water slowed her muscles, froze her lungs, and she sucked in small gasps of air. Faint moonlight beckoned her to the other side of the overpass. She was shivering like mad, but the sound had stopped for a moment. Out of fright, she dove underwater, but a moment later broke the surface.

That's when the floating beast surged toward her from every shore. She paddled back toward the bridge, teeth chattering so loud she couldn't hear the strange sound anymore. Her legs retreated sluggishly in the mud until she was directly under the archway, hyperventilating and muttering to herself.

Help me. Oh God, help me.

A black speck fell onto Sarah's cheek. She peered up at the bridge, no longer able to breathe, and a million ants rained down on her.

CHAPTER 14

"I'VE BEEN DOING QUITE a few experiments but getting nowhere." Paul stood in front of a glass tank and pried off the lid, releasing the putrid odor of dead rat.

Kendra peered into the tank, holding her breath. Swarms of ants smothered the remaining fur and flesh of a single rodent. They tunneled deep into its guts and black holes that used to be pink eyes.

"Plain-old African Siafu," said Paul, seeming less repulsed than Kendra. He sealed the lid tight. "As expected, they killed their prey in minutes. So what about this new species—Siafu Moto? Since I'm using rats in my experiments, we should get the same reaction."

He snatched an empty plastic tank off the counter, strolled to the back of the lab and stooped down in front of a small knee-high door. When he opened the latch, another pungent smell wafted into the room: cedar chips and food pellets. Inside the closet were a couple of metal cages filled with common white lab rats. He chose a fat one that nearly bit him before he dropped it into the tank.

"*Rattus Norvegicus*," he said. "A nice juicy one."

Paul brought it back to the counter and picked up a bottle of brown ants. He unscrewed the lid, dangling the bottle over the tank. "Now here's what happens when you introduce a yummy meal to Siafu Moto."

Kendra gave a look of disgust as he poured the enormous ants over the rat. Nothing happened. A few took a leisurely stroll down the fur, but mostly they stood still. One ant crawled along the tail and was quickly eaten by the hungry rodent.

"All the specimens have responded the same way," he said. "They don't eat or hunt. Just scurry around in a daze."

"Why don't they attack?"

"I'll tell you why," he said, raising a brow. "Ready for this? They don't have alarm pheromones. I tested all of them for every pyrazine. Shook them till they were nearly dead, but not a drop of fighting chemical."

"That doesn't make sense. They're attacking people."

"None of this makes sense."

"So maybe the ants don't communicate with chemicals."

"Actually, they carry all the other normal pheromones: primer, signal, trail, aggregation. Not to mention they have extremely sensitive antennae. I ran an EAG using trail phero-mones and their response was off the charts."

Paul set up an electroantennogram by removing an antenna from one of the Siafu Moto. He lodged it between two elec-trode devices and sent the antenna a whiff of pheromone ex-tract, secreted on a test strip. An enormous electrical activity registered. Paul tried it with other test strips. "As you can see, the antenna proves highly sensitive to all colony pheromones, as well as rat and human odors."

Kendra nodded. "So they have all the functions of normal ants, except they can't attack."

"But they do attack." His fingers tapped the glass tank, but it failed even to startle the docile ants. "Perhaps they've been de-signed to fight as a group, not individually—and only at tasks they were programmed for."

Programmed for? Kendra thought. Ants couldn't be taught

how to walk a straight line. They weren't trainable. They acted on instinct and chemical secretions. Working for the needs of the colony, not some group of ecoterrorists, was an uncompromising principle ingrained in their DNA.

"I know it's crazy," said Paul, reading her thoughts, "but I'm well past crazy. We have to assume they've done it somehow. Laredo and his scientists must have found a way to program behavior down to the DNA level."

"They just get freakier every minute," said Kendra. "If only we had access to Laredo's experiments."

Paul was thinking the same thing. He didn't believe the army destroyed all the files on the Siafu Moto, and he couldn't imagine the ants were created by ecoterrorists. The amount of time, money and resources would be enormous, and they would have employed the most brilliant entomologists in the world. Paul had never even heard of Dr. Laredo.

Kendra cocked her head, thinking out loud. "The army claims they eat only rats and people, so maybe we can starve them. Kill off the rats and evacuate the people."

"Those ants are eating more than rats and people," Paul replied. "I've been doing some digging of my own and I don't like what I found."

"What's that?"

"Nothing. Not a single living thing."

Three days ago, Paul had enlisted the help of a buddy, Jack Carver at the USDA's Department of Urban Entomology, and a bunch of his newfangled field study equipment. Paul regarded the older entomologist as the best in the business, next to himself. Jack was a laid-back kind of guy who had taken to wearing flannel, blue jeans and a canvas hat full of fishing hooks, to remind him that retirement was less than a year away. His white trailer had pulled into Battery Park, loaded with computers and a six-wheeled explorer, which looked vaguely similar to a Martian rover and was able to drill through pavement and quarry soil. Its robotic arms were equipped with life sensors and a video ANTCAM that gave close-up views of insect activity.

The sun had set over the grassy field. Inside the trailer, Paul sat stiffly in a three-piece suit. Jack slouched at the control panel with his feet up, fishing hat over his eyes, peering down at the monitor as the explorer dug up the park lawn.

A couple FBI agents had parked next to the trailer. They had been following Paul around for days, which annoyed him no end.

Two other entomologists were assisting in the dig, young women who eyed Paul as though he were a god. They had read all his books, attended every lecture and followed Paul's career as if he were some rock star. They kept sneaking glances while working the rover controls.

"Don't gawk, ladies," Jack warned them. "Staring at such brilliance can burn your retinas."

They laughed, but Paul clenched his jaw in embarrassment. The last couple of weeks he had learned nothing useful about the ants. Having to call upon his most respected colleagues was grossly upsetting. Paul tried to focus on the video screen—the black silhouette of the New York City skyline, the floodlights and camera boom and heaps of dirt being lifted by the excavator and poured out in dusty heaps. Once the pit was three feet deep, the robotic arm lowered a life sensor. It could distinguish heat, movement, noise and chemical secretions at a micro level. Any living tissue would appear as an infrared glow, with colorful rings of red, yellow and blue. It could detect every worm and beetle, down to the smallest egg of a mite.

The team was expecting to sift through a huge assortment

of specimens. It was the time of year when all the parks would be teeming with an explosion of life: birds, tiny mammals and crawly things. They started in Battery Park at a spot known for its fertile soil. If they were lucky, the rover would unearth a Siafu Moto colony, possibly a coveted queen. At the very least, they hoped their intrusive equipment would coax the ants into an observable attack that might lead to an important discovery about their behavior.

Everyone in the van was silent as the sensor moved slowly across the pit. It picked up good reception on the video screen. The rocky crust, dense soil and specks of glittery particles appeared in various tones of black, gray and white.

That was it. No color. No Siafu Moto. No sign of life— anywhere.

Jack bolted upright and scanned the pit, fumbling with the controls. "That's astounding. In thirty years I've never come across lifeless soil. Not in any city we've studied."

"Keep digging, Jack." Paul turned to his friend, pale-faced, eyes bloodshot. He hadn't slept for three days and his hands were shaking.

"You look like doo-doo," Jack told him.

"Just keep digging."

The excavator swung around and the robotic arm dug deeper into the soil, finally hitting bedrock. The life sensor showed no change in the image.

"Not even a pill bug," Jack gasped. "Impossible."

Paul gritted his teeth. "We'll find another spot. It's a big island. We can dig all night."

Jack shrugged. "You better cut me in on the reward, Kemo Sabe."

The trailer followed the rover all across Manhattan and the FBI agents followed the trailer. The ANTCAM was lowered again and again: Central Park, Bryant Park and all along the riverfronts. Each time they watched the image on the monitor Paul's breath would stop with a sense of anticipation, but each time his hopes were dashed.

Jack was flabbergasted. "A city with no bugs? This could destroy the whole ecosystem, maybe even collapse the town."

"We keep digging," Paul insisted. The hours went on and Paul grew impatient, and then frantic. Worst-case scenarios filled his head and a feeling of incompetence he'd never known. It just wasn't possible that he'd sat in a trailer all night, looking at nothing, knowing nothing and unable to answer the most basic questions about the ants.

What the fuck?

All week long these beasts were emerging, attacking New Yorkers, and yet he couldn't find a single egg. He was chewing on white knuckles, staring at the black monitor, and began to wonder if this was some act of God. Perhaps this was personal. Some kind of punishment for dealing with the devil, looking for fame and glory under the guise of helping humanity.

The women were staring at Paul, murmuring to each other with a look of concern, as he fell into the grip of a severe panic attack. He shot up like a rocket, threw open the trailer door and raced across the grass, his jacket and tie flittering in the wind. He headed for the rover, which was digging a wide pit.

"Gosh darn it," Jack bellowed. "Shut it down!"

One of the women pulled the plug and the robotic arms dropped lifelessly.

In wingtip shoes, Paul dove into the pit and burrowed frantically into the earth. The heat sensor picked up the warmth of his body and Jack watched Paul glow infrared on the monitor, arms flailing in blue, yellow and red rings like some demonic alien.

Paul heard nothing but his own breath as he plowed through the cold, damp ground. He didn't notice the headlights splash his face, the FBI agents getting out of the car or the sounds of doors slamming. His hands were raw and fingertips numb and he realized he'd hit upon a sharp object. Paul pulled up the skull of a small mammal, stopped only briefly to look at it, and then excavated a dozen more skeletons, all picked clean and gleaming white in the glare. He was panting hard, digging fiercely, and seemed completely unaware that he was muttering a sting of profanities.

"Dr. O'Keefe!" someone shouted.

Paul abruptly turned around, his chest rising and falling.

In the headlights of the sedan was an FBI agent, legs spread wide, fists clenched at his sides. He had an authoritative voice. "Sir—could you get out of that hole? Please."

Paul sunk down in a pile of dirt. His trembling fingers cradled the skull of a rabbit. At his knees were the bones of numerous squirrels, moles, birds and a dog.

"Paul?" Jack gazed down at his friend with kind eyes and held out a hand. "Get up, Paul."

"You didn't find a single ant?" Kendra asked. "I imagine the mayor loved that bit of news."

"Oh yeah." Paul narrowed his eyes. "The ants must have tunneled down deep, but they're in that soil, eating everything in sight."

"Why not just rats, like they were designed to eat?"

"Like all living creatures, they learn to adapt."

"Well, you can't eradicate a hundred million years of instinct in a twenty-five-year science experiment."

"There's only one question we have to answer." Paul strolled over to the tanks, thinking hard. He leaned over the Siafu Moto and tapped the glass again. "What makes them attack?"

Kendra collapsed onto a stool with her elbows on the counter. She stared at the ants, palms pressed to her forehead. An idea was forming and she pondered it out loud. "For two years they've been dormant, living on rat meat and furry creatures. Now suddenly they're surfacing, killing people. Why?"

"Running out of food, perhaps."

"What if they're just getting . . . *antsy?*"

"Oh, that's bad."

"Think about it. What makes ordinary Siafu surface?"

Paul's wheels were spinning too. He moved to the first tank, pointing a finger. "Siafu move out to hunt when the queen reaches full maturity. And then *bam,* first rainfall and they hit like a tidal wave, killing everything in their path."

"So if the queens mature this spring—"

"They'll hit all at once. Consuming a hundred thousand animal prey in just one night."

"You mean people," Kendra corrected.

"So let's hope it doesn't rain."

Kendra folded her arms at the disturbing thought. "Rain. The tides. The sun. It could be any natural trigger."

"Or we may be jumping to conclusions," Paul rubbed his beard, looking doubtful. "Hopefully those reports tomorrow—"

"Reports?" Kendra scoffed. "Reports are crap. The only way to destroy ants is by killing the queens." She walked into the closet and emerged with two Bug Out suits, tossed them on the table. "That means we have to go find one."

"Too dangerous."

"Same old Paul." Kendra sighed. "Try to think back to the actual work you did before you traded in your hiking boots for Italian leather."

Paul's voice was steady, but the tips of his expensive shoes retreated beneath the table. "Field study without research is kids stuff, Kendra. It's just playing in a sandbox."

"Well, I've been killing off colonies in that sandbox." Kendra let out a breath of frustration. "Paul, listen to me. I've discovered a combination of pheromones that entices the workers into killing off the queens, and then killing off each other."

"Really?" he asked, sounding only slightly interested. "Pheromone manipulation is hardly new. It's fraught with inconsistencies."

"It works, Paul. I focused on the queens' chemicals instead of the workers', and the entire colony responded. We wiped out nearly a dozen colonies in four months."

Paul's expression told Kendra he wasn't quite convinced.

"I'm pretty sure if we can find a queen by daylight, we can create enough synthetic duplicate to blanket the city and destroy the ants in two or three weeks. Maybe sooner, if we get Jack and the USDA involved."

He narrowed his eyes, mulling over the proposition.

"Are we here to kill ants or what?"

"Of course," Paul replied. "And I'd be more than happy to try your experiment, but capturing a queen is harder than finding a beetle in a haystack."

"Do you have any other ideas?"

"Actually, yes." He checked his watch. "We have a meeting right now with someone who might be able to locate those queens for us."

"Who's that?"

"Jeremy Rudeau."

Kendra was shocked. "Oh, Paul, you didn't."

"Don't blame me. The army wanted Jeremy on this." He sounded defensive. "You think I'd bring you two together myself? Hopefully he can add something useful to our efforts." Paul was suddenly vexed and started for the door. He glanced back at Kendra. "Coming?"

She exhaled and walked with Paul to meet the man who had put the final nail in the coffin of their marriage.

CHAPTER 15

JEREMY RUDEAU HAD ALL the makings of a movie star. He was tall and broad-shouldered with high cheekbones that always looked sun streaked, a strong jawline and a mane of black wavy hair. His pale gray eyes picked up every color in the room like a prism and his deep baritone voice added nicely to the package. Yet it wasn't just stunning good looks that sent Kendra's heart pounding, as she walked into the conference room and found Jeremy talking to the mayor. Seeing Paul and Jeremy together felt like getting caught with her hand in a cookie jar.

Jeremy paused midsentence and stood to greet them, extending a hand. "Paul, so good to see you." He noticeably brightened and said, "Kendra, I didn't realize you would be here as well. That's wonderful, wonderful."

He leaned in to kiss her. It was the casual cheek kind, but she noticed Paul straighten. Kendra was well aware that Paul and Jeremy had been bitter rivals since prep school. At Georgetown they had competed in fencing and the debate team. At Harvard, they became associate professors of entomology and vied for department chair. They wrote scientific papers disproving each other's theories. However, their biggest rivalry by far was Kendra. She had been dating Jeremy when she fell hard for Paul.

"Glad you could make it." Paul's voice sounded strained.

"Too happy to help, really. This is the craziest thing I ever heard. " Jeremy took his seat. "I was just about to explain the fundamentals of swarm intelligence to Mayor Russo."

The mayor waved a dismissive hand. "No offense, but you're a computer guy. How do you plan to kill real ants?"

"While it's true I haven't chosen the same route as Paul, studying ants down in the dirt," Jeremy smirked, "I am quite a shark at catching them. Or so I've been told."

"Don't be so modest, Jeremy." Paul's voice was laced with sarcasm. "You're by far *the* leader in the field of ant tracking." He turned to the mayor. "Jeremy uses computers to make simulated ants so he can figure out where the colonies nest. Sort of like a computer game developer. Really, he's the best in the business."

Jeremy smiled, seeming unaware of any mockery. "I don't know about that, but my company has had great success in all areas related to swarm intelligence."

"Swarm what?"

"Let me explain." Jeremy leaned in, his hands moving gracefully, accentuating each word. "The amazing thing about ants is that they have no leaders, no manager, no one giving orders. Yet they're able to accomplish all the complex tasks of a highly developed community, like food gathering, cleaning and defense. It's called self-organization and it's a concept that's hard for humans to fathom. Just imagine a football team with no coach, a ship with no captain, an army with no general. So how do they do it?" Jeremy held a dramatic pause. "Through a highly efficient method of chemical secretions called *phero-mones.*"

"Pheromones," the mayor repeated. "I knew that."

"Sure. It's a Greek word meaning 'carrier of excitement.'" Jeremy grabbed a pen from his shirt pocket and began drawing visual aids to illustrate his point. Kendra noted it was the silver Montblanc she had given him as a birthday gift years ago, and it made her feel edgy yet oddly touched. Inscribed down the barrel was a series of ones and zeros: *01101100 01101111 01110110 01100101 00100000 01101011 01100101 01101110 01100100 01110010 01100001*. Binary code for "Love, Kendra."

"Ants communicate thorough odors," Jeremy continued. "For example, an ant finds food and returns to the nest, leaving a tiny scent on the ground." He marked the paper with dots and arrows. "The smell leads other forager ants down the same trail, which they reinforce with new markings, making it stronger. By repeating the process with many ants in many different directions, the best route to the food is found."

Kendra leaned back in her chair, hoping to stay out of the conversation, all the while watching Jeremy's sexy dimples blink on and off as he spoke. There was no denying the killer body, and although he had proven quite adept in bed, he fell short of all other expectations. She turned to Paul and his dark brooding eyes under thick lashes, large fingers quietly drumming the table. It was never a contest. Ever since she'd met Paul, no man seemed to stack up.

"That brings us to the term swarm intelligence," Jeremy said. "By creating algorithms based on ant efficiency, my company saves other companies billions of dollars. For example, we developed computer programs for the United States Air Force, modeled from ant behavior, which can figure out things like how many drones are needed to swarm an area and take out ninety percent of the targets in half an hour."

Russo looked impatient. "That makes sense from a technology standpoint, but how can it solve our problems with real ants?"

"Let me tell you," Jeremy answered. "For the past twenty

years, the global infestation of deadly ants has skyrocketed, so we've been using these computer programs to figure out ways to destroy them. Five years ago, a supercolony of fire ants in the Yucca Valley had grown to over a hundred and fifty miles long, all the way up to Bakersfield; cut right though Edwards Air Force Base. Using supercomputers, we modified the swarm intelligence programs to emulate the ants—all from data gathered by Kendra and her company, Invicta."

Uh-oh, here it comes. Kendra slumped in her seat as Jeremy threw her a wink.

"Invicta has been supplying us with statistics on fire ants for years. We studied and analyzed video, charts and graphs, every piece of data from Kendra's field studies, then created millions of computerized ant models based on things like behavior, soil, weather, geography—*mating habits,*" he said, raising a brow.

Kendra could feel Paul glaring at her. She wanted Jeremy to *just stop talking,* so she blurted out, "Ants are very predictable in their habits. We were able to figure out which direction they would travel, colony size and, most important, the location of the nests. At that point we were able to dig up the queens."

"Kill the queen and you kill the colony," Paul said, looking at her.

"In other words," Jeremy said, shooting Paul a glance, "know your enemy and you can destroy him."

"Well, that is rule number one in the military," Russo replied.

"Exactly," Kendra said. "So using Paul's DNA samples and Jeremy's supercomputers we might be able to figure out the locations of the Siafu Moto nests."

"*Might,*" Paul stressed.

"Still, even if you find the nests," the mayor reasoned, "what good will it do? You said these ants are indestructible."

"Nothing is indestructible," Jeremy said. "It's just a matter of finding the right method to kill a particularly nasty opponent." His eyes lingered on Paul. "And of course, finding the right man for the job."

"Or woman," Kendra added. "I might be able to kill the queens with a technique I've developed. It has more to do with the manipulation of natural chemicals than creating a toxin. It's sort of like tricking the colonies into suicide."

"Is that right?" Russo asked. "Paul didn't mention it."

"Paul isn't too familiar with research outside his own," Jeremy said. "But Kendra has already killed off quite a few colonies with this method. It's very promising, very promising indeed. I'm certainly going to incorporate it into my business practices."

Kendra could almost feel Paul steaming, and suddenly wished she hadn't kept Jeremy so informed on her progress— but then quickly reconsidered: Why shouldn't she tell a colleague about her work when he was so interested, so *supportive* of her efforts?

The mayor turned to Jeremy. "You said that colony of ants you found was a hundred fifty miles long. What did you call it, a supercolony?

"That's right," Jeremy answered. "And we're looking at the same behavior in our New York variety. The largest supercolony ever discovered is a single colony of Argentine ants that stretches through Italy, France and Spain and then spans thousands of kilometers throughout Japan and California."

"Across continents?" the mayor asked, surprised.

"Yes. When scientists put the Argentine ants together with any other species, they fought to the death, but when they put the European variety with the species from Japan and California, they acted like old buddies. Even though they were separated by vast oceans, they had formed a global supercolony."

"Ants wear a waxy substance that they can smell on each other," Kendra added. "It's like those ants in Europe, California and Japan were all walking around in the same team uniform."

"So these ants could technically spread across the nation, and the world."

"Technically, yes," Jeremy said.

"It's even more frightening than you realize," Paul warned. "A supercolony is genetically homogenous. They recognize each other and cooperate with each other, and they kill off all the native insects in the area. From what I've discovered in the past few days, these ants are doing the same thing. Not just annihilating rats and people, but every living creature they come in contact with."

"Is that so?"

"Actually," Kendra said, "if we hope to kill the colony with pheromones, a supercolony might be easier to hit as a single unit."

"Especially if I can locate the nests," Jeremy added.

The mayor looked skeptical. "In my day, a bug crawled by and got the old boot stomp. But if you think this computer stuff might work against these freaks of nature, then you have my support."

Jeremy nodded with confidence. "It certainly can't hurt."

The mayor stood up, stretching an ache in his back. "Paul, can you stop by my office? I've got these confounding lab tests from all over the world that I'm anxious to unload."

"Sure." Paul gave Jeremy a weak nod and followed Russo out the door, not even glancing back at Kendra.

She wanted to follow Paul, but her legs felt like rubber. On top of that Kendra was hungry, starving, actually, and exhausted. It was hours since she'd devoured a small bag of pretzels and her blood sugar was in the basement. She longed for a shower, a nap and a serious conversation with Paul, but felt a pang of guilt at such selfish desires while a citywide crisis was lurking.

Now she was alone with Jeremy. She watched him whistling and unpacking boxes and was certain no lack of comforts would ever stop him from saving the world. He could probably go for days without anything but a computer and some hair gel.

"So, what did they tell you about this new species?" she asked.

"Siafu Moto?" He chuckled. "They told me it was some kind of ecoterrorist experiment that escaped. Apparently all the research was destroyed, and if I breathe a word of this I'll be thrown in prison."

"You believe all that?"

"The prison part, maybe. The rest, who knows?" He pushed aside a box and sat down next to Kendra, smelling clean and faintly of musk. The back of his neck flushed, a reaction to being near her, and his deep voice dropped to a coarse whisper. "Been a long time since Bakersfield, Kendra. The desert is fine, but robotics is the future."

"I'm sure you're right."

"It's not too late to get back in. We really miss that brilliant mind of yours." His fingers playfully flicked her short locks and he smiled as if pleased with the new look. "I miss you too."

Kendra turned from his gaze.

"So, I guess you're back with Paul," Jeremy said, standing up and busying his hands inside the box again.

"You guess wrong. I'm a consultant, same as you."

"Yeah, right." He clicked his tongue. "When are you going to realize Paul's work will always come before any woman. You deserve better, Kendra. You can't replace love with the social order of *Solenopsis Invicta*."

"What is it with you two? Why do you have to disagree about everything?"

Jeremy frowned and then snarled, "It's that blasted Paul and his stupid theories about ants. I hope this disaster proves him wrong, once and for all."

Kendra sighed, weary of their endless bouts.

"Any scientist in his right mind knows that ants are savage warriors, not to be admired. Let's be sensible. Other than man, ants are the only creatures on the planet that go to war. They fight for territory, food and sometimes no reason at all. They show no mercy. They take prisoners and make them into slaves. Kendra, ants are no better than we are."

"You're talking about a small number of species. Most ant colonies get along fine."

He shook his head vehemently. "If this catastrophe proves anything, it's that Paul O'Keefe is full of crap."

She forced a smile. "Let's just hope you can find those queens."

He seemed to calm a bit. "My technicians are setting up Gwendolyn now."

Kendra figured Gwendolyn was one of Jeremy's supercomputers. He had a habit of naming them after women he fell in love with. She wondered if he still owned the prized Cray-2 that he renamed Kendra when they were dating.

"We should have the entire DNA strand soon. You want to sit in?"

"No thanks. My focus is anatomy. You know—the actual ants." She stood, ready to leave, but he caught her wrist.

"If Paul hadn't come between us . . ."

Kendra could see the hurt in his expression. Things were never right with Jeremy. His jealousy of Paul could be maddening, but there was something sweet underneath his bombastic nature. Kendra realized she had failed not just one relationship but two, and touched Jeremy's cheek. "I'm sure it would have been wonderful," she said and headed toward the door. "See you around the watercooler."

"Looking forward to it."

CHAPTER 16

PAUL SAT IN THE mayor's office, across from Russo. It was a perfect replica of his study in Gracie Mansion, adorned with cherrywood walls, leather furniture, marble tables and a collection of antique guns in gilded frames. It gave the appearance of a stately office, one of a mighty municipal warrior, instead of an underground hideout padded with six inches of steel.

Paul shifted uncomfortably in his snug wooden chair. In any laboratory field or lecture hall he was a voice of authority, a tutor among colleagues. But now he had the feeling of being back in the principal's office. A nine-year-old caught with a locker full of spiders, ladybugs and termites, forced to sit in front of a domineering man listening to lectures on the dangers of bringing vicious animals to school.

Russo pushed a stack of papers toward Paul. "Here you go."

Paul stared, daunted at the reports, but didn't pick them up. No doubt they all had reached the same conclusion. Besides, he'd finally mustered enough courage to confront the mayor and didn't want to lose momentum. "I think Kendra is right about evacuating the city. We're gambling with a lot of lives."

"Now, Paul. We've been down this road before." Russo waved a dismissive hand. "It's my gamble, not yours. This is my city, my people and my responsibility." He leaned back with a trace of sympathy. "I'm a military man, you know.

Served four years in Iraq. I understand the casualties of war when you're facing an enemy, human or not. It's painful, sure, but you don't risk the lives of many just to save a few."

"What if it's not a few? What if things get worse? We should be preparing for a possible disaster. Kendra and I have a theory that the ants might actually launch—"

"Whoa, whoa, slow down, Paul." Russo held up a palm. "Why do you think we're all down in this bunker? We *are* following emergency procedures. I'm fully staffing this place. By Monday we'll be able to completely run Manhattan from underground. But evacuating civilians? We'll cross that bridge when we come to it."

"I think we have come to it."

"Hey, you're the one who told me you could get rid of these bugs. I've given you all the authority, unlimited resources— just do it."

"It isn't that easy. We haven't even been able to figure out *why* they attack."

"Well, that's why I hired you. To figure them out and kill them. I didn't hire you to run around the city like those other lunatics, panicking the public. You're different, Paul. You understand business and finance."

He said it so offhandedly. Paul was taken aback at the idea that the mayor would put money ahead of human lives. He tried to sound more forceful. "I have to insist that you're grossly underestimating the threat to this city. We need to make the facts public. At least that will free our consciences if anyone else gets hurt."

"Free whose conscience? I don't have a problem with mine."

Paul blinked back his anger. He fought off his role as a scientist always to reveal the truth. What exactly was his role? It was all so confusing. He was part of a team, brought in by the mayor to solve a crisis without causing a citywide panic, yet he was tired of the lies, the cover-ups, evading the press. "We have a moral obligation to tell people the truth."

"What truth is that?" the mayor asked flippantly.

"That New Yorkers are on the dinner menu of a trillion insects, thanks to the United States military."

"That's funny, Paul. You have a real gift for comedy—if you think going public is an option."

Finally, Paul appealed to the bottom line. "What about our legal obligation? If you have no moral qualms, then consider the enormous liability to the victims."

"Our asses are covered by the Homeland Security Act. This falls under federal jurisdiction, notably the United States Army, and believe me, I'm getting plenty of pressure from those bozos to keep the lid on this."

"So that's it? You're rolling over for the general?"

Russo was losing patience. "What do you propose we do? You want to be responsible for the stampede out of town? It took me four years to get our fiscal house in order, now you want to balance a ten-billion-dollar deficit next year?" He stood up and strolled around the desk with a hearty grin. "Come on, Paul, you said so yourself, these deaths are probably isolated incidents. You didn't find a single colony."

"I was wrong. We know they're out there. Hoards of freak insects created by some ecoterrorist experiment that I didn't even know about."

"Well, now you do. So take a look at these reports and think about it for a couple of days. Then I expect you to come back with some real solutions. If you can't kill these ants, I don't know who can."

Paul walked out of the office feeling the mayor's hand on his back. Russo nearly pushed him past his secretary. As they reached the hallway, Paul started to speak but the mayor shoved some folders into his hands. "Don't forget the reports, huh? I'm sure there's something useful in there. And we have dozens more coming in tonight."

The door slammed shut and Paul stood alone in the hall-way, once again feeling like he was back in the third grade.

CHAPTER 17

KENDRA WALKED INTO THE laboratory, where Paul was feigning deep interest in a computer screen. He immediately forgot his trouncing by the mayor and replaced it with thoughts of jealousy.

"So what were you and the illustrious Rudeau discussing?"

"Usual ant chitchat." Kendra busied herself with an assortment of glass slides. This was not the time to be making marital confessions, but she felt an overwhelming need to confront Paul, to talk about the affair, get it out of the way once and for all.

Kendra took a breath. "Paul. Jeremy and I—"

"Let's not go there." He stopped her with a raised palm.

"Fine." She moved closer, but he eased back. "So tell me, why is he here?"

"Jeremy? I told you, to help us find the queens."

She gave him a sideways glance.

"Like I said, the army wanted him here."

The lab was suddenly stifling and Kendra felt a need for unsterilized oxygen. "Is there a way out of this tomb?"

"We're not supposed to leave."

Her eyes were pleading.

Paul held out a hand. "Let's see that map."

* * *

It felt like they were walking in circles. Paul continually turned the map of the bunker upside down and then right side up, scratching the side of his head. "Right . . . no left," he kept muttering. Kendra fought the urge to confiscate the map, having learned that men had fragile egos when it came to directions. Choose your battles, she told herself as they headed toward the south end, the deepest part of the bunker, composed mostly of bedrock tunnels with few working lights. It was dead quiet, musty and dark, but according to the diagram this passage was the only place, besides the elevators, marked with an exit sign.

"That must be it," Paul said. At the end of the tunnel was a steel door cut into bedrock and a sign marked NO ACCESS— AUTHORIZED PERSONNEL ONLY. A sensor for a card key was placed beside the door, along with a final warning that entering was strictly forbidden without authorization. Paul took out his ID.

"Sure you're authorized?" Kendra asked.

"We'll know in a second."

He slid the plastic through the scanner and the light blinked red. He tried again; still red. He turned it around, upside down, rubbed it on his pants and bent it straighter; red, red, red.

"Damn." He sat down and leaned against the cold metal door.

Kendra took the card from his hand and glided it gently through the slot. The light flashed green. The door slid open with a *swish*.

"Ah. Must have loosened it," he said, as they crouched through the doorway.

They were at the bottom of a circular pit dug from the earth. A black light in a metal cage gave their skin a blue zombie-like sheen that matched the glistening surface of the rough bedrock walls. Kendra's white shirt and Paul's lab coat glowed bright violet. There was a damp, clammy texture to the air, along with the sound of a slow water drip somewhere.

"Where the heck are we?" Kendra asked, her voice rising into an echo.

"The end."

"The end of what?"

"The end of the bunker," he said, looking at the diagram. "I suppose this is the way out for any survivors of a nuclear catastrophe."

"There's no elevator or even a door."

"No. Just a hatch, way up at the top."

"Where?"

"Up the ladder," he said, pointing to the map. "Far end of the wall."

She walked over to a steel ladder painted red and looked up into the darkness, already feeling dizzy. "Wonder how high it goes?"

"Mayor said we're three hundred feet below sea level."

"Great."

"I can promise you sky at the top. It looks like all we have to do is open a hatch door and you're out in the cool air."

"Yeah, like you opened the last door."

"Hey, we could go back to the ant maze, hunker down in the laboratory and share a bologna sandwich."

"Now you're being an ass. Let's go."

They began to climb.

Night had fallen. The horizon was a marvelous smear of pink and lavender, the sun just a sliver between two skyscrapers.

Paul and Kendra emerged from the bunker onto the roof five stories above the streets. She was out of breath and shaking from the climb. A cold wind chilled the air but the blacktop was still warm and spongy. Kendra breathed deeply into the breeze, relieved to be outside again.

"How does it feel?" Paul shouted over the wind.

"Great. But it's cold."

He took off his lab coat and swung it gently over her shoulders. Kendra turned from him, feeling suddenly self-conscious, but Paul wrapped his arms around her waist. He leaned over her warm cheek and smelled the scent of honeysuckle and desert sand in her hair, touched the short blond locks and examined them curiously.

"New look?" he asked.

"New everything," she answered.

"Well . . . I like it."

Kendra was fairly sure he hated it, but was glad he hadn't said so.

"I missed you," he whispered.

"So what happened, Paul?"

"I don't know. My job. Your job. I guess whatever we had just slipped away."

No, she thought. Not for me. Kendra walked to the edge of the roof. Below, the East River shimmered like glass and to the west endless smokestacks stood against the deepest blue.

"Eight million people," she said. "What if the ants really do launch an attack? It might happen any day. Next rainfall, next high tide or some other trigger."

Paul followed her to the ledge. "We're going to destroy these monsters. Then maybe we can put us back together."

"I can't play second fiddle to your career again."

He nodded, knowing he'd screwed up the first time.

Kendra's gaze drifted to the skyline. Twilight brought out the stars in the east and they twinkled.

"I'd forgotten about the lunar eclipse." She was staring at the moon, an oversized sphere of orange, slowly darkening to red. "My students will have some crazy day with the ants. An eclipse always sends them into a . . . frenzy."

Kendra gaped at Paul, his face as stark as her own.

CHAPTER 18

THE FIRST SOLDIER APPEARED on Ninth Avenue, along a strip of soil lined with dogwood trees. From the center of a mound, a hole sprang open. The ant peered out, her over-sized head pivoting right and left like a water sprinkler. Over jewel-cut eyes stretched long antennas, wiggling fingers assessing wind currents and ground cover. Her exceedingly long jaws were shaped like elephant tusks and could pierce through a rattlesnake.

Like a leviathan from the deep, the ant emerged. Her sleek black body was immaculate, as she was compulsively neat and incessantly cleaning herself. The ant stood on hind legs and her head sprang up toward the cool night sky like that of a hunting dog sniffing for scent.

Prey was detected in every direction. It was a go.

In an instant, holes burst open and soldiers poured out like a treacherous river, at a rate of six hundred thousand per minute, swallowing the soil and small tufts of sprouted grass.

The regiment didn't have to go far. A man, known only as Phil, was passed out in a nearby alley with an empty bottle of vodka in his soiled lap. The procession gathered at his feet and spread around his body like the chalk tracing of a homicide victim. They climbed up his dirty tennis shoes and into the pant legs. They charged up his neck and across his torso, raiding a flimsy undershirt.

Phil was nearly covered in ants by the time the first bite was taken. Like razor-sharp hedge cutters, mandibles snipped and slashed, repeating the process again and again.

The old man stirred, and then groaned, as smaller soldiers rushed into the bloody area quickly, strong jaws chewing the softer inner flesh. Even 90-proof alcohol was not enough to anesthetize the pain. Phil flailed helplessly under a growing weight across his chest. But such thrashing was useless and brief. While the sensation from a thousand living stings was excruciating, paralysis from the toxins set in quickly, and all he could do was shriek inside his mind as the agony continued.

Ants spilled across his bloated face, searching for the most succulent flesh. The thin skin of the eyelids was a delicacy and they sliced it up quickly, boring into the soft eye tissue.

Some tunneled into nostrils, all the way to the sinus cavities and down the throat, while others pushed through parched lips, engorging the mouth and continuing down passageways to the lungs and esophagus.

Once these fragile areas were reached, the ants inserted their tubes and pumped their liquefying agents into the flesh. A new round of formic acid was released, drawing thousands of other ants. As the enzyme traveled through his body, Phil lost all movement and faculties. Brain cells were bursting. Liver and kidneys ceased functioning. Every muscle broke down to a rubbery mass, and thick blood passed through veins as soft as noodles. The entire torso was marbled a dark purple from pools of massive hemorrhages under the skin.

Finally, a ripping sound came from Phil's trousers like a burst of flatulence. It wasn't air he expelled but an explosion of his stomach and intestinal lining and a tremendous amount of blood. It seeped out through his baggy pants and trickled down the alleyway.

After Phil was blinded, asphyxiated and nearly skeletonized in about nine minutes, the army moved out. Partly through instinct and partly through genetic mangling, Siafu Moto were programmed to exterminate; feeding the colony was crucial but secondary. The ants set off on their next mission, heading toward a brick apartment building and leaving a deadly pheromone trail in their wake.

They knew brick buildings were like giant refrigerators.

As they neared the entrance, the ranks broke off in a hundred directions. They scurried up the face of the building and burrowed under doorways and into windows, air vents and cracks in the walls, following pipes, ducts and stairwells.

Within minutes, they blanketed the building.

CHAPTER 19

IN A CRAMPED STUDIO apartment along Twenty-ninth Street, Donny Peltzer lay in bed wearing nothing but striped briefs and a Fender guitar slung across his chest. He picked up the roach clip in the ashtray and sucked in the last of the joint, thinking how expensive it was to live in Manhattan just to keep the creative juices flowing properly.

Donny was practicing "Crossroads" for the gazillionth time. It had to sound perfect. If he got this gig at B. B. King's he could give up his dog-walking business. Donny hated dogs. He licked a scrape on his knuckles, where Scotty-the-ugly-schnauzer had bit him, and then pressed the triangle pick to the wire strings.

It was the slow and easy Robert Johnson rhythm, not the upbeat version by Cream, and the melody drifted nicely through the room, lingering with the stench of pot, dirty laundry, soaking dishes and the mustiness of a sagging purple sofa that was always damp for some reason. Most everything in Donny's apartment was old and dingy—except the posters. Hanging from the walls were dozens of chrome-framed Broadway theater posters. *A Chorus Line. Grease. Hairspray. Mamma Mia! Wicked.* All the classics. Theater was Donny's passion and each time he played a sleazy club, he felt one lick closer to an orchestra pit.

Just as he reached the second verse, the part that goes *"I'm going down to Rosedale, take my rider by my side,*" Donny paused midstrum and looked at the front door. Muffled voices were shouting in the hallway. But there was something else. A hissing sound in the kitchenette. It was a bit late in the year for steam to be rising from the radiator, especially since the heat was turned off in February, but hey, this was New York.

The sounds abated and Donny played the first chords again—and then his fingers suddenly lost their grip. The pick fell to the mattress. He froze with fear.

Donny stared at the wooden bedpost by his foot and the massive silhouette of an ant crawling across the top. It was the biggest, blackest ant he'd ever seen; big as a water bug, almost an inch long. He put the guitar on the bed and tucked his legs to his chest.

Instinctively, his eyes moved to a copy of a newspaper lying on the floor. There was a caricature of a scary ant on the front page. What did the articles say? They traveled in packs.

Oh great. Donny's heart was pounding as his gaze shifted over the room and bare carpet. Finding no buggy friends, he settled once again on the ant, which was now spiraling down the bedpost. It ran along the mattress, straight for the guitar. It vanished under the instrument and Donny held his breath. He was too scared to move.

The ant appeared again, having eclipsed the guitar, and stood out boldly against the spruce grain. It seemed to be staring at Donny, who reached down to the floor and grasped the newspaper. Slowly, he rolled it into a heavy tube and raised it high in the air, ready to strike. But he didn't. Instead, Donny leaned in closer to the creature. It was cleaning its face and antennae with nimble front legs. It stood very still for a moment and then it moved an inch to the left, then to the right, then cleaned some more. It appeared to be sort of—harmless.

Donny's heart slowed and he chuckled. It's an ant, he thought, quite correctly.

With the tip of his index finger, he gave the critter a shove. It flipped upside down, kicking its wiry legs above the smooth wood. Feeling more courageous, Donny rolled it back onto its feet. With a slight pinch, he plucked the insect off the guitar and dropped the little fella into his palm.

The ant didn't move. It seemed rather powerless against the mighty force of a human hand. Still, Donny had never seen an ant this size. It may have been abnormal but certainly not dangerous. Suddenly the hysteria in the city seemed ridiculous, and Donny curiously inspected the tiny suit of armor. It had a bulky helmet head that reminded him of Darth Vader and made him smile.

"I am your father, Luke," Donny said in a raspy voice and then breathed through his teeth, sounding like an air regulator.

A sudden pain ripped through his hand, as if a searing-hot skewer had pierced straight through the center of his palm. Donny howled and tried to shake off the ant as another burst of pain hit again, so acutely he fell to the carpet.

The ant was still hooked to his skin, slicing and stinging again and again. Donny stared wide-eyed and raked his nails over his palm, until all that remained was one pincer embedded under the skin.

Caught between a wave of shock and pity, Donny lay on the floor, crying like a baby and rubbing the wound, which was trickling blood. His hand burned red and swelled so much that his fingers looked like hot dogs. It hurt to make a fist, but Donny found a rolled-up sock and squeezed it to stop the bleeding.

Then the lights went out.

Donny bolted upright in the dark, holding his breath and

wondering if the ant was still alive, looking for him with one missing claw. He heard the steam growing louder and that's when he realized it didn't really sound like the radiator after all. Didn't the newspaper say the ants made a buggy noise? This wasn't good, not good at all. Donny wanted to get out of the dark, *badly*.

With a quick and cautious hand, he reached under the bed for a flashlight and patted over familiar objects. Baseball bat. Rollerblades. Stack of *Hustler*. Bong. The carpet felt rough and irritating to his overexcited nerve endings. He squirmed farther under the box spring, until his hand hit the wall.

Then the hissing stopped.

Donny shimmied out from under the bed and sat in the dark, dumbly listening to nothing but his own irregular breath. His bare foot touched something cold. Small. Metal.

Donny snatched up his lighter. With one trembling hand he flipped open the cover and pressed his thumb to the trigger that spun wheel against flint.

It sparked. It sparked again. *Come on, come on, man.*

The flame lit and relief came to his face. Now there was a soft glow to the room. It was brighter yet somehow darker. What was different? His posters were missing. The walls were completely black. Holding the lighter over the bed, Donny backed away and screamed. He sprinted to the door, but never got past the triple dead bolts.

Not that it mattered. The murky hallway was packed with frantic neighbors, covered in blood and ants, screaming and crying out in pain. Shaking candles and flashlights revealed flickering images of insects crawling over ceiling and walls, down to the elevator. Desperate crowds headed for the emergency exit, but like most of the buildings in Manhattan, the stairwell was completely infested.

CHAPTER 20

"NĬ ZÀI NĂLĬ?"

Chen Jinsong, a fragile old man with a red pinched face, stumbled to the top of the storage cellar and cried out to his wife, who was sweeping the back of the bodega.

"Dào zhèlǐ Lái!"

She hurried to him, clutching the broom. "How I know! Go see yourself!"

There was commotion in the street. High-pitched screams, breaking glass and shouts of alarm carried Chen back to the terrifying nights of his childhood when the Chinese army would invade his village, and summoned images of fleeing men and women grabbing their meager belongings.

Chen stepped into the street.

The outdoor market of Chinatown's Mott Street was in chaos. Pedestrians ran wildly in every direction, knocking down tables of brightly painted dolls, silk fans and slippers. They sprinted past strings of bright red paper lanterns and Chinese signs in neon green, as the smell of fear mixed with the usual odors of spices, fish and smoked meats.

The street was packed. Chen could see long lines of cars blocking the road, some abandoned, others crammed with people honking and yelling and going nowhere. Tourists held fast to their children, fighting their way out of restaurants, past windows of hanging duck and roast pig, as fellow merchants shouted to each other in Mandarin. Frantic commuters poured out of the subway entrance, stepping over slower-moving victims while trying to escape the underground assault.

Chen watched in horror as a screaming Asian woman, swatting a baby carriage, was knocked to the pavement by a man in an expensive suit. The woman crawled to the curb and sat down crying, as ants covered her legs and blanketed her bright yellow dress.

A wide ribbon of insects flowed across Chen's fruit bins like the billowing black silk of the New Year's Dragon. He doubled back, knocking over carts of mangos and apples until the sudden blast of a car engine spun him around. Hurling toward him was a dark vehicle painted with ants. The monster truck jumped the curb as pedestrians scrambled out of the way. It struck a homeless woman, her shopping cart and two teenagers zigzagging in its path. Chen froze as the headlights hit his face. He shut his eyes and the engine roared.

Crrrrkkkk! The sound of crashing metal nearly shattered his eardrums as the car hit a concrete wall of the bodega. The horn blasted steadily and the man behind the wheel was still, his face pressed against the broken windshield, covered with ants and blood.

"*Li Mei!*" Chen cried, running through a cloud of plaster to the back of his general store.

"Here!" she yelled over her shoulder, frantically beating away ants with a broom as they swarmed from the cellar. Chen grabbed his trembling wife around the waist and half dragged her to the back exit.

The alley was dark and motionless as Chen and Li Mei walked with quiet feet and shifting eyes to the far end of a six-foot fence. Behind them, a militia of ants carpeted the ground and invaded the walls of surrounding buildings.

There was nowhere to go but over the top. Chen helped his wife up the fence and onto a dumpster, but could not scale it himself.

"Go! You go!" he cried.

She shook her head, clasping his hands tighter.

"For the children. For the children," he pleaded again.

Li Mei nodded and clumsily pitched herself over the jagged wooden fence, falling through darkness onto the lid of another dumpster. Unable to balance, she slid inside the metal cave, and into a nest three feet deep with ants, trash and rat bones.

CHAPTER 21

THIS CANNOT BE HAPPENING, Kendra thought, but it was happening.

She and Paul had returned to the bunker fearing the worst, but hoping they were wrong. Finding no one around, the halls eerily quiet, Paul headed for the lab while Kendra veered off toward the control center, only to find intense panic among a crowd of people crammed into a large television lounge, staring at a screen. Kendra watched the news report and silently prayed it was some sort of horror flick, or perhaps a cable news simulation, at the very least *Candid freaking Camera*.

". . . What is going on in Manhattan right now is cataclysmic and unbelievable." News anchor Michelle Scott fumbled nervously with her earpiece, anxious eyes darting between two unsteady cameras. At the bottom of the screen a ticker ran: *CNN SPECIAL REPORT—DEADLY ANTS ATTACK NEW YORK CITY.* "We have on the phone Ray Lowell, a noted entomologist at Florida State University," Scott continued. "Can you tell us, Dr. Lowell, what is going on here?"

"I'm not entirely sure myself." The voice of authority was shaky at best. "These aren't like any insects we've ever seen. These ants are organized, marching in columns by the millions, like you would see in some African species. Maybe in Tanzania, but certainly not in New York—"

"Excuse me, Doctor," Scott interrupted. "Right now we

have a report from John Seaver who is standing in Times Square. John, what's the story there?"

The once dashing and confident reporter stared wide-eyed into the camera, his jacket torn at the shoulder and his silky black hair windswept as he ran backward, shouting over the furor and trying to stay in the shifting spotlight of the cameraman.

"Well, Michelle, it is *utter chaos*! There are reports of attacks all over the city. We're hearing the same thing from everyone—this is *surreal*. The police are telling everyone not to panic, which of course is ludicrous. If you look right down this street—Brett, get a shot of that. If you look right there, you can see *bodies*. Those are dead bodies and some, well, some still alive—"

"John, maybe you should get out of that area."

"Yes, yes. That's what we are planning to do."

"You go ahead, John. Right now we just received an appeal from the police commissioner that all residents of Manhattan should be tuning in to the Emergency Broadcast System, if they still have power—apparently these ants are destroying power lines—or they should follow the evacuation routes posted in their buildings. Most importantly, don't panic. Leave your belongings and get out of the city as quickly as possible. Do not attempt to go to the police or fire departments because it appears they are being overrun. Fire trucks have been hosing down streets—"

"That may not be going on, Michelle," John Seaver cut in between wheezing breaths as he continued to flee in long backward strides. "The gridlock down here is atrocious. Everyone we've seen, and that includes myself and my cameraman, we've been walking, or I should say running—Brett! Brett!"

The camera suddenly tumbled to the ground. It rolled a few times and stopped, still broadcasting a sideways view of the enormous Times Square intersection at night. Under billboards flickering a dazzling array of colors, bodies were scattered in heaps like packages fallen off a delivery truck. Some were still fighting for life, most were not. Shadowy figures sprinted over them in aimless directions.

Kendra broke from the television. She darted through the labyrinth of halls with one hand pressed against a stabbing ache in her side, past a stream of contorted faces, blurred from tears that stung her eyes.

Just hours ago, she'd been arguing with Paul in the lab, casually talking to him on the roof, wasting so much precious time. Overcome with guilt, all she could think was, Why didn't we do something? At the same time, she was filled with fury. This wasn't her fault. After all, she had just arrived, while Paul, Mayor Russo and other so-called guardians of the city had known about the ants for weeks. She remembered the mayor's callous words in the control room: *Do you have any idea what such an undertaking would cost?*

Angry voices resonated from the control center, sounding like a party that wasn't going well. Kendra reached the enormous room and found the place crammed with UN delegates in colorful costume, racing across the floor, slamming into one another, their voices exploding into a single multilingual drone.

Overhead TV screens were broadcasting attacks all over the city or giving instructions via the Emergency Broadcast System. *This is not a test . . .*

John Russo stepped to the podium with a sturdy gait. He

had spent the first few shocking moments alone in his office, flipping through news channels and muttering to himself, worried about where the blame would fall. Within minutes, however, he sprang into action, barking out orders to his staff and city officials, who were quickly congregating in the bunker. Without a doubt, this was the major event he'd prepared for his entire career. Now his only job was turning himself from villain into hero.

He cleared his throat in the microphone and feedback blasted to the ceiling. TV screens went black, phones were hung up and the room quieted. Ambassadors fumbled with their earpieces.

"First off, I want to assure everyone you are perfectly safe down here. While I realize you'd rather be with your families or assisting coworkers on the ground, you're here because you are not expendable. The only chance this city has is to keep you safe." Russo felt it was best to start a doomsday speech by flattering the audience, assuring their safety and then deferring to a higher authority. "I have a message from the president of the United States that was taped just minutes ago."

As the president began to speak, Kendra started for the doorway, knowing for the first time since arriving where she was headed. With or without Paul, she was going to find a queen.

CHAPTER 22

NEWS OF THE ATTACKS blasted through the bunker PA system as Kendra rushed hastily through the maze, unable to find Paul's laboratory in so much confusion. She stumbled into the computer room, where Jeremy and his programmers were rushing between various computer stations.

"Kendra," Jeremy gasped. He seemed to have lost some of his cool. "I was just about to look for you."

"Tell me you found something useful."

"Come with me."

He led Kendra to the back of the large room, filled with high-end computer servers that rose from the floor like an industrial garden. The chilly air smelled like fresh paper and plastic. Kendra recognized the loud humming that emanated from an ABI gene sequencer, an enormous stainless steel machine connected by satellite to the IBM Sequoia supercomputer at the Lawrence Livermore National Laboratory. It processed information at lightning speed, 20 petaflops, or the equivalent of twenty thousand trillion calculations per second, meaning it would take 120 billion people armed with calculators nearly fifty years to process what Sequoia could do in a day. It was one of the few computers in the world capable of sequencing the Siafu Moto DNA within hours.

Jeremy rolled up a chair for Kendra beside him. She flinched when a twelve-inch ant crawled over the desk. Then her heart slowed when she realized it was just a hologram; an oversized 3-D Siafu Moto image floating over a platform. It was the first time Kendra had seen one of these space-age, screenless computers up close. They were all the rage in techie circles, cutting-edge scientists like Jeremy who could spare a few hundred grand.

Jeremy swiped a finger over the image and it froze. "We've been working on this all night," he said, jittery with nervous energy. The single ant began spinning in circles, a perfect replica of the Siafu Moto, down to the heinous stinger. The hologram seemed so tangible, Kendra thought she could reach out and touch it.

"The DNA sequencing is complete," he told her, and the long, colorful strand of molecules spun gracefully in front of her. "I've never seen anything like it. It compares to no other ant on a molecular level. It's a monster."

"What can you tell me?"

"They have an overabundance of pheromone-binding proteins."

"Yes, we know from the EAGs that they're highly sensitive to odor."

"According to their gene, Gp-nine, these ants are monogynous and have only one queen to each colony."

"Like Siafu, not fire ants."

"They're a fierce hybrid." Jeremy was revved with excitement. "Check out these powerful legs. From video footage on the news stations, we clocked them at nine miles an hour. They have two speeds—stop and go. When they reach their prey, they attack like a single unit, like some demon from hell. Unbelievable."

Kendra was growing impatient. "Can you find the queens?"

"No. They're on the hunt. However, we did locate the

nests." A model of a park floated in the air. "We started breeding the first colony in Riverside Park. We set the computer to the exact date and place that the FBI believes the ants were released. Then we let nature take its course, watched them multiply for two years and spread across the city." The angle pulled back and Manhattan floated like an island in space. Hundreds of blue dots lit up like a Christmas tree. "The blue lights represent nesting sites of the queens. If the program is right, we're facing forty thousand subcolonies in Manhattan, over nine hundred billion ants."

"So the military was right on target."

"First for everything." He brought up a series of grainy aerial images of the city, taken by satellite surveillance cameras with night-vision capabilities. "The army just released these photos and they seem to confirm my findings. Wherever you see clusters of bodies, those are likely nesting areas where the colonies emerged."

"Where the heck have they been hiding for two years?"

"Check out this view of underground Manhattan." Jeremy pulled up a map, an enormous tangled web of colored lines. "Below this city are twenty-nine million miles of subway tunnels, cables, sewer lines, gas and steam pipes—the length of which could circle the earth twelve hundred times." Over the colored lines was a pattern of black lines connected by circles, like a constellation. "These lines represent each subcolony and the circles show where they intersect. Like any supercolony, they spread out, but they stay together."

"So they're an easy target for my pheromone formula."

"If you can find a queen." Jeremy tapped at the keyboard. Numbers and charts flew by. "According to my data, they're subterranean like Solenopsis, but once they surface—they're Siafu all the way."

"So much for digging up the nests. Siafu are nomads." She sighed, knowing driver ants could leave their nests for months. They hold nightly raids and rest during the day, building living nests with their bodies. The gigantic balls, called bivouacs, are often found in hollow tree trunks. Members hold on to one another's legs to form various passages and chambers that contain food, eggs and larvae, and of course, the coveted queen.

"Unfortunately that's what my program suggests," he agreed. "The colonies will attack at night and set up camps during the day, maybe in the walls of buildings."

"Then that's where I'm headed."

"Better bring a sledgehammer."

Kendra thought of Paul. "Think I'll just bring the bait."

Jeremy clicked his tongue knowingly. "It is amazing the great Paul O'Keefe didn't see this coming. He's been studying these ants for what—two weeks? I've only been here a few hours and already I've found the nests. Too bad I wasn't brought in sooner."

Kendra ignored the comment. She stood to leave. "Wish me luck."

"You aren't going out there yourself?" Jeremy said, alarmed. "It's too dangerous, Kendra. Let Paul go—it's the least he can do."

"No time for that." Kendra looked at the enormous city floating like a planet in space and rubbed her weary eyes. They felt dry and scratchy.

Jeremy pressed a warm hand to her forehead. "Looks like you're about to crash."

"I have other plans," she said, and squared her shoulders. "Keep at it, huh?"

"I'm not going anywhere."

CHAPTER 23

KENDRA REACHED THE LABORATORY, ready for an argument. She found Paul staring into a microscope looking panicked. His hair stuck up in odd directions and his shaky hands were clumsily turning knobs and adjusting slides. There was a chaotic mess of printouts strewn across the counters.

Paul snapped to attention when he saw Kendra and fanned out several loose sheets of paper, stammering out his findings. "The reports are not good. Results are coming back from every institute on the planet. They all say the same thing. *Indestructible.*" He fired off the data. "Negative to fungus and disease. Negative to parasites. Negative to natural enemies. Strepsiptera, Orasema, nematodes, mites, phorid flies. They tried high-pressure oxygen. A hundred pesticides." He smacked the pile of reports. "Those damn corporate suits just hightailed it out of the city, for chrissakes."

Kendra stormed across the room and snatched the papers from his hand. She threw them in the air and they rained down like ticker tape. "Are you insane?" she shouted. "We're dealing with weapons. Monsters. Creatures from the deep!"

"Oh, I see. This is my fault." Paul said it like he wasn't thinking the same thing.

"Wasn't that your job? Didn't the mayor put you in charge? Why didn't you demand he evacuate the city?"

Paul was flustered under the barrage of questions. "Don't

you think I blame myself? Of course I do, but who would ever . . ." He was becoming angry; his cheeks reddened. "You saw them yourself. I believe the words you used were 'preposterous' . . . 'ridiculous.'"

"I didn't mean . . ." Kendra wasn't sure what she meant, but hurling insults wasn't part of the plan.

"This study of yours," he said. "Will it work on these ants?"

"It's possible. But we need to find a queen if it stands a chance."

Paul reached across the counter to a couple of boxes marked BUG OUT. He tossed one suit to Kendra and threw a rucksack over his shoulder.

"So let's get the damn thing."

The two moved swiftly to the mayor's office. A new sense of urgency weighed heavily on their shoulders, along with the bundles they carried, filled with supplies.

Paul wanted details. "So tell me about your research. How did you kill the colonies?"

Kendra kept a steady pace. "It all goes back to your experiment on brood pheromones. Remember how you saturated grains of rice with extracts from newly hatched larvae?"

"Of course." Paul nodded. The well-received study was cited in every major science journal. As a college freshman, Paul had unwittingly revitalized a movement in integrated pest management with his first published paper. "The workers hauled the rice back to brooding chambers and tended to the grains as if they were real offspring."

"Right. You showed that ants could be fooled by their own chemicals. So I started playing around with different concentrations of various queen pheromones, and injected the formula into the nest."

"It must have caused extreme agitation in the colony," he commented.

"More than that. Within hours, I had hundreds of queen corpses."

Paul stopped short. "Your theory?"

"The high concentration of the sex pheromone caused the workers to kill off the queens."

"Quantitative pheromone effect."

"If you want to get technical. Then I added the queen's alarm pheromone to the mix, and the whole colony started killing each other off."

"So you're saying you found a way to synthesize pheromones into a formula that causes the workers to kill off the queens and each other?"

"That's what I'm saying."

Paul started walking again. "Impossible. Nothing like that has ever worked."

"Not in sixty years of trying."

"Do you realize the implications of your findings? Fire ants terrorize twenty-two states."

"Twenty-four."

"If you can apply this method to other insects, you could save farmers millions of dollars."

"Billions."

"You could prevent crop depletion across the nation."

"Across the planet."

"You might wipe out the insecticide industry."

She grinned. "I can live with that."

They reached the mayor's office. "It sounds very promising.

Still, Siafu Moto aren't normal ants. They might not respond to your cocktail."

"Paul," Kendra groaned.

He held a finger to his lips and reevaluated his position. "I like it."

"You like it?"

"Okay, I love it."

"And?"

"And your radiance blinds me. I'm not worthy to carry your microscope."

Kendra smiled with satisfaction. "I do like the new you."

CHAPTER 24

MAYOR RUSSO SEEMED HOPEFUL for the first time that day, listening to Kendra and Paul divulge their plan to capture a queen. Kendra explained that if the pheromone operation was successful, it would trigger two immediate reactions. The workers would kill off the queens and then destroy each other.

General Dawson was interested in hearing the specifics of the chemical synthesis, asking questions about how it was done, the results of Kendra's own experiments in the desert. He took notes and occasionally spoke into a small recorder.

Colonel Garrett was entirely skeptical. "My team of top scientists spent months trying to find a way to kill these ants. You waltz in here the day you learn about them and tell us you have some magic formula?" He shook his head vehemently. "General, you know as well as I, these ants are indestructible. Nothing that kills ordinary insects will kill Siafu Moto."

"We don't have a clue how to destroy them," the general replied. "But their idea is far safer than any I've heard today."

"We agreed on the solution, an infallible plan. Not some half-witted theory that hasn't been tested."

"I haven't agreed to anything, and neither has the president. I'm willing to give the pheromones a try—if it can be done quickly. That means twenty-four hours."

Garrett started for the door. "As far as I'm concerned, this matter has already been decided." He left the others in silence.

"He's right, you know," the general told Kendra. "This is a long shot, isn't it?"

"Yes, it is," she admitted. "But I'm sure it stands a chance."

"What do you need from us?" Russo said.

"We could use some help finding a queen. Perhaps the army, or National Guard."

Russo shook his head. "I'm afraid the Guardsmen are too busy with the chaos on the streets, evacuating the city."

The general concurred. "Besides, none of my men know the first thing about finding an ant queen."

"It takes a trained professional." Paul nodded to Kendra. "Guess we're it."

"You'll need a gun out there. People are going nuts. Agent Cameron will issue you a weapon."

"That won't be necessary," Kendra said. "Our only concern is the ants."

"We have nothing to protect you from those insects or help you find a queen."

"We'll be in full gear, searching the city for nesting sites," Kendra told them. "It doesn't take a lot of fancy equipment, just good instinct."

"Where will you look?" Russo asked.

"I hate to sound morbid," Paul replied, "but we should check the biggest food supply. There are plenty of residential buildings in Midtown. I'm going to assume these ants are like Siafu. Attack all night, rest in tree trunks—or I should say buildings—all day."

Kendra wondered if she should mention that Jeremy's computers predicted the same thing. She decided not to.

"What are your odds?" Russo asked Paul.

"Better than one in a million."

"So let's say, by some miracle, you find a queen," Dawson said. "What then?"

"We synthesize enough pheromones to cover the city," Kendra replied.

"How much do you need?"

"Not as much as you think. This is potent stuff, and insects have highly developed receptors in their antennae. Just to give you an idea, it takes less than one tablespoon of trail pheromone to lead an ant around the world five thousand times. Just a few molecules can stop a colony."

"We'll hit every street in Manhattan," Paul said. "After that, we can pump the chemicals into the sewers and subways where they hide."

"Of course, we should spray all the buildings as well," Kendra said, and her expression darkened. "We have to consider alates."

"What's that?" Russo asked.

"Something we don't want to think about but have to be prepared for," Paul replied.

"It may happen soon." Kendra explained to Russo the mating ritual of ants. During the flight of the alates, winged virgin queens take off in a nuptial dance with the males, filling the sky with billowing gray clouds of swarming insects. Then the newly pregnant queens fly away to begin new colonies. "They can fly thousands of miles. It would be devastating."

"It usually happens once the queens reach full maturity," Paul said. "Hopefully we're not too late."

"So you can make these pheromones in the lab?"

"No, we can't. We can isolate and identify the molecular structure, but we'll need at least a metric ton of the synthetic pheromone to kill the colony."

"Where will we get that?"

"I have a friend, Jack Carver, at the USDA. One call and he can whip up enough base for this pheromone right in his laboratory."

"I've got a direct line out," Russo said, and picked up a phone with a heavy cord snaking to the wall. He handed Paul the gold-plate receiver.

Paul dialed the Washington number, waited for a connection. He was relieved to hear Jack on the other line.

"Good Lord, Paul. Don't tell me you're still in New York City? Somewhere safe, I hope."

"Can't say exactly."

"Well, it's good to know you haven't been eaten. Guess the ants have better taste than that."

"Jack, this is no joke. I'm here with Kendra and she's possibly found a way to kill these crazy beasts, but I need your help." Paul relayed a short version of their plan.

"I'd like to help you, but I've been snubbed by the Pentagon. Tried to send out a team after our last excursion, but they pulled the plug on our whole operation. They don't want the USDA involved."

"I have a United States Army general here who can give you all the clearance you need."

General Dawson gave a nod.

"He'll be calling you as soon as we find a queen. In the meantime I need you to whip up a metric ton of base for the pheromone. Maybe soybean oil. Nothing that can evaporate. I need at least forty-eight hours of nondiluting odor."

"A metric ton? You're talking millions of dollars."

"Don't worry about it, Jack. It's not on your tab."

"How long do I have?"

"No more than six hours."

"You're not serious."

"Never more so."

"I'll have every synthetic chemist on it, Paul."

"Thanks."

"Tell Kendra if her experiment works, she'll have my job."

"Doubt she wants it. She'd just wind up a sarcastic old geezer like you."

"You just get me the breakdown."

Paul hung up the phone. "We need a way to spread the chemical over the city."

General Dawson nodded. "I can get a fleet of aerial firefighting aircraft. The Green Sweep C-130 is a converted cargo plane capable of dropping twenty thousand gallons of liquid. It's been instrumental in cleaning up the oil spills in the Gulf and putting out the Los Angeles fires. It will be perfect for widespread areas and buildings."

"Terrific. Get me a couple of those. And a few crop dusters for the smaller streets."

"I'll have them deployed immediately." The general spoke into his handheld recorder. "Jack Carver, USDA." He winked at Kendra and started for the door. "Good luck out there and remember, you've got just twenty-four hours. By sundown tomorrow I want this city completely evacuated."

Kendra furrowed her brow, unsure why the statement sounded so foreboding.

Mayor Russo waited for the general to leave. He gestured to Paul and Kendra, waving them over surreptitiously. They leaned in close as he spoke quietly, a dire look in his eyes. "There's been talk of dropping low-yield nuclear bombs on Manhattan."

"Nuke the city?" Kendra gasped. "Whose dumb idea was that?"

"Colonel Garrett has been telling everyone at the State Department with ears that radiation kills the beasts."

"Do you think they would actually do it?"

"I think the colonel is blowing smoke, grasping at straws to save his own hide. Can you imagine the president authorizing such a thing?" The mayor huffed. "As long as I'm alive, there won't be any bombs falling on this city."

Kendra started for the lab to gather equipment for the trip. Paul tracked down Agent Cameron, who wasn't pleased about issuing a gun to a scientist with no training.

"You'll probably shoot yourself," he said, and reluctantly led Paul to a small room with a large closet that was loaded with weapons locked down tight.

Cameron grabbed a pistol and opened a file cabinet that was full of magazines. He eyed Paul suspiciously. "You're wasting your time out there."

"No one else is doing anything productive."

"That's because they want to save their weapon," he muttered.

"What weapon?"

Cameron bit down hard. "Never mind."

"Do you know something about these ants, Agent?"

Cameron slammed the file cabinet, startling Paul. "That's the problem. No one does. This was an FBI investigation from the beginning. I was *this close* to exposing whoever was funding this operation, until the plug was pulled by Military Intelligence. My sources disappeared, the money trail evaporated, we were thrown off the case. So Garrett rushes into Bolivia and destroys the entire laboratory without gathering any evidence. His technical crew didn't bother to investigate who created these monsters, how they did it. You're a scientist; don't you find that odd?"

"I find your suspicion odd."

"You didn't see what I saw. Those bodies in Bolivia were completely mutilated. Liquefied. The people who created these ants are extremely dangerous. Garrett doesn't seem to care about finding them."

"Maybe the army knows more than they care to share with the FBI."

"Maybe." Cameron gave Paul a stern look. " Now I'm stuck following two bug scientists around."

"You think I have ties to ecoterrorists?"

The agent didn't answer.

Paul shifted uncomfortably. "Are you going to issue me a weapon or what?"

CHAPTER 25

FIVE HOURS TILL DAWN. A large moon cast a veil of light over the city, picking up thin wisps of smoke and speckled ash, white ash like snowflakes blowing in the breeze from small, scattered fires. Kendra emerged from the hatch onto the roof, where she had just been hours before, but now the cool air had a bitter stench of sulfur, and she could see a fleet of army aircraft spewing extinguishing foam from their pregnant bellies over Midtown. News choppers dashed over the city like mosquitoes at a campout. In the distance, sirens blared from emergency vehicles going nowhere and store alarms wailed through hundreds of broken windows.

Paul emerged from the hatch right behind her, dropping a Bug Out suit at her feet and stepping into his own. He glowed white like a space alien. Neither of them spoke.

Kendra climbed into the gauzy material, which seemed paper thin but felt heavy, like a bulletproof vest. The lining was metallic and stiff: new breathable steel from DuPont. It would be an uncomfortable field trip. Paul zipped her headpiece and checked the seal. It was immediately cramped and hot inside the suit and Kendra threw off the hood, wiping her brow.

Paul knelt on the blacktop, checking the contents of the knapsack. There were specimen bottles, flashlights, blowtorches and a medical bag, along with a pistol.

"A gun?" Kendra blinked hard.

"Not just a gun, a Beretta 92f."

She balked.

"You heard the general. There are desperate people out here." Paul closed one eye and aimed at the moon. "Cameron didn't want to give it to me. Thought I couldn't handle it."

"He's probably right."

"All I needed was a quick lesson. He showed me how it works. This doohickey here is the magazine release." Paul ejected the magazine and found it empty. He checked the chamber. "Jackass gave me one bullet."

"And I'm sure you're an expert marksman. All that training in . . . ?"

"Eagle Scouts." He replaced the magazine. "Although that might have been a flare gun."

"Right."

They headed for a small steel hut in the center of the roof. Once inside, they descended five flights down a narrow stairwell to the first floor. They were facing an office with the words UNITED NATIONS BUREAU OF PUBLIC OF AFFAIRS lettered in gold on frosted glass.

"What is this place?" she asked.

"Looks like the same as below. Emergency headquarters for the UN, FBI, CIA, all the biggies."

They moved quickly down the turquoise carpeting. In every office, lights were on and televisions crackled with static or instructions from the Emergency Broadcast System. Phones were off their hooks. Spilled coffee cups and papers were strewn about the floor. These people had left in a hurry.

Paul heard voices and motioned to an office, where he and Kendra discovered a small television with cable coming in clear and they stopped to watch a few seconds of a news report. Camera shots of Manhattan revealed an endless stream of refugees packing the George Washington, Williamsburg and Brooklyn bridges, where helicopter spotlights guided them to another borough or the shores of New Jersey. SWAT teams from the Tri-state area were evacuating parts of the north in armored buses. South of Midtown was barraged by cruise ships, military boats and carriers along ports east and west.

A seasoned newscaster was talking over the footage: "I haven't seen images like this since Hiroshima. Right now the Department of Defense is estimating up to one hundred and forty thousand fatalities and twice as many wounded . . . skin eaten away . . . blinded . . . just horrendous."

He called it "the worst natural disaster in the history of mankind," but Paul knew there was nothing natural about it.

"Come on," he whispered.

At the end of the hall was a swinging door marked CAFETE-RIA. Paul and Kendra eyed each other before blowing their way inside. The eatery was a mess. Chairs were tipped over and tables were filled with plates of stale sandwiches, dried-up stew, noodles, rice and beans. Tidy cuts of decaying fish lined a sushi bar.

"Is it wrong to grab a snack before saving the world?" he asked.

"We'll need our strength," she replied.

Paul stretched the long leg of his white suit over the velvet rope to the buffet, where steel counters and glass shelves displayed sandwiches wrapped in cellophane, fruit and Jell-O, cereal boxes and cans of soda. They were both starving. Paul handed Kendra a turkey on whole wheat with mayo and bean sprouts.

She flung the sandwich over her shoulder and reached for a slice of chocolate cake. "Damned if sprouts are going to be my last meal."

Paul unwrapped a roast beef on rye, taking great bites and closing his eyes with a satisfied grin, and then washed it down with a can of Coke. He watched Kendra alternate bites of cake with spoonfuls of fudge pudding, her mouth moving in ecstasy. He had forgotten how beautiful she was: the way her nose crinkled up and the little crescents that formed in her cheeks whenever she smiled or frowned.

"Still eat chocolate for breakfast?"

"Still eat bees?" she replied.

"That was a dare." He winced at the memory.

"You didn't have to do it."

"I was trying to impress you."

They smiled at each other. It was the same warm smile Paul remembered from years ago.

Kendra tossed the empty plates on the counter. "You ready?"

There was no putting it off anymore.

Paul crushed his soda can. "Let's go."

CHAPTER 26

THERE WERE NO PEOPLE. Anywhere.

Kendra gazed over First Avenue as though it were a movie set for a disaster film. Towering buildings loomed in darkness; the electric had shorted out from insects gnawing on the wires. Store windows had been shattered by looters and folks just out of their minds. A yellow cast from an overhead streetlight spilled across smashed hoods of tightly packed cars that all looked the same shade of rusty brown.

There was not a lot of sidewalk space. Kendra moved alongside Paul, snaking around vehicles and climbing on bumpers. Pieces of glass and debris lay scattered at their feet, along with photos, letters and mementos people had grabbed as they ran from their homes, irreplaceable items they couldn't live without. It was the dolls and teddy bears that got to Kendra the most, and the clothes: pants, shirts and undergarments frantically torn from people being eaten alive.

Kendra had never witnessed so much stillness outside of the desert. At the same time, there was an uncanny feeling of movement all around her. Shadows fluttered in doorways. Even the concrete sidewalk appeared to quiver with life.

"I wonder if we're going to be swarmed any second," she whispered.

"Probably not," Paul answered. "The ants are looking for people and its pretty slim pickings around here."

The two scientists navigated the street, shrouded in white, except for their heads sticking out of the bug suits. They decided to forgo the hoods, which could be flipped and zipped in a matter of seconds if necessary. With added white shoe mitts and gloves they felt reasonably protected, but quite conspicuous. That worried Paul. There was definitely a risk that someone might steal their suits. He had one bullet in his gun, which would be useless against a mob of looters. Paul was an entomologist and to him, swarms of angry ants—even deadly mutant ants—were far more controllable than street thugs. Humans were unpredictable and irrational, driven by self-preservation, and there was no telling what stupid thing a person might do. He unconsciously reached for the pistol to check his response time, and then recoiled, aware of his own primitive instinct. He tried to focus on the task at hand.

They headed west and turned the corner of Fortieth Street, where the intersection had clogged up quickly and the street was mostly clear. After vaulting over cars and obstacles, it felt good to walk on pavement again, but it was dead quiet. Sirens fell silent as entire city blocks lost power. Not a soul was on the street. Manhattan was becoming a ghost town.

The quiet was broken by a police squadron bursting out of a diner. The men were armed with shotguns and wore menacing hoods like ninjas and sleek black uniforms with NYPD across the chest. They marched past Paul and Kendra, who halted their journey until the pounding of heavy boots grew faint. Then the two scientists continued toward Midtown, turning the corner onto a narrow lane where the buildings were old and expensive. There was a deceptive feeling of sanctuary among the flowering gardens and iron benches, old-fashioned gas lamps and cobblestone courtyards.

Then they saw the first body.

It lay curled on its knees and bloated in tightly stretched clothing with arms tucked beneath the chest and a bloody face pressed against the pavement.

Paul rolled the man over and found no pulse in his neck. His skin was bone white and when he lifted the man's under-shirt, the entire torso was marbled in dark purple blotches: pools of thickened blood with nowhere else to flow. A pen-light showed much of the skin was in motion, peppered with black bumps of ants tunneling just under the first few layers.

Kendra rose to her feet unsteadily and stared down at the man's pasty complexion. He stared back at her with protrud-ing red eyes. It was a familiar memory that eased her into dark waters that she'd had no intention of wading in again. She began to shiver violently and cursed herself to keep it together, stepping back with arms wrapped tight around her waist.

"Kendra?" Paul was looking at her with acute worry.

She didn't answer him.

He walked slowly toward her, trying to make eye contact, but she seemed to look right through him. Paul grasped her shoulder, gave a firm shake and Kendra's eyes snapped into focus.

"Let's keep going," she said and turned on her heels, as if nothing had happened.

Then they noticed the others.

Lining the street were corpse after corpse: some curled up in the middle of the road, and others sprawled over steps and bloodstained walkways.

Kendra stood rapt in front of a dead woman in a white slip, kneeling with her hands clasped in prayer around a NO PARK-ING sign. Globs of dried blood hung from her eyes, nose and lips.

"I believe we've gone to hell," Kendra barely whispered.

"No," Paul replied. "Hell has come to us."

Rounding the corner, a bearded old man walked in long strides, rising up and down like a carousel horse. His soiled raincoat flapped open with each step, revealing nothing but a jock strap. Over his shoulders, like a sack of rice, was a young naked woman, gray-skinned and obviously dead. Blond hair swung from side to side, out of sync with her limp arms. Bright red lipstick was her only trace of color.

In the beam of Paul's penlight, the man grimaced and stopped abruptly, making the young woman's head flop back. She had pale eyes and a gash along her forehead.

"You ought to pick up one of these bodies, mister," the old man croaked. "If the ants come, you just throw it at them. Works better if they're still alive, but the dead ones are all right." He laughed as he passed them. "Trust me, it works."

CHAPTER 27

DARK CLOUDS THICKENED LIKE sludge across the moon, blocking out precious light. The New York skyline was black against black. Paul and Kendra could barely see where they were going, but followed the ghostly white glow of the sidewalks. Paul paused on Second Avenue and dropped the heavy backpack on the ground, rummaged blindly through the front pouch and pulled out a couple of military-grade flashlights.

Kendra turned hers on high beam and Paul set his on lantern mode, which illuminated the surrounding neighborhood in soft lavender. They walked in silence past high-rise office buildings, which soon gave way to older brick tenements and deserted fast food eateries, electronics and clothing stores.

Paul's mind was still on Kendra's vacant eyes, staring at the dead man.

"Do you want to talk about it?" he asked.

Kendra pretended she didn't hear him. He was going there again, after she'd made it clear so many times that it was not a point of entry. She was rubbing the smooth, delicate spot on her wrist as if dabbing perfume. It wasn't a conscious habit, but a reaction to the fluttery feeling of wings on her skin. *Eyelashes.* Butterfly kisses her mother gave her every night before bed. She still felt them, rather often. With that single image engraved in her mind, the haunting eyes of the dead man, Kendra rubbed her wrist on the kissing spot but it neither erased the fluttery feeling nor blocked out the memories that were so relentless.

They were in Argentina. Kendra was seven years old, lying in a field of high grass under the plentiful shade of floss silk trees, which grew in clusters: green leaves shaped like fingers on a hand and trunks covered in thorns. It was hot, muggy like the tropics, with the occasional screech of wild birds and howler monkeys.

Kendra could see the worksite from her perch on a small knoll. The fire ant mound must have reached over three feet high, because it came well past her father's knee. He was an exceedingly tall man who reminded her of Abe Lincoln, with his narrow face and Amish-type beard. He had an overbearing presence, but was gentle and prone to clumsiness. Kendra took after her mother, who was blond and small-boned with light, playful eyes and even features. The two adults stood at the base of the mound in full gear, cutting a wedge out of the dirt and throwing the ants into a frenzy.

Kendra was occupied as usual in a tenacious search for rare butterflies, an obsession since the age of five, but every so often she looked back reassuringly at her parents. She caught sight of a Malachite, hardly rare, but not yet part of her collection, so she snapped the net over its wings and plowed across the field on sturdy legs to show off her find.

Her father was arguing with a man and two other men in a jeep. They were locals from the village where they were staying. Kendra's mother pulled off her white hood. She had a worried expression and shooed her daughter away. Not used to being ignored, Kendra retreated with a scowl. She didn't like hearing adults argue either, so she trotted back into the field and sat down and studied the incandescent green wings of the Malachite.

She talked to it, played with it and named every part of its body. Then she explained to the insect that butterflies live only for a few days but not to be sad because three days aloft on graceful wings was better than seventy years of walking on boring feet. When it finally died she would stick a pin through its body and hang it on a board.

This is where things got fuzzy for Kendra. There were several loud popping sounds and she may have heard a scream or maybe not. But something frightening made her look back at the worksite. She stood up straight, and the Malachite soared into the clouds. Kendra watched the jeep race away. She could barely see her parents lying on the ground by the ant mound, the grass was so high. Only the tips of their shoes and the thin white lines of their protective suits peeked over the green blades. Kendra wondered if they had fallen, and she became frightened and anxious to reach them.

The site was not more than fifty yards away but it seemed like miles and now her legs felt heavy and hard to lift as she moved slowly toward the mound.

The puffy white face of her mother stared up at Kendra and her swollen lips were slightly moving, telling her something. Her father too had open eyes, but expressionless. Neither of them wore head gear or gloves. Both were covered in ants and bleeding across their chest, or maybe the neck, or the hands; it was always different.

Then someone grabbed Kendra and swung her over large shoulders. The last thing she remembered was the sound of her own scream, as her parents moved farther away.

"You can't deny the similarities," Paul was saying and it snapped Kendra back to the present. "There's such a thing as post-traumatic stress disorder."

"And there's such a thing as bad psychology, Dr. Freud,"

said Kendra, irritated. "My parents were killed over a few dollars. What we have here is the most catastrophic event in human history. I have every right to a freak-out."

He nodded, watching her rub her wrist, and decided to drop it.

They crossed Thirty-eighth Street to what sounded like a street festival with no music. Halfway down the block, hundreds of people moved in the glare of police searchlights. Residents of the Emily Harding Home for seniors were being evacuated. There were no vehicles for transport so they had to settle for wheelchairs, gurneys, stretchers and even a few shopping carts, all pushed by a long procession of rescuers.

A skinny, dark-eyed boy about twelve years old held the arm of a woman as she plodded toward a wheelchair. She was embarrassed, complaining about moving so slowly, and the boy kept saying, *"No problemo. No problemo."* He eased her into the seat and set a bulky pocketbook on her lap. For a brief moment, his eyes locked with Paul's. The boy smiled, and then rolled the woman down the street with the others.

"Come on," Kendra said in a low voice, and they continued down Second Avenue.

They reached an enormous intersection by the Queens Midtown Tunnel where throngs of pedestrians clambered over cars and buses that clogged the arched entrance. Along the skyline, smoke poured from tall building fires as if from burning matchsticks. A fleet of military choppers were flying through the smoke and landing somewhere in Central Park.

Paul and Kendra reached Thirty-sixth Street and found a long stretch of old brick residential buildings.

"These look like ant hotels to me," she whispered.

"So we sneak up on them?" Paul asked.

"Just close enough to grab a queen," she answered. "Before they tear us apart."

"No way," Paul said confidently. "These suits are top of the line. Jack the Ripper couldn't get through."

She raised a brow. "Think so, huh?"

"Maybe."

"I just wish we had some kind of warning."

"Perhaps we do. Some of the survivors say the ants make a chirping noise."

"Ants don't make audible sounds."

"Maybe it has something to do with how they signal attack."

"Or maybe they bred them with crickets."

"Listen." He paused and they heard a muffled tapping. Paul orbited his flashlight around the empty street. "Let's not spook ourselves. What were we talking about?"

"Our plan."

"Right. Find the best building and check out the most likely nesting spots."

"So, what's the best building?"

"I suppose whichever one has the most bodies around."

CHAPTER 28

Washington, D.C.

IT WAS A FORTY-FIVE-MINUTE helicopter ride from the United Nations to the White House lawn.

General Dawson and Colonel Garrett were to lead an emergency meeting in the situation room at 3:00 A.M. Gathered around the table were President Andrew Davis, Attorney General Joseph Hastings, White House Chief Counsel George Bennington, Cabinet members and Joint Chiefs of Staff, the heads of Homeland Security, along with majority and minority party leaders.

In front of each person was a black bound report lettered in red: OPERATION COLONY TORCH. The president and attorney general sat beside each other, red-faced and flipping through pages while Colonel Garrett summarized damage, projected casualties and estimated worst-case scenarios. Garrett's mission was to get everyone in the room thinking alike. The ants in Manhattan could never leave the island. The lives of 300 million Americans were at stake. The colony had to be contained.

Both Garrett and Dawson had agreed that Kendra's pheromone formula would not be mentioned at the meeting. It was too much of a long shot and could delay approval of Operation Colony Torch.

Hastings would be a tough sell. He was known as the president's Doberman, guardian of the administration. Any proposal that showed the slightest trace of controversy was sniffed out by Hastings and snapped off with ruthless jaws. The election year was fast approaching and the president's ratings were dropping even faster, ever since the ant attacks in New York. Something drastic had to be done, but as far as Hastings was concerned, Operation Colony Torch was political suicide. "Who the hell are you!" he bellowed at Garrett. "I don't even know you." He turned to the president. "These guys walk in here, tell us some South American secret weapon has gotten loose in New York and they want this administration to clean up their colossal mess?"

President Davis was pensively leaning back in his chair, hands steepled under his chin. "I think we're past the blame game, Joe. We have to take some kind of action."

Hastings was furious and vowed that he would die or be the last voice of reason. He slid his copy of the report to the center of the table and sternly reproached the two army officers. "Let me say this: even the suggestion of using nuclear weapons on our own country may be grounds for treason. You'd better have a damn good reason for recommending such an undertaking."

The statement was followed by a lot of head nodding.

Dawson cringed at the monumental task in front of him. He barely had the support of his own colleagues at the Pentagon. No one wanted to touch this with a nine-hundred-foot pole. His fellow generals and commanders had jumped into action, focusing on evacuation, flying in supplies and medical needs, but no one wanted to be involved in the containment.

Just hours before, Secretary of State Howard Sherwood was fuming that Dawson had put Garrett in charge of the operation: "You put a colonel in charge of coordinating logistics, coming up with a plan and recommendations to save America's greatest city?"

Dawson cringed at having to defend Garrett, but he was knee deep in the turmoil with no allies. "Colonel Garrett has more knowledge about these ants than anyone. Frankly, we need him."

Garrett addressed the group with confidence, summing up the first section of the report, which explained that no other means of destroying the ants besides nuclear bombs had been discovered.

Hastings called for an immediate motion to bring the discussion to the Senate floor. "We need to get approval from the proper channels and clear this with both the UN Commission and the Atomic Energy Agency in Vienna. The president needs documentation, very detailed documentation, outlining all our options. At the very least it will take a week to get clearance on even considering your proposal."

"You don't seem to understand," the general stressed, "We don't have a week. We don't have a day. These ants are moving quickly. Even if we blow up the bridges and tunnels, there are juvenile queens ready to take flight. They can fly thousands of miles. The ants can cross water by joining together and making huge balls that carry them downstream, possibly across rivers or even oceans."

Senator Denise Sheldon of New York slammed both her hands on the table. "New York City!" she shouted at the general. "The most densely populated county in the nation. The financial and cultural capital of the world. Home to the New York Stock Exchange, NASDAQ, Madison Square Garden, Lincoln Center—not to mention outstanding museums and universities, along with nearly every major radio and television station, newspaper and magazine." She was going to make a show of this and there was nothing stopping her. "Times Square. Greenwich Village. Central Park. These are places known by every person in civilized society. You're talking about New York City, damn it!"

Garrett shot back, "No, ma'am! Excuse me, ma'am, but it is not New York City. It's Siafu Moto City. These insects have taken over, with no plans of ever leaving."

The outburst was startling and the group stopped breathing as Garrett's eyes scanned the table. "Each of you must understand that we will *never* save Manhattan. Our only option is bomb it now or bomb it later. You need to start thinking about saving Long Island, New Jersey, Connecticut and the rest of the nation." This was Garrett's stage moment. He was enjoying this, Dawson could tell, and he was revolted. The colonel had the floor and scrutinized each worried face, speaking in a patronizing tone, "This is one city, in one nation, on one planet. Right now, we have to consider the only feasible action to save the United States of America—and beyond."

There was a period of silence, and then the president cleared his throat and asked, "How many casualties are we talking about?"

Garrett flipped opened his black folder, but kept his eyes locked on the commander in chief. "There are approximately one hundred and forty thousand people already dead from the ant attacks. Out of the three million commuters and tourists, almost all of them have left the city. Out of the one point six million residents, there are roughly one hundred thousand left. Most have gotten out on their own, by train or foot, by bridge and tunnel, fleets of ships and helicopters. We are still evacuating at a rate of twenty-six thousand civilians per hour. Hospital workers, doctors, nurses and patients, emergency crews, police and military will be the last to leave."

On the wall was a large map of the borough. Garrett rose

from his chair and pointed to evacuation sites. He explained, "If we begin bombing at seventeen hundred tomorrow, there will be approximately six thousand lives lost—those civilians too wounded or too incapacitated to make it out."

He was actually talking about *doing it,* and his words swept panic over the room. Each set of terrified eyes shifted from one person to another. The smell of fear was erupting off bodies like steaming volcanoes, yet Garrett continued, unruffled, "There are going to be people we simply cannot reach. But everyone who is physically able will be flown or shipped out of the city, well outside range of any nuclear fallout. Right now we're focusing on evacuation of the surrounding communities."

"Let's talk about that," the president said. "Damage at the hypocenter, and the extent of nuclear fallout."

This time Dawson walked over to a map of the Tri-state area, where colored rings showed a bull's-eye that centered on Manhattan and radiated outward. He pointed to targets as he spoke. "We're talking about dropping no more than four precision, extremely low yield neutron bombs. These are called Enhanced Radiation Warheads, meaning they produce a minimal blast and large amounts of radiation.

"Yes, we all know about *clean bombs,*" said Hastings. "They leave the buildings standing and vaporize all the people. They're the scariest motherfuckers on the planet, which is why they've been banned by every country, and why they've never even been tested."

Dawson returned his focus to the president. "The W-70 has a one kiloton of explosive yield, confined to an area of only a few hundred yards in radius. However, it throws off a massive wave of neutron and gamma radiation, which will penetrate every building and the earth itself, destroying all living tissue.

Taking into account the expected weather and wind velocity, we believe the fallout will be minimized, and certainly contained within the areas we've already evacuated. Any radioactive dust will be blown out to sea in a southeasterly direction, where it will dissipate rather quickly.

"These red areas are blast zones, absorbing forty percent of total energy and causing the most structural damage, so we plan to detonate the bombs over these four areas: Riverside Park, Washington Square, Central Park North and Central Park South. The orange areas depict the massive wave of radiation that will kill most if not all of the ants, while penetrating structures, ground surface, any place they might be nesting underground, and leaving most of the buildings intact. This blue area is the ionized and residual radiation, confined to Manhattan, although we'll have to test some pockets of Queens, New Jersey and the Bronx. Within a generation," he added, "Manhattan will be livable."

"How do we even know this will work?" the president asked. "What if we nuke the city and the insects aren't destroyed?"

"Exactly," chimed in the majority leader. "Maybe it will even make them harder to kill. Doesn't radiation do weird things to insects?"

"I believe you're thinking of Godzilla," chided the minority leader.

"You think this is funny?" scolded the president.

Dawson had dreaded this kind of thing. He told the group, "We know for a fact that radiation kills the ants."

"I don't believe this," the New York senator gasped. "It's a bloody nightmare beyond our wildest dreams. We'll be the laughingstock of the world."

"Correction," cried Hastings. "Our *military* will be the

laughingstock of the world, which I think is a fitting depiction, considering—"

"Just a moment," Garrett interrupted. "Do you honestly believe that possession of the single most deadly weapon in the history of mankind is something to be ashamed of?"

"General, get that man out of this room!" Hastings cried.

"I apologize, sir," Garrett said mildly. "This is no time to be congratulating ourselves." His nerve returned with his voice. "However, you mentioned how we'll look to other nations. Did you think about how we will look if we don't do anything about these ants? I'll tell you. Weak. Fearful. Easily strikable."

Dawson knew this was coming. They had discussed it on the flight to Washington as their best line of defense. "The colonel is right. If other state leaders think these ants are out of control, that the insects are spreading across the planet, how long do you think it will be before they take matters into their own hands? And it won't just be New York but all the surrounding states. There are nations just waiting for an excuse to blow us up. Surely, you all remember the global panic over the last pandemic. This is a thousand times worse."

The room fell silent, everyone thinking the same thing, and Dawson knew he had won them over in fifteen minutes. He had given the president an out.

"So you're saying," the president said slowly, "if other countries insist we take care of the problem immediately, we're defenseless to argue. It's not in our hands."

"I can guarantee you, there are heads of state preparing their own nuclear arsenal in the name of global security," Dawson replied.

As he spoke, Garrett used a remote to turn on a television screen that began flashing photos of New York City victims, chewed to the bone, inside an abandoned city. It was the most startling testimony yet of what the entire country might face in just weeks. There was no doubt that stopping this heinous enemy warranted extreme measures.

Garrett added, "If you turn to page thirty-four of the reports in front of you, it's clearly outlined that there is a zero percent chance of containing the ants if we wait twenty-four hours. That goes to ninety-eight percent if we hit them before nightfall."

The president nodded thoughtfully. He would be phoning his closest allies in moments, Dawson was certain. If they were in agreement, he'd give the green light.

The attorney general had one last question, and his voice cracked over the silence. "What will we say to the rest of the world, after we drop the only neutron bomb in the history of mankind?"

The words rolled off the colonel's tongue. "You're welcome."

There wasn't a body not soaked in sweat. Heads were spinning and no doubt every person in the room wanted to run and hide in a closet. Dawson was asking for the unthinkable, and succeeding in convincing the powers that be that there was no other option.

In his mind, however, he was praying for one, and wondering if two scientists had found their queen.

General Dawson and Colonel Garrett left the Situation Room with a green light on Operation Colony Torch. Garrett was elated, bursting with pride at what he regarded as his own personal victory: setting the American military on a new course in history. However, Dawson felt sick to his stomach, and spoke not a word until they reached a military jeep waiting with a driver to take them to the Pentagon. He stopped and looked off into the distance, to a helicopter landing behind the White House.

"I'm going back to New York," he told Garrett.

"What the hell for?"

"There are Americans who know nothing about this bombing, people in the city—our own soldiers—trying to help others get out."

"A few thousand lost souls is not a great sacrifice considering—"

"Those are bogus numbers," the general said. "Shit, Tom, do you think I'm an idiot? You may be able to fool those people in there, but I know there are a hell of a lot more casualties we're facing. You'll never get the military or the medical workers out on time. There are a hundred thousand wounded that need to be reached."

"They're dead, Leonard! Anyone in Manhattan after nightfall is dead. The only reason they're still alive is that the damn ants rest during the day. After tonight there won't be a soul left in Manhattan. We're giving them a quicker, less painful death."

"We'll just see about that." Dawson started toward the South Lawn, with Garrett quick on his heels.

"Hold on, General." They stopped in a face-off. "By dusk that insect army will be on the march, spreading out by the billions to the rest of the world. I don't want to lose those people, but there's nothing else we can do. The president has ordered we proceed with Operation Colony Torch and that's the end of it. Problem contained."

"You don't know that," the general argued. "If we bomb the city, and even one queen escapes, it will be a free-for-all. Bombs dropping everywhere a fucking ant pops up." He jabbed a finger in the colonel's face. "We've seen them flying, Tom. *Winged juvenile queens.*"

"They won't get far." Garrett straightened in his uniform, nodded to a passing senator. "Stop worrying. Everything's taken care of."

The general shook his head and continued toward the Rose Garden. "I'm going back to New York. Maybe those scientists have found a blasted queen and can save both our asses, along with the city."

"Not a chance, General. The president will never sign off on an untested solution. We have our orders. Don't waste any more time in New York."

"You can come with me if you like, or stay here."

Garrett shrugged and followed the general. "What do you hope to get out of it?"

Dawson replied, "My soul."

CHAPTER 29

IT WAS WELL PAST midnight and the streets of New York City were lifeless and somber as a mortuary. Paul and Kendra walked along Thirty-sixth Street, past the procession of old apartment buildings that were built above small shops and cafés. They crossed Second Avenue, passed a dry cleaner's and Paul stopped abruptly.

"Take a look at this." He moved his flashlight beam up the sidewalk where dozens of corpses were sprawled out like X's, as if they had been arranged in a line. A man lay facedown in a T-shirt and checkered briefs. Paul gently rolled him over. The side of his skull was smashed, the eyes pushed back in their sockets. All the front teeth were chipped inside his bloodied mouth. Kendra noticed a portion of cartilage ripped through the knee, and she gasped when Paul bent the bloody forearm in half.

"Broken," he whispered, zigzagging the flashlight beam up the face of the building. Nearly all of the windows were thrown open or shattered. "He's a jumper. Maybe they all jumped. That would explain the formation."

"Shit. This is the worst."

"Yeah. This is the building."

He lit up the front doorway, where number 268 was printed in white letters.

Another soft tapping sound made Kendra orbit her flashlight. "Is it them?"

"No," Paul answered. "Sounds like a person banging." He stepped into the street to get a better view. "Up there."

The beam hit a window on the fifth floor.

Banging on the glass were the hands of a small child, her face stricken white with terror. The little girl turned away briefly and then looked back, letting out a silent scream and banging faster.

"She can't get out," Kendra cried.

Paul ran to the fire escape and reached for the ladder, but the bottom rung was at least a foot too high. Kendra returned her flashlight to the window.

The girl was gone.

Come back. Come back. Kendra stared until her eyes burned. Seconds later, the child appeared, yelling so loud that the window seemed to vibrate.

Paul was clanging garbage can lids. "Kendra, I can't see, dammit! Give me some light."

Reluctantly, she turned the flashlight toward Paul.

He dragged the garbage cans below the fire escape and hopped onto a shaky lid. Balancing like an amateur surfer, Paul stood up slowly and raised his arms, flipping the metal catch and releasing the ladder to the ground. At that same moment, sharp blows hit the window. Kendra pivoted the beam and saw a flash of silver that came with an explosion. In one incomprehensible moment, she watched a metal toaster tumble through a shower of broken glass. It seemed to spiral downward in slow motion and then crashed onto the pavement.

Kendra frantically whipped the light back to the window. Behind the gaping hole, caught in the bright beam, was a woman. She was stark white and naked, with an unruly mess of long dark hair. Kendra squinted with disbelief. Parts of the woman's face were torn to the muscle and her eyes were dripping with tears of blood. An oxygen mask, placed over her mouth, was covered in ants like the beak of a crow, and more insects dangled from her outstretched arms like delicate wings of a Greek mythological Siren: half woman, half bird.

The woman stooped down and raised the little girl, wrapped in a blanket. Kendra gasped when she shoved the child through the ruptured window and dropped her into the night air.

The body landed with a thud. Paul rushed to her side.

Kendra half expected to see the woman jump, but the figure was gone. She rushed to the girl, kneeling by Paul, and took the tiny hand in her own. There were no marks on the child but she let out a small moan. She had a slightly round face, skin as smooth and white as porcelain. As Paul put his ear to her chest, Kendra smelled the faint aroma of baby shampoo and Cheerios. She ran her fingers over the soft cheek.

"She's moving," Paul said, watching her leg jerk slightly. "Her spine's okay."

Paul and Kendra both got to their feet and painfully contemplated the situation in silence. The dilemma of what to do next was no longer obvious. The world had been turned upside down, the line between right and wrong blurred.

Paul flung the backpack across his shoulder and shifted hesitantly on his feet. "Kendra, we have a choice to make here."

She could tell from his tone that his decision was already made, and she shot him a stern expression.

"It's almost light," he reasoned. "We have to find the queen now if we're going to—"

"We're not leaving her," Kendra said flatly.

Paul took a deep breath and stooped down. He shook his head and delicately scooped the girl into his arms like a fragile bouquet. "New York Medical is close by."

The electricity along East Thirty-fourth Street had been knocked out for hours and the clouds were unforgiving. Kendra had the frightening sense of being one of the last souls alive, and wondered what had happened to the alarms, helicopters and police sirens. Somehow, silence seemed louder than all that chaos. She tried to concentrate on the comforting rhythm of the little girl's breaths and the violet glow from the flashlight on the pavement.

Paul took even steps and held the child carefully, trying not to jiggle her too much. Kendra noted the gentle touch and the way he kept making sure the girl was still breathing, the hopeful look on his face when she stirred. She had been ready for a fight, assumed the great and practical Dr. O'Keefe would try to ditch the child and resume the search for an ant queen, but in fact, he was intensely focused on the little girl.

For six blocks they walked in silence, until the child suddenly roused from a fitful sleep, flinging an arm around Paul's neck and burying her face in his chest.

Kendra caught the smile on Paul's face and felt a warmth move through her own body. The child stirred and opened her eyes. Paul looked down at the girl.

"Uh, hello," he said awkwardly.

"Momma?"

"I'm Dr. O'Keefe," he said, putting his sweaty face close so their noses almost touched. "What's your name?"

"Hannah," she whispered, and then asked, "Why is your head so big?"

Paul frowned and whispered to Kendra, "She must be hallucinating."

"Actually, I think she's rather perceptive."

Hannah closed her eyes with a yawn and fell back to sleep.

It was getting cold, as they continued down the block. Dampness hung in the air and a light breeze kicked up the smell of blood. Kendra's eyes were stung from the smoke and debris. Her contacts were drying up but the bottle of saline was zipped inside her ant suit.

They passed the abandoned playground of a school, where all the windows were broken. Kendra didn't want to think about that, but a screaming in the distance brought her to a halt. She couldn't tell if it was a man or a woman but the sound faded and she continued.

They still had another few blocks to go and she tried to concentrate on the child, keeping her eye on Paul and wistfully imagining him walking with their own child someday. Calmness settled over her body. It was a feeling that lingered for only a moment.

Paul abruptly stopped. "Turn off the light."

"Why?"

"Turn it off."

Kendra reluctantly flipped the switch. Darkness shrouded the street like a black veil, making Kendra feel light and unsteady, and she leaned against Paul.

"Listen."

There it was. A slight buzzing noise rushed toward them like a gust of wind. It was a hauntingly inhuman sound, yet it had a melody.

Kerka kerkosh ker kerkosh kerka kerkosh ker kerkosh

It resonated like waves of angry crickets in an orchard, growing louder and closer until it surrounded them. Kendra threw her hand to her mouth.

"Quiet," Paul said under his breath.

The little girl became stiff in his arms and Paul looked down to see Hannah's eyes wide, her face frozen in a mask of terror.

As quickly as it started, the noise began to fade, receding like the evening tide. Hannah closed her eyes again.

Kendra didn't know if it was cold sweat on her face or the sudden mist of rain.

CHAPTER 30

TWO SEARCHLIGHTS SHOT UP like geysers a thousand feet into the air behind New York University Medical Center. Paul and Kendra followed their beckoning call to a stadium-sized crowd gathered in a parking lot outside the emergency room, under a steady shower of horizontal rain.

Blinding rays from halogen lights spilled over the scene and Kendra realized it wasn't a mob waiting to get inside, but a triage unit. There seemed to be as many medics as victims. Doctors and nurses worked swiftly and expertly in biohazard space suits, kept on hand since two airplanes changed New York City's landscape and its definition of "emergency."

Thousands of wounded ambled like zombies, pale and bloody with telltale red eyes and blackened lips. They lumbered like the living dead, minds less intact than their bodies. A toe tag dangled from each wrist listing name, address, injury, priority level and medications. Cadavers were wheeled on stretchers to an abandoned lot overlooking the East River. They lay in bunches stacked like kindling on top of plastic sheets.

Kendra bristled at the sight of so many bodies. Her protective suit now felt rigid and steamy, as the rain weighed down her shoulders. She and Paul searched for a medic, but it seemed like every emergency worker was far too busy with the critically wounded to help the little girl.

Paul approached a nurse who was bandaging a tattered arm. "Is there anyone who could help us with this child?"

The nurse didn't look up. "You're better off taking children to the front."

He hoisted the child higher, wiped the dampness from her face and set off in a new direction, beckoning Kendra to follow.

They proceeded down a path to the main entrance, stepping carefully over the wounded, and then crossed a narrow green lawn full of dandelions and writhing bodies, but the number of living waned. Soon they were walking through a field of scattered corpses, like a pumpkin patch.

For a moment, carrying a single child past so many dying victims seemed ludicrous to Kendra. Here they were trying to find a queen that might save the entire city, yet they had stopped to save one solitary life. She wondered if Paul was thinking the same thing, and worried that he might place Hannah down any second with the rest of the victims, but he showed no sign of letting up. He continued the trek to the hospital entrance, face pinched with worry. He looked relieved when Hannah stirred and again threw an arm around his neck.

Yellow tape blocked off the front of the hospital. Friends and family of the dead and injured stood beneath a hand-painted bedsheet labeled WAITING AREA, their wistful faces begging for the slightest information.

Soldiers were everywhere. They stood armed and kept order, in muddy boots and uniforms covered with some kind of clear plastic.

Paul scanned the nondescript faces and touched the sleeve of an elderly man in scrubs walking briskly by. "Excuse me. Are you a doctor?"

"I am," the man answered curtly, continuing his hurried pace toward the entrance.

"Please. This child fell from a window."

The doctor stopped and looked at Paul, confused. Then he checked the girl's pulse, then pupils, and made a quick examination of her body.

She moaned and crinkled up her nose.

"Slight concussion," he grumbled. "Lacerations, maybe a fracture. Come with me."

Relieved, they followed him through the shattered glass doors into chaos. The lobby, spacious on any other day, was now packed. A circular visitor's desk was staffed with aides scrambling to sign in a steady flow of doctors and nurses, who had flown in from all over the country. Injured children were being admitted and anxious parents were shouting and refusing to leave. Everywhere victims were sprawled out and bleeding, too close to death for assistance, not close enough to be tossed. The expensive leather furniture and Persian rugs were now just comfortable places to die.

Paul and Kendra followed the doctor through broken fire doors into a brightly lit hallway. Massive generators in the basement vibrated under their shoes. Corpses sat upright against the walls next to patients, making it hard to distinguish between the living and dead.

The doctor shook his head in disgust and flagged down an intern. "Get these bodies out of here. This is a hospital, not a morgue."

"Yes, Doctor." The orderly chose a body that didn't flinch when he kicked it lightly with the tip of his shoe, and then threw it over his shoulder.

"Damnedest thing," said the doctor. He grabbed a pen off

the counter and wrote a few notes on a pad. Paul noticed sting marks on the back of his hastily bandaged hand.

"Are the ants here?"

"Not yet." The doctor ripped a sheet from the pad and handed it to a nurse. "Just came from Bellevue. It's completely infested."

"I was afraid of that," said Paul. "What about the patients?"

"I have no idea. I go where I'm needed and there's nothing that can be done there now." He spotted an orderly with an empty gurney. He whistled loudly and said, "Bring that over here, please."

The young woman changed directions, spinning the gurney toward the doctor.

"Tag this girl," he instructed and asked Kendra, "Do you have her name?"

"Her first name only. We don't know if her family is alive."

"Well, she is, and quite well, considering." He pulled a toe tag from his pocket and handed it to Kendra with a pen. "It's not often we see someone we can save."

Paul set the child gently on the gurney, hesitating just a moment, and then watched the orderly cover her with a blanket. The toe tag simply read, *Hannah, 268 E. 36th Street*. It was placed around her tiny wrist and the girl was carted away. Paul stared blankly as his hopes sunk to a new low; logic and reason seemed to evaporate from the universe, sucked into some backward dimension. Right now anyone could tell him the earth was flat after all and he'd believe it.

From the loudspeaker came a booming voice of the military that filled the hallways and stopped the frenzy of people in their tracks. "Attention, all hospital staff and patients. By order of the United States Army, all persons are to evacuate this hospital immediately. There will be no new admittance.

Doctors and nurses are to assist as many patients as they can to evacuation locations, and those not able to move should be transferred to the lower levels of the hospital. We will have further instructions as the day progresses."

There was a new rush of emergency personnel through the hallways, shouting and wheeling patients. Paul and Kendra stood like statues in the wind of a hurricane. Without saying a word to each other they walked back to the lobby, out of the hospital and away from the cries of victims, until there was only silence and the empty street again.

CHAPTER 31

"FUCK FEMA!" MAYOR JOHN RUSSO yelled into his private line to the governor. "This is a war zone, Bob. I need military guys. Marines! Send me fucking Marines!"

Russo slammed down the gold-plated receiver, disgusted at being the only person left in New York who had any balls. The only official willing to make the hard decisions from the front lines. He stared down at the mounting list of callers, famous names from around the world offering useless assistance: celebrities, politicians, heads of state, wealthy private citizens.

And then there was the media. *The damn media.* Calls were coming in from every TV and cable news station, reporters from *The New York Times, The Washington Post, Time* and *Newsweek. Nightline* and *Meet the Press* were hounding him. *Dateline NBC* and *60 Minutes* wanted to nail him. The list was endless.

Everyone wanted to know how he was going to kill the ants. When would the city be evacuated? Is it true that the only way to destroy the beasts was nuclear radiation?

There was no way to avoid it any longer.

U.S. Army Public Affairs was setting up TV cameras in the control center for the mayor's first televised news conference, broadcast from an undisclosed location.

"Olivia! Find out if Paul O'Keefe is back yet," bellowed

Russo, and his secretary appeared in the doorway. "And those damn people from federal. I want up-to-the-minute reports. Those interviews start in an hour and I need answers."

"Yes, sir."

"And what about the president?" he added. "He hasn't returned any of my calls."

"I'll keep trying." Olivia closed the door gently.

Russo pressed his palms against his temples and rubbed them down the sides of his cheeks, feeling the coarseness of two-day-old beard. That was unacceptable. He had seen the faces of other bureaucrats in disasters, their ridiculous attempts to look as if they were doing the work of the true rescuers. Digging out survivors from a bomb blast, pulling bodies from a flood, hosing down a four-alarm blaze. They all spoke to the cameras from a safe distance, with their sleeves rolled up and their twenty-four-hour stubble. That was for actors.

From the top desk drawer, he pulled out a silver-plated electric razor with engraved initials and a matching hand mirror. He ran the humming blade over his beard and blew the stray hairs from the desktop. He nodded approvingly at his reflection and leaned back in his bulky leather chair.

Focus. Focus. Focus, John.

The mayor knew the next few hours would make or break him and he wasn't about to take any chances. Russo returned to his computer, linked up with the Siafu Moto command center in Baltimore. The screen read:

BREAKING NEWS . . . U.S. PRESIDENT DAVIS SEEKS CONGRESSIONAL AID FOR IMMEDIATE EVACUATION OF ALL NEW YORK CITY BOROUGHS, AS WELL AS SOUTHERN NEW YORK STATE AND NORTHERN NEW JERSEY . . . 3,000 ADDITIONAL MARINES HEADED TO MANHATTAN.

General Dawson walked into the office.

"Where have you been?" Russo demanded. He flicked the message onscreen. "It's about time we got some more troops on the ground. I can't exactly clear the city with what's left of my police force—"

Dawson cut him off. "Those Marines won't be coming. There's been a change in plans."

"What are you talking about?"

"Have you heard from Professor Hart and Dr. O'Keefe?"

Russo shook his head.

The general replied gravely, "I've deployed a special task force to the bunker immediately. They'll be arriving within an hour to keep order and begin a steady evacuation by helicopter."

"Just wait one minute." The mayor scowled. "Down here I'm in charge. You're in my territory. This is still New York City, and what I say goes."

"This is a military operation. I get my orders from the commander in chief."

"So do I," Russo angrily retorted

Dawson was in no mood for a stalemate. He laid it on the line. "Look, we can help each other, but that means supporting the president one hundred percent, and as of now his plans have changed. We'll be hitting this city with a series of low-yield nuclear bombs."

The mayor was aghast.

Dawson looked him in the eye. "Plan is to cut off all bridges and tunnels with thermal air strikes, then hit Manhattan with four missiles."

"I don't believe this. Nuke the city?" The mayor's thoughts hit a wall.

Colonel Garrett entered the office and announced to the

general, "They're loading up the planes, we're getting clear-ance." He gestured toward Russo. "Is he on board?"

"Are you insane?" Russo shouted. "No, I'm not on board! I was never informed . . ." He stammered, "On whose authority . . . ?"

Garrett didn't even blink. "We are under direct orders of the president." He threw a copy of *Operation Colony Torch* onto the mayor's desk. "We *will* stop these ants by nightfall, before they attack and spread even further, and we *will* bomb these bastards to kingdom come—as planned."

"This is my city!" the mayor shouted.

"Your city has eight hours."

CHAPTER 32

THE FIRST LIGHT OF morning was returning to the sky, but everything looked colorless and gray, like the battlefields of war. The rain had stopped, but the cool air settled and lacy wisps of fog danced gracefully over the pavement. Manhattan was lifeless and nearly out of power. There were bodies everywhere, and Kendra was disturbed by how quickly she'd gotten used to the sight of them. She stepped over a partly devoured cat.

"You were right," she said to Paul. "The ants are eating more than rats and people. They're learning how to survive out here. Falling back on natural instincts."

"There's nothing natural about a planet ruled by insects."

They were both exhausted but the evacuation announcement at the hospital had put an anxious spring in their step. "Do you think the army would actually nuke the city?"

"No way. They can't be that stupid. I'm pretty certain if they dropped a nuclear bomb on Manhattan, the only thing crawling out of the rubble would be these damn ants."

"Still, we better find that queen. Fast."

Paul flipped on his flashlight. Once again they were standing in front of number 268 East Thirty-sixth Street.

"Go time," Kendra said, and they headed for the entrance.

* * *

Rectangular sunlight stretched from two narrow windows that bathed the laundry room in a pinkish glow, electrified the beige walls and added sparkle to the line of steel dryers. It looked like any other laundry room in New York City, except for a pair of large Nikes sticking out from under a wash basin.

Paul and Kendra followed the feet to the body of an enormous man curled up under the sink. Paul squatted down to examine the corpse. "Body's cold. Only a few bites and stings," he said. "Yet his extremities are swollen and his pupils dilated. Maybe a heart attack."

"The ants probably snuck up on him," said Kendra, walking across the room to a table of half-folded clothes, size XXXL. She eyed a bottle of blue laundry detergent that had spilled all over the floor. "Must have scared him to death."

"That's odd," Paul said and strolled to a back door leading out to the street. "Why didn't he run to the exit instead of the sink?"

"I don't know," she shrugged. "Does it matter? All we need is a queen."

Paul scrutinized the back of the room, which was featureless except for the airtight fire door and two windows painted shut. "The ants had to come from the hallway in front of the room." He spoke with the befuddled tone of a TV crime-scene investigator as he followed the man's soapy sneaker prints. "These footprints go to the washers. Then they stop and go to the sink. Why did he walk to the washer instead of running out of the building?"

"Yo, Sherlock," Kendra said. "You're an entomologist, remember? Think Ant."

"Right." Paul nodded. "Ant."

She let out a weary breath. "It's morning. We must have

missed them." She felt hot and zipped open the heavy white suit. Something caught her attention, and Kendra pointed with her chin. "Paul, check out that washer near the body. I hope I'm wrong, but it looks like a head."

A mop of reddish brown hair was pressed against the circular glass. Paul walked to the washing machine and tugged on the handle. Out flopped the snout of a dog, curled up tight inside the metal drum.

"Collie," Paul said and looked over at the dead man. "He must have been trying to save Lassie here from the ants." He lifted the dog's limp head. "Suffocated, I guess." He bristled and then refocused his thoughts on the room. "So I guess we look for pipes, vents, holes. If they're hiding in the walls, this is probably the best place to find them."

Kendra nodded and pressed her palm against the wall. She put her ear against the cold plaster and listened for any sounds of activity.

Paul tracked a pipe that stretched across the ceiling to a dark alcove by the hallway. Below the pipe was a wall vent, about six feet from the floor. He called to Kendra, "Hey, over here."

She followed him into the shadows.

A four-foot ladder splattered with paint was folded up in the corner, and Paul pried it open. He dragged it under the vent, climbed the rungs and removed the iron grating with a hard shove. The opening was small, but he managed to reach an arm inside and then tried to fit his head. Dust rained down on his hair.

"Forget it. This building must be a hundred years old," he said, coughing. "There won't be any passageway big enough to fit the two of us."

"How about a colony of twenty-two million ants?" said

Kendra, drumming her fingers on her cheek. "*Think*. They may have been bred to attack a city, but they can't escape their nature."

Paul sat down on the stepladder and closed his eyes. He considered everything he knew about Siafu and then said, "So where in this building do we find the equivalent space of a fifty-foot hollow tree trunk?"

Kendra's face brightened. "I'll tell you where."

CHAPTER 33

DING. THE ELEVATOR BELL broke the ghostly silence in the lobby as the gilded doors parted, revealing a roomy interior paneled in chestnut brown. Paul and Kendra stepped hesitantly inside, relieved to see that the small light fixture was still working.

Paul unhinged the stepladder and positioned it under the trapdoor screwed to the ceiling. "Are you certain about this?" he asked.

" 'Certain' will not be in our vocabulary today."

Paul shook his head and climbed up to the escape hatch. He used a penknife to turn the screws. The lid dropped and dangled from its hinges. He stared up at the darkness, listening to the quiet, then peered down at Kendra. "You ready?"

"I'm fine. You're the one about to risk a face full of killer ants," she joked.

He flipped his hood, not amused, and zipped it tight. "Gimme the flashlight."

She handed him a bug vacuum as well. It was a pistol-shaped device, but when extended, it looked more like a *Star Wars* light saber.

Paul poked his head through the opening. The elevator shaft was dark and he strained his ears, listening to the silence through the plastic head cover and raising his flashlight skyward. The bright beam dissolved in two hundred feet of darkness. He lowered the light and it settled on the walls.

That's when his cheeks lost color and for a long moment Paul didn't dare move, or even blink. Millions of ants covered the elevator shaft. Their black armor shined like marble in the shaking light of the beam, as the colony moved slowly and methodically in wavy columns like slithering deadly snakes.

Paul blew out a breath of air and ducked inside the car, slammed the door and held it closed with all his might. He was beginning to hyperventilate. The bug vacuum dropped to the floor and he threw off his hood.

"What?" Kendra asked.

"They're in there! All over the place. *Jesus*." He tightened the first screw with trembling fingers.

"I knew it," she declared. "Well, get up there."

"Get up there! Are you crazy?" Paul backed down the ladder and wrung his hands together, willing them to stop shaking.

"Did they react to you? Show any signs of aggression?"

"I don't know, Kendra." He closed his eyes and breathed through his nose. In the dark recess of his mind he could see them crawling, slowly. His brow furrowed. "No, actually, they didn't seem to notice me."

"Then they're in down mode, right? Like the ants in your lab?"

"Maybe." He cast a troubled eye at the hatch door. "We can't really be sure."

"You seem to forget why we're here," Kendra said, zipping her suit. She flipped her headpiece and started up the ladder herself.

Paul grabbed her wrist and eased her back down. "Okay, okay," he gave in. He climbed to the top and turned the screw, gazing down at Kendra through the crook of his elbow. "But if I hear even a lip smack from those buggers, I'm out of there."

She reached up and handed him the bug vacuum. "Fair enough."

Paul slid the vacuum through the hatch, along with the flashlight, and zipped his hood once again. "Wait till I get up there. If it seems safe, I'll tell you to press the button. We'll look for the queen floor by floor."

Arms braced, Paul hoisted himself onto the roof of the elevator, landing on his chest and skimming across fifty years of dust and grease. He got up on his knees in the filthy white suit, surrounded by darkness and millions of imaginary legs racing toward him. He shivered and flipped the flashlight to lantern mode. The shaft became awash in light.

Paul stood ready to retreat, but the ants were fairly still. At least he saw no outward sign that they were preparing to attack, so he began looking around. The elevator roof was less than ten feet across. In the center, two thick cables operated the car from an electrical box at the top of the shaft, while four thin wires secured each corner for balance. The air was musty with a metallic odor of gears and machinery.

Paul grasped the grimy cable and moved to the wall, close enough to reach out and touch the ants if he wanted to. He didn't. Yet fear turned to fascination when he observed the colony up close. The ants were passing bits of food, carrying eggs to a nest made from their own bodies and disposing dead ants into a makeshift burial site, formed by thousands of legs linked together. They were busy with all the duties of ordinary ants but Paul was watching them from inside the colony, and he found that extraordinary.

"What's going on?" Kendra's voice came from the elevator.

"Shhhh."

"What do you see?"

"Would you hush?"

Paul shifted his attention back to the ants, with a glint in his eye and a growing sense of excitement. He examined them closely through the plastic window of his hood. At that moment, the Siafu Moto were not a weapon but a colony like any other. It's what he wrote about, spoke about; it was his passion. A society based on equality and cooperation. If people could emulate ants in this regard alone, they could be saved from certain extinction. He wondered to himself if perhaps the ants were here to teach us a lesson.

"Do you see the queen?" shouted Kendra.

Paul's thoughts evaporated. "Hold on."

He orbited the beam of light over thick layers of insects. If they were anything like ordinary Siafu he would find the queen laying eggs under a large mound of protective soldier ants. The mound would be easy to spot. Sometimes they were as big as soccer balls. Paul surveyed the area for another minute, until he was satisfied that the lobby level was clear.

"Start her up," he yelled softly down the hole.

Kendra pushed the button for the first floor. Instantly, sparks exploded from above. Like shooting stars, they soared gracefully through the air and then burned into cinders halfway down the shaft. Ants scrambled out of the electric box, where they bit wires and crammed gears.

Unaware of the malfunction, Paul rode the elevator car on his knees. When it stopped gently, he climbed to his feet and lifted the lamp to the wall, when a noise startled him. He turned to find Kendra pulling herself through the hatch.

"What are you doing?" he asked.

She got to her feet, equally covered in grime. "You didn't think I was going to miss this, did you?"

"No." It was an honest answer.

Wide-eyed and mouth gaping, Kendra strolled across the roof of the car. "Just look at them," she gasped. "This is what it's like, being on the inside."

"Yeah, I feel it too." He smiled like a young boy finding the most remarkable bug for his collection. "I'd forgotten the allure of nature's most coveted secrets."

"Too busy cashing checks."

"Ouch." His face pinched. "That hurt."

Kendra crouched lower, examining them closely. "They seem normal enough."

"Yet for some reason, they're oblivious to us."

"So much for your theory they attack in groups."

Kendra held up her flashlight to a nest, where hundreds of ants linked together to form an oval bed three feet across. There was no sign of a queen, but thousands of eggs were being coddled and licked clean by nurser ants: small, delicate capsules, waxy yellow in color, yet transparent enough to distinguish the wormlike larvae inside.

"Paul, take a look."

Below the nest were broken eggshells and a multitude of pink, squirming newborns. Adults crawled over the brood, checking each one like a new mother trying to find her only child in a sea of look-alikes.

"Trophallaxis," Paul said with a sense of awe. The ants were regurgitating liquids into the mouths of the juveniles. "Not something you see in the field every day."

Kendra nodded. "Maybe if we observe them long enough, we'll learn something useful."

"I think we're better off finding a queen and getting the hell out of here."

There was a sudden knot in his stomach and he backed

away. The light spread over a mass of crawling winged ants. They moved restlessly in circles over one another, occasionally lifting their wings and catching air.

"Alates," he said anxiously.

Kendra took a closer look. Although the ants were indeed future queens, they were useless for her purpose, as their glands wouldn't secrete the proper pheromones until the nuptial flight. "It won't be long before they take off."

"So now we have to worry about flying monsters."

Both of them scanned the elevator shaft with renewed alarm.

Kendra stood on her tiptoes, trying to get a better view of mysterious movement along a section of wall. "Bring the light closer. There's something here."

Paul held the lamp over her head, illuminating a mound of ants in the shape of a football. They moved slowly, in a tightly packed huddle.

"Hallelujah. It might be a queen," Kendra said.

"All right. You get ready with that bug vacuum. I'll try to sweep them off."

"Seriously?"

"That's why we're here, isn't it?"

She nodded and stepped out of his way.

Paul held up a gloved hand, pointed like an arrow ready to strike. He took several deep breaths and raised the lamp higher. Kendra swallowed hard and held the vacuum in a tight grip to steady her hands.

Paul struck swiftly into the center of the mound and scooped out a layer of ants. They felt soft and light against the white glove. He winced and danced on his feet as they all sprinkled to the floor like sand.

Ants scattered from the mound and the prize they coveted came into view.

It was a hand. A left hand, adorned with a platinum wedding ring. It was cut ragged at the wrist, the flesh chewed off and bones pulled apart.

Paul gagged and dropped the flashlight.

Kendra fell back in silence.

The hand plunged down the shaft.

"Well. That was fun." Paul checked his glove for stragglers. He tried to wipe the sweat from his brow, but instead left a smear of grease on the plastic window of his hood. He walked to the hatch. "I'll take us up a floor. You keep an eye out for Her Majesty."

Kendra nodded, speechless, as Paul lowered himself into the car. She braced her knees and steadied herself as the elevator began to rise. She picked up the lamp and the bug vacuum, as the car passed the third floor, then the fourth, then the fifth.

"Paul, stop!" she yelled.

The car didn't stop. In fact, it was gaining speed.

Paul was pushing every button.

"It's not stopping, Kendra!" he yelled back.

Suddenly sparks were shooting everywhere. Kendra ducked as they pelted the elevator. Five floors from the top, Paul noticed the bright red *Emergency* button and pounded it with his fist. The elevator screeched to a bumpy halt.

They both fell to their knees.

"Shit," he winced.

Kendra could hear pain in Paul's voice, but it was another sound that kicked up her heart rate. It started at the top of the shaft and traveled down in waves: the same angry chimes she'd heard in the street.

Kerka kerkosh keka kerkosh kerka kerkosh kerka kerkosh

In a flash, ants were streaming down the walls, the entire

colony on the move. The sound bounced through the shaft and became deafening. Kendra pressed the hood against her ears and looked up to see ants spiraling down the heavy twisted cable, straight toward her. A few dropped to the floor, right by her knee, and she kicked them, brushed them away with her shoe mitts. She scrambled backward like a crab and her hand clipped the flashlight. It rolled to the edge and down the shaft, taking the last bit of light and leaving her in darkness.

Something grabbed her ankle. It was Paul, reaching through the hatch door and shouting something, but Kendra couldn't hear anything over the ants. The elevator buckled and swayed and then there was the straining sound as the cable's hanger began to give way. Smoke poured from the engine and then it shorted out with loud popping sounds and a burst of flames.

"Hold on—we're going down!" Paul shouted.

Kendra held her breath, trying to make herself lighter. There was a thunderous snap as the pulley broke loose and the elevator began to free-fall.

Two corner wires snapped under the tremendous weight and the bulky car jammed against the narrow walls, metal against brick, slowing down its plunge and sending more showers of sparks into the air.

The ladder shot out from beneath Paul's feet and his legs kicked helplessly in the air. His body halfway through the hatch, he held tight to the center cable and pulled Kendra toward the hole, dragging her across the roof and over broken cable wires.

Kendra cried out, tumbling through the hatch with Paul and hitting the floor, just as the elevator slammed to the bottom with a crash.

CHAPTER 34

PAUL AND KENDRA LAY flat on their backs in utter silence. The light flickered twice but didn't go out. Paul was badly bruised, but remarkably, nothing was broken. Kendra too was banged up, but in one piece. They sat up nursing their aching bones. Paul unzipped his hood and flipped it from his sweaty head.

A shot of pain hit Kendra in her lower spine and she arched her back with a grimace.

Paul crawled to her. "You okay?"

"I think." She threw off her hood and blinked hard. "Great. I lost a contact lens." With a hopeless breath, she patted the floor.

Paul slowly got to his feet and limped to the door. He pressed all the buttons on the wall, but the elevator moaned like a beached whale. He tried to pry the doors apart but they wouldn't budge. "We might be stuck here a—"

"Unnngh!" Kendra cried.

Paul dropped to her side. "What?" he cried. "What's broken?"

She rolled onto her stomach, one hand reaching toward her lower back. "*Here*," she winced. "*Shit. Shit. Shit.*"

There was a thin tear in her suit, about the length of a pin, where the piece of cable had caught exactly onto the wrong spot, right along the zipper. It was the only part of the suit not made of woven steel.

Paul released the zipper and lifted her blouse. There was a streak of blood and . . . something else. He could feel his eyes bulge. "Listen to me, Kendra," he shouted over her moans. "There are a whole bunch of ants on your back."

"Well get them off, damn it!"

Paul reached for the backpack, knowing that any attempt to scrape the insects off by hand could leave the stingers intact. He took one huge breath to steady his nerves and fumbled through the pouch for his medical bag as his calm-doctor demeanor took over. He pulled out a scalpel.

"I need you to stay as still as possible." He tried to steady her writhing body, climbing over her hips and straddling her legs, pressing a hand down between her shoulder blades.

Six ants were gathered in a row across the lumbar spine, clamped tight, as blood trickled between the vertebrae. A red rash covered Kendra's back like welts from a flogging.

Paul could see the stingers working frantically up and down, and sprayed the area with an antiseptic that numbed the skin. The plan was to scrape the ants away with the edge of the blade, but the little bastards clamped on like Gorilla Glue, metal lodging between armor and skin. Three of the ants had already tunneled their way inside. He'd have to slice them off. Holding tight to the scalpel, Paul pushed the point a quarter inch into the flesh.

Kendra groaned as he started cutting, scooping out small chunks of tissue. She hissed through gritted teeth while Paul scraped the flesh into a glass vial, along with the ants, which locked on tight with a scissor-like grip. After the last of the ants was removed, Paul tried to control the bleeding with gauze and closely inspected the wound, making sure he removed every last bit of stinger. Even detached from the ant, a stinger could continue pumping poison into its victim and kill an allergic person in minutes.

And Paul knew Kendra was allergic to fire ants.

Gently, he turned her over, and immediately he knew there was a problem. Kendra's pale face was feverishly hot and her eyes were droopy.

"Look at me, Kendra," Paul mouthed the words loudly. He grabbed the medical bag and pulled out a syringe and two glass vials. "Don't close your eyes, baby. Talk to me. I need to know—have you been taking your shots?"

He wasn't getting any response. Cold sweat dripped from her forehead and her teeth chattered from severe chills. "Have you been taking your shots?" he yelled in her face. He tapped her cheek lightly and her eyes fluttered open.

She nodded and whispered, "Yes."

Kendra had been giving herself shots of H-1 blockers for years, but it seemed to offer no protection against the Siafu Moto toxins. Her breathing became labored. Anaphylaxis was setting in fast.

Paul filled the syringe, striking the glass with two quick pings to get the bubbles out. The normal dose of epinephrine was .3 milligrams but he gave her twice the amount. He filled another syringe with an antihistamine. It was a dangerous thing to do, mixing large amounts of medications, but it was a last resort if she didn't respond to the first dose, and she hadn't.

As the needle jammed her arm, Kendra's lips were turning blue and a hissing like a tire leak sounded from her mouth, signaling her throat was swelling shut.

All at once Paul was enraged with himself. How could he have taken such a risk? The truth was, he never seriously believed the ants could hurt them. That kind of thing happened to amateurs, not award-winning scientists. Paul knew ant behavior like the back of his hand and could anticipate any situation. But this time, things were different. They were dealing with something paranormal. Again, ego had gotten him in the worst predicament of his life.

"Stay with me, honey!" Paul took her pulse. It was 140 and rising. She was slipping away. Paul was not a religious man but he found himself praying, hard. He cradled Kendra in his arms and pressed his cheek against her forehead, feeling her skin burn with fever.

Come on, baby. Don't do this to me.

Paul was panic-stricken. There was nothing he could do if she slipped into a coma. He laid Kendra gently on the floor and stood up, tense, shaking his fists with frustration, and let out an angry grunt. He began kicking in the door with all his might. He pounded the metal with his shoes until a sharp dent cut the door and the soles of his feet burned.

Paul gave up his fight and fell to his hands and knees. Kendra's body lay still beneath him and he turned from her swollen white face. It was over, he couldn't believe it. This was how it ended, right here, so suddenly. Tears filled his eyes.

There was a gasp of air.

He turned to her, startled. Kendra was breathing. Not just breathing, but moving.

Paul was overwhelmed with relief as Kendra curled up in a ball, hacking on a sudden influx of oxygen. He lifted her head and reached into his bag for the inhaler, and then shot two doses of antihistamine into her lungs.

She took hungry breaths.

Paul brushed the tangled hair from her wet face. The swelling began to subside and color came to her cheeks.

"Was I . . . dead?" she asked.

Paul shook his head with a smile, relieved beyond words.

Kendra inhaled deeply through her nose and began to breathe normally. Paul helped her to sit up against his chest and their hands clasped tightly together. She nestled against his shoulder, suddenly freezing, teeth chattering, but his chest felt warm.

She asked, "So now what do we do?"

"We wait. I hold you and we sit here together. We wait until the drugs finish working."

She nodded, not wanting to ask, *What if they don't?*

"Let's make a deal," he said. "You don't die on me and I won't die on you."

"Ever?"

"At least for today."

They sat for a while, saying nothing.

"Hey," she said at last, and plucked something off the ground. "I found my contact lens."

Paul laughed and blew off the lens, helped put it back in her eye.

"Friggin' ouch," Kendra snarled, reaching behind her suit and drawing back fingers laced with blood.

"I had to cut the ants off your back."

Kendra caught sight of the scalpel on the floor, smeared red with bits of flesh. She picked it up and raised a brow. "You enjoyed this, didn't you?"

"What—playing doctor with you?" He pressed his fingers into her abdomen, looking for signs of soft tissue, and whispered, "I always have." He sprayed the wound again with a soothing antiseptic and put on another layer of gauze and tape. "No sign of internal bleeding, but you're not in the clear yet. Do you feel dizzy? Weak? Thirsty?"

She shook her head, squeezing her hands together to keep still. His warm breath sent chills up her neck.

"Nausea? Chills?"

"Yes. I mean no. I'm fine."

Paul finished dressing the wound. He put several layers of surgical tape over the rip in Kendra's suit.

She watched his hands tremble as they packed away supplies.

"That should hold."

"You were worried." Kendra smiled.

"Yeah," he said and turned serious. "I thought you were gone. It's the worst thing I ever felt in my life."

She smiled and her fingers stroked his cheek.

"Don't ever scare me like that."

Kendra suddenly jumped to her feet with fluttery movements. "You know, I actually feel great. So much *energy*." Not able to keep still, she shifted on her feet like a boxer, blowing out long breaths.

"What's the matter?" Paul asked with concern.

"Nothing," she said, her eyes shifting wildly. "I feel great. Really, really, really great." Her pupils were dilated and she seemed hyper-alert.

Paul was a little worried, baffled by her quick recovery. He wondered if it was the immunotherapy or the drugs he administered, or maybe some kind of miracle. He decided he didn't care.

She slammed the door with both her fists over and over and then thrust her knuckles into the panel of buttons on the wall.

Ding. The elevator doors parted to the bright lobby, and the sound of Siafu Moto.

CHAPTER 35

THE COLONY POURED DOWN the stairwell like black torrential rain. Churning rivers of ants slid down the steps and dangled in ropes between the railings. A second army shot up from the basement and joined forces at the front entrance.

Paul stumbled to his feet and slammed the button to close the door. It didn't. He knelt down and shook the backpack, scattering supplies all over the elevator floor. The gun spun into the corner. "We'll have to make a run for it! As fast as we can! Right over them! Out the front door," he said in rapid fire over the noise of the ants.

Kendra zipped her hood and grabbed the bug vacuum. She looked angry, revved up, raising her chin with defiance and pointing the nozzle straight ahead. She stepped out of the elevator. "Not without a queen."

The drugs are making her loopy, Paul thought and flipped his hood. He followed Kendra into the lobby, but then retreated, still unnerved by her accident. Realizing there was no way he could chance losing her again, Paul took a breath and stepped out of the elevator, easing up behind Kendra.

She hit a button on the bug vacuum and the nozzle elongated.

The ants suddenly surged toward them like a tsunami.

Paul prepared for the most terrifying experience imaginable. He closed his eyes and knelt down with his hands on guard, but the suspense was too great. So he turned to Kendra, who was staring wide-eyed through the plastic window, unable to believe what she was seeing.

The ants parted. They broke into regiments and formed a wide ring around the two stunned scientists. The colony began circling them in unison.

New reinforcements filled the lobby and swarmed the elevator. The room darkened as ants covered the track lighting above and two lamps on a table. They spilled across sofas and chairs and a large framed wall mirror, where Paul briefly caught his reflection before it disappeared. The wallpaper, a pattern of pink roses, became black. He squinted through the plastic window of his hood. Beads of sweat covered his face and stung his eyes as he braced for the onslaught.

Just don't panic, he told himself, hoping he didn't do something crazy again, like rip off his suit. "Kendra," he said aloud, "don't panic!"

She wasn't listening, but was intensely focused on the only corner in the room completely undisturbed by the crazed colony. A potted dwarf palm stood under the bright beam of a single bulb. Paul followed her line of vision and saw it too.

Kendra was staring at one leaf, and on that leaf, something was staring back.

The mammoth queen stood motionless, except for the slow snapping of her mandibles. It was her enormous size that made her so conspicuous, like the tail of a rattlesnake, along with her threatening stance, as if she were standing on hind legs, like the striking position of a praying mantis. The queen stretched her abdomen and opened her mandibles in a roar, as if straining to smell her prey through their thick white shells.

"Is that—?" Kendra signaled to Paul, pointing the bug vacuum at the plant.

He blinked away the sweat in his eyes. "It can't be."

"But it is," she replied. "Just hold steady. We won't see luck like this for the rest of our lives." Kendra stepped forward, toward the queen.

The colony surged.

The assault was so quick Paul thought the ants magically appeared on him. He had barely sucked in a breath when they covered his legs. They swarmed the body of his white suit to the zippered neck without giving him a second to react. By the time Paul let out a gasp, they blanketed the head cover. The sound rang in his ears as they raced across the window, inches from his face. Paul staggered backward, crying out to Kendra, but he could see only bits of light between flurries of a thousand legs. The weight of the ants, over eighty pounds, was unexpected and he dropped to his knees. He managed to brush the window free long enough to see a five-foot mound of ants in front of him. Then he realized it was Kendra, encased by the colony.

Kendra staggered blindly toward the potted palm. She could feel the heaviness of ants on her shoulders and held tight to the insect vacuum while one hand frantically swatted the plastic window like a windshield wiper.

The queen was still perched on the leaf, undisturbed, mandibles wide open.

Kendra could no longer brush the multitude of ants away or hear her thoughts over the buzzing. A blanket of Siafu Moto smothered the suit, four inches thick. Her neck strained at the burden of the bloated hood. Unbalanced and disoriented, she fell to her hands and knees.

The suit became stifling and Kendra sweated in darkness, as tiny vents in the material sealed shut and the air inside thinned. She attempted to stand, but 130 pounds of excess matter clung to her body. At the same time she was losing strength, a rage was building inside her.

This is not how I'm going out. Adrenaline exploded through her veins and she reached behind her neck for the zipper, tearing the hood cover from her sweaty face.

Her eyes focused. The queen was right in front of her. Ants crawled up her hair and she raised the length of the vacuum, pressing the button. Suction whirled. They scurried across her neck as she aimed the nozzle.

Kendra sucked up the queen.

Instantly, she felt a rush of cold air as the intense weight lifted from her body. Brightness stung her eyes and she knew right away what was happening. Ants were pouring off the suit and the entire colony was vanishing. They scurried off lights and furniture, headed under doorways, down stairwells and into every nook and cranny in seconds. The room brightened. The wallpaper was once again pink. Kendra saw the reflection of her glistening face in the mirror.

Paul was sitting on the floor clad in white, peering out of the plastic window with terrified eyes. Kendra sank to the cool marble tiles beside him.

The two scientists sat dumbstruck all alone in deafening silence. Paul uncovered his soaking wet head. "What the hell just happened?"

Kendra held up the trapped queen. "We got her."

"Great." Paul looked at the tiny prisoner. "But what the hell just happened?"

"They disappeared," she said. "It doesn't make sense. The second we trapped the queen, the whole colony took off."

Paul was silent, processing this information, wondering if it meant something useful.

Kendra studied the queen in the glass chamber and grimaced. There was more to this queen than anyone had been told. Her voice was laced with promise. "Maybe we just found our signal. Let's get back to the bunker."

CHAPTER 36

BY 9:00 A.M. MOBS OF civilians were making their way to the United Nations, drawn to a fleet of army helicopters that circled the roof, landing and taking off in quick succession. The streets became a surging human river, and Paul and Kendra were caught up in the current. They drifted with the crowd in every direction, bodies pressed together like floating debris. National Guardsmen had taken position around the perimeter of the building, visors down, rifles ready.

Swirling in a whirlpool of panicked refugees, Kendra felt someone grab her hair from behind. A couple of men were clawing at her white suit, yelling something with an accent. The larger one latched onto the dangling headpiece and pulled, choking Kendra around the neck, while the younger one, practically a kid, grasped her shoulder trying to unzip the back.

"Ant suit! Ant suit!" he cried "Give me, please—for my mum."

"I'll pay you!" the other man said and held up a wallet.

Paul tried to slap the men away, but the big one caught his gloves and tried to snatch those too. Paul looked back at Kendra, practically being strangled. "Unzip—!" He choked on his own words as the large man grabbed his hood as well.

Kendra punched her fist into the man's face and he fell back, only to resume the fight.

Paul unzipped his own headpiece and the man grabbed it

in his hand and ran, waving the white hood like a winning lottery ticket, leaving Paul angry and bewildered why anyone would want a piece of an ant suit that was useless by itself. He ripped off his gloves and threw them at the youngster, who was still struggling with Kendra. The kid grabbed the mitts, equally excited, and took off. Another idiot, Paul thought.

The two scientists were still churning along the streets and were nearly separated trying to make their way to the entrance. Paul considered firing his gun, but these maniacs would probably try to steal that too. The mob reached the brink of the barricades but held back, seeming to sense if they came any closer, shots would be fired.

Paul and Kendra hurled themselves onto a walkway, where they spotted a soldier with sergeant stripes. Paul tried to explain that they needed to get inside the UN.

The young sergeant was dizzy with frustration, his crew cut soaked in sweat. His bellowing answer seemed to be directed at everyone. "The building is closed! Go back to First Avenue and head north to the park. There are helicopters landing and plenty of boats leaving by the Queensboro Bridge and Roosevelt Island."

A strained voice broke through his walkie-talkie, shouting commands. The sergeant once again yelled to the crowd, "Please, folks! The ants are headed this way, they'll be here any minute. You've got to get out of this area!" He threw his arms out to the crowd but no one moved.

"We need to get inside the bunker," Paul demanded.

"What bunker?" The sergeant seemed genuinely clueless and Paul figured even at this crucial hour, not everyone was privy to the city's secrets. He tried to explain, but the sergeant just shook his head, and then finally pushed his way through the crowd, escorting them to his commanding officer at the main entrance of the UN.

The moment Paul mentioned the underground bunker, the officer became alert. He slid both their ID tags through an electronic scanner and allowed them back into the building.

Paul and Kendra quickly retraced their steps through the cafeteria, down a hallway to the stairwell leading to the top floor. As they neared the roof, they heard the thunderous sounds of helicopter engines and shouts of commands.

Choppers were taking off from the blacktop, evacuating the last few civilians from the bunker. All of the UN delegates had been hastily assembled over the course of three hours and forced to make the three-hundred-foot climb up the ladder. Those physically unable were airlifted by a harness.

"That's the last of them," a captain shouted to the pilot and then scowled at the approaching scientists. "Where did you two come from?"

"We have to see General Dawson," Paul said.

The captain vehemently shook his head. "Everyone is to be evacuated immediately. Those are the general's orders." He turned to the pilot, "Can you take two more?"

Kendra wasn't about to board any helicopter. She broke for the hatch with Paul. The captain grabbed her arm. "Get your ass in this chopper, lady—now!"

Paul pushed the officer aside and reached into his bag. As the man drew his gun, Paul withdrew the queen, displaying it plainly. "Do you know what this is?"

"I have my orders, sir."

"This is a queen ant. It may hold the key to killing off these insects. The general is waiting for it. Do you wish to keep the general waiting?"

The captain stared at the enormous ant for a long moment. "The last evac is coming at seventeen hundred. That's five o'clock. You be on that flight." He frowned at Paul and got into the helicopters with the others. The civilians buckled up, and he yelled to the pilot, "Let's go!"

As the helicopter tore into the sky, Paul and Kendra headed for the bunker.

Kendra held tight to the rungs. The pounding in her head had returned, along with nausea and body aches. Below her wobbly legs, Paul stayed close, talking her down. They hit the dirt floor and collapsed against the bedrock, dirty, bruised and exhausted. Kendra clenched her chattering teeth. She could almost feel the poison still lingering in her body, a living surge of heat through her veins.

"You need another dose," Paul said, fumbling through the backpack for his medical bag. "Something's wrong. You might be falling back into shock."

"Nothing is wrong. I haven't slept for days. We took the *Twilight Zone* tour of the city. I missed being an ant hor d'oeuvre by two seconds." She had other examples but the truth was, she felt terrible. Kendra stood up with a forced grin, refusing the shot and taking the medical bag from Paul. "I'll be fine."

They started through the bunker, but pretty soon she was losing strength and fell behind Paul as they headed toward the lab. She nonchalantly pulled an EpiPen out of the bag, pricked her arm with the needle and pinched her eyelids shut, imagining the chemicals filling her body.

This better work. If there were something to worry about, they would know soon enough. Meanwhile, there was no need to throw Paul into another anxiety attack. There was plenty of work to do and not a lot of time.

The Siafu Moto queen was bumping around inside the rucksack, not appreciating the hurried ride. For most of the trip, she'd scurried furiously around the glass. Having gotten used to the bottle, she appeared much calmer. Kendra imagined how long it would take to extract her pheromones and create enough serum to blanket a city. But would there be time to stop the colonies before they spread? Would her breakthrough research even work? She felt suddenly full of doubt and wondered how many other scientists were trying to come up with an antidote. What were they doing while she and Paul were scouting for a queen? Perhaps some entomologist in Australia, South America or right here in the United States had already found a solution or discovered there was none at all.

The hallways were eerily silent. The bunker was almost abandoned and there was no longer anyone running the city's power, water and security systems. The heart of Manhattan had fallen under the order DO NOT RESUSCITATE.

Paul and Kendra reached the control room. It loomed empty, like a forgotten cathedral shrouded in darkness, except for the flickering blue screens overhead. Mayor Russo slouched at a podium in a rumpled black suit, looking solemn and somewhat befuddled, like a minister who had lost his parishioners.

His hoarse voice was barely a whisper: "The ants are moving across bridges and tunnels. The president has given orders to speed up the evacuation of New York, destroy all passages to Manhattan and bomb the island with nuclear missiles. We have just hours left."

Kendra gasped, "You can't be serious."

Russo had a far-off gaze. "Tens of thousands of people are

still out there. Some of them badly injured. This city . . ." His voice trailed off. "Everything is moving so fast."

"Where's Dawson?" Paul snapped.

The mayor shrugged. "The decision has already been made."

Paul put the queen into Russo's hand. "Maybe this will change their minds."

The mayor looked down at the ant and folded his hand around the bottle. He turned to Paul and Kendra, steely-eyed. "Follow me."

CHAPTER 37

PAUL AND KENDRA SPENT the next thirty minutes in the laboratory setting up computers, analysis equipment and preparing the queen for the painstaking operation. The extraction and isolation of her pheromones would not be an easy task, and it had to be performed perfectly. The slightest error would result in failure.

News of the queen's capture was met with guarded optimism. Mayor Russo stood anxiously behind the scientists, listening to them exchange concerns as they began the procedure. General Dawson, too, regarded Kendra's every move like a hawk, recording the entire undertaking with some handheld military device. The general had bought them some time by delaying the bombing operation till 6:00 P.M.

Colonel Garrett watched impatiently from the back of the room, his expression grim. "Assuming the experiment fails, there will be a helicopter landing on the roof at eighteen hundred," he warned. "We will all be on it."

Kendra noted the clock on the wall read 1:45. They were in good shape. It would take about an hour to extract the correct pheromones and come up with the molecular structure. The formula would be handed off to Jack Carver at the USDA, where the queen's scent would be synthesized and mixed with a metric ton of a soybean oil base. It would take another hour to load the aircrafts that would fly over the city and drop their loads. There was no doubt they'd be cutting it close, but certainly the planes could reach the city by nightfall.

The thrashing queen had been calmed inside a cooler and placed under a microscope. Kendra handled the insect with utmost care, as strictly instructed by Colonel Garrett. The queen must be kept alive, he told her. As the last of her kind in captivity, she was vital to national security.

Kendra used a syringe to withdraw liquid from her poison sac, where the queen-recognition pheromone was located. In their haste, Paul could only conduct a speedy exam of the queen's morphology—and she was outstanding. Everything about her was enormous and strangely different from any normal insect. A quick ultrasound showed her brain size to be at least one hundred times larger than any other ant's on earth, and Paul found himself wondering if any intelligence lurked inside that cranium.

"Ridiculous," he mumbled.

"What?" Kendra asked.

"She's ridiculously large."

"She's lovely," Kendra replied, carefully depositing the drop of venom into a vial with solvent for analysis. Within fifteen minutes, the mass spectrometer software was able to distinguish the correct compound from other substances in the poison sac by comparing them to a library of all possible monounsaturated compounds related to known pheromones.

"We've got it," she said, downloading the data.

Jeremy entered the room. "Can I help?"

"We've just isolated a pure version of the queen's recognition pheromone," she told him. "We could use another computer."

"What can I do? Just tell me," he said eagerly.

Paul handed him a flash drive. "You can send this over to Jack Carver at the USDA."

"Good old Jack," Jeremy chuckled. "He still around?"

"Yes," Paul said. "And he's waiting for these results with barrels of base solution, ready to synthesize it into a mix."

"What about the alarm pheromone?"

"Working on it," Kendra said over her shoulder. "We need to hit them quick before nightfall. It would help to know the locations of the entire colony."

Jeremy shook his head. "Like I told you, these ants have been too genetically mangled for my computers to predict their direction."

"Then we saturate the entire city." Paul shrugged. "It would be helpful to know their locations, but it's not imperative."

Kendra bit her lip and eyed the general. "How about the army?"

"What about the army?" Dawson replied.

"Don't you have special equipment that can see through buildings and underground?"

The general folded his arms in contemplation. "Our satellites can give you aerial views of the streets, but they can't penetrate walls or the earth."

"GPR," Mayor Russo said with a brisk nod. He held up a finger. "The bunker is equipped with its own ground-penetrating-radar system. It can detect any object from twenty meters below the bunker, all the way up to the surface."

Kendra shook her head with doubt. "We need something that can locate the ants across the entire island of Manhattan."

"Still, it might give us an idea of how they travel and congregate," Jeremy said. "How do I get into the bunker computer system?"

"I can give you access," Russo told him.

"First get that formula to Jack," Paul said.

"I'll follow you," the mayor said to Jeremy, and the two men headed for the computer room.

"You should get started on that second pheromone," the general told Kendra. "The clock is running."

She nodded hesitantly and stared down at the queen, wringing her hands. It would be incredibly difficult to identify the alarm pheromone from a single queen using gas chromatography. The principal method was the same as the one she used in the desert: shake the queen and capture pheromones released from the gland opening above her mandibles. Then run a computer analysis to isolate the pheromone. The problem was, there was only a single specimen. Kendra typically needed a dozen queens to come up with enough extract to isolate the pure pheromone.

As the queen came out of her cold slumber, Paul placed her carefully in a specimen jar. "You ready?"

Kendra nodded. He gently shook the jar, then a bit more vigorously.

"Careful," Garrett said sternly.

Kendra prepared the syringe and pushed it through the top of the specimen jar. She held the tip of the needle directly above the queen's mandibles. The jaws barely opened, which wasn't a good sign. The queen had gotten used to all that bouncing around inside the bottle and wasn't much alarmed. Still, Kendra drew the plunger, soaking up her scent, and removed the needle.

"It's not going to be enough," she muttered to Paul and he nodded.

"We have to at least try."

The sample was analyzed by gas chromatography–mass spectrometry, but it proved to be inconclusive. The trace amounts of pheromone did not register a signal above the background noise.

"The numbers aren't there," Kendra said under her breath.

"Follow your instincts," Paul whispered back. "They've gotten you this far."

Kendra squared her shoulders and turned to the general. "The gas analysis didn't work. I need to dissect her glands."

Her words hit a wall of silence. Dawson and Garrett eyed each other for a moment.

The colonel spoke, "Under no circumstances can you destroy that ant. It's the property of the United States Army."

Dawson seemed more compromising. "Is it absolutely essential?"

"Dissecting her mandibular glands is the only way to get enough of the pure pheromone that I need."

"General, we have no way of knowing if this experiment will work," Garrett protested. "It probably won't, and then what? The colony could spread and this queen might be the only key to destroying them."

Dawson gave a slight nod. He told Kendra, "Do whatever's necessary."

Garrett huffed and retreated to the back of the room.

As Paul prepared the queen for dissection, Kendra felt suddenly exhausted and her vision blurred. She chugged down some water and tried to stay focused.

The clock on the wall read 2:30.

The queen was frozen in a dry ice acetone bath and placed on a watch glass under the microscope, dorsal side up. The top of her head was punctured and the cuticle layer peeled away toward the front. The remaining part of the head shell was held back, and one of the mandibles was pulled out gently, transferred to a clean probe and placed in a vial.

This time the chromatographer came up with a pure form of the pheromone.

It was minutes before Jeremy returned for the information. Kendra washed up in the sink and handed him another flash drive.

"Get this to Jack," she said.

Jeremy took off, with a small salute.

Garrett shook his head in doubt. "It will never work in the field."

"It's our only hope," Russo said.

"Our best hope is still Operation Colony Torch. Unless you can prove this method will work, the president will not change our strategy," said Garrett.

"You may be right," the general replied.

"How on earth will we test it?" the mayor asked. He turned to the general. "We need more time. You'll have to call off the operation until tomorrow."

"He can't do that," Garrett answered for his superior. "These ants must be stopped before nightfall. We've been given a green light by the president and there's no turning back."

The general told Kendra, "Hold on to that queen. Don't let her out of your sight." He started for the door.

Paul said, "So I guess there's nothing to do but wait."

"Pack up your belongings," the general said before heading out. "Get ready to evacuate. Pheromones or bombs, I want everyone on the roof by eighteen hundred hours."

CHAPTER 38

COLONEL GARRETT WAS ALONE with Paul and Kendra as they placed the dissected queen in a specimen bottle. She might have been dead, but she was still precious cargo, a valuable commodity that Garrett eyed curiously, biting his lower lip.

"So you managed to find a queen," he said. "They aren't easy to spot, lost in a sea of twenty-two million."

"It wasn't that hard," Kendra replied sternly. "This queen was isolated, all alone on a leaf while the rest of her army was trying to kill us."

"Don't you find that strange?" Paul asked, equally intense. "In every ant species, the queen is the source of life. In the field, the guards engulf and protect her."

"I wouldn't know about that."

"Why do I get the feeling you do?"

Garrett didn't answer.

"Come on, Colonel, we're in this together," Kendra said. "Maybe we can help each other." She tilted her head back and smiled at the colonel, batting her thick lashes, awkwardly running her fingers through her blond locks.

Paul rolled his eyes at Kendra's obvious attempts to woo Garrett. "Don't be ridiculous, Kendra. This guy's no scientist. He's just an army pawn, as clueless as the ants."

Garrett stroked his chin in thought. Then his expression

shifted and he was beaming as if he'd struck upon an idea. "All right, Doctor. I will admit we recovered some of the genetic information from the laboratory. It's highly classified, but I'm willing to share some of data—if you're willing to make a deal."

Paul stared with a dubious expression. "I'm listening."

"You are correct, these are not ordinary queens. Laredo programmed their DNA for specific behavior and selectively bred them over twenty generations. The queens, in fact, control the whole colony. "

"Why didn't you mention this before?"

"Because these ants are a weapon. A very important weapon that now belongs to the United States military. Shall I continue?"

Paul nodded.

"The workers have no fighting pheromones. Laredo isolated the alarm pheromone and removed it from all the ants. Without the queens, they won't attack. You see, it's the queens' alarm scent that sends the armies into battle, while the workers merely repeat her orders through stridulation, that chirping sound you hear."

"In other words, Laredo turned an ant species from a cooperative society into a murderous dictatorship."

"You obviously don't understand the implications of this colony. These ants are a weapon to end all wars. There isn't a nation that would use nuclear bombs after seeing what these insects can do. Not as long as America has possession of these ants." Garrett approached Kendra with a look of expectant applause. "Siafu Moto are the perfect weapon: all the power of an atomic blast without the radioactive mess."

The room fell silent.

"So what's the deal, Colonel?" Paul asked.

"I want your cooperation," he said, with a hint of desperation. "There are things I know that would send you screaming into the night. For twenty-five years I've worked with the CIA. I'm one of the few people who know how close this planet is to extinction. Iran and Iraq, their secret alliance formed with Russia. They've enriched enough uranium to blow up Israel, Britain and America ten times over. Then we have North Korea and China teaming up to beat them to it. The end of humanity is inevitable. It's just a matter of who will be the last to go."

Paranoia, Paul thought. An unavoidable consequence of working too long for the CIA. He looked at Kendra and rolled his eyes.

Garrett continued with a hazy expression, "Don't you see? The Siafu Moto changed *everything*."

"Why don't you cut to the chase?" Paul said.

"Tell the general you were mistaken, that your pheromones cannot work."

"Colonel, no disrespect—but fuck you."

Kendra put a hand on Paul's shoulder. "So you're asking us to help destroy a city, kill thousands of people for a weapon that's so unstable it should never have been developed in the first place?" She shook her head. "Forget it. In a couple of hours we'll have enough formula to stop the bombing. We'll kill these insects and your weapon will be lost forever."

The colonel gave a rakish smile. "You think the president of the United States is going to change his strategy on a hunch? Unless you can prove your formula works, Operation Colony Torch will stand."

Paul looked at the clock. They had less than two hours. No one said a word, until someone cleared his throat, and they all turned to the doorway.

"Operation Colony Torch is finished," General Dawson announced. "The formula has been analyzed and approved by our scientists. They ran preliminary tests and they're certain it will work."

Kendra looked shocked. "I'm glad to hear that, General. But how can your scientists be so sure?"

"Because they know these ants. The Siafu Moto were not created by terrorists. There is no such group as Earth Avengers. The entire project was funded by the United States military."

CHAPTER 39

GARRETT BELLOWED AT HIS superior, "This is outrageous! Revealing top-secret information to civilians! Why, it's *treason*."

General Dawson stood with fists wound tight at his sides. "This has gone far enough, Tom. We've been waiting for a method to destroy these ants for twenty-five years."

"You can't assume their feeble experiment will succeed. The entire world is at stake."

The general's face reddened. "I'm relieving you of all duties regarding this mission."

Garrett ignored the comment. "The decision has already been made by our commander in chief to evacuate and bomb the city."

"That was before we had a way to destroy the colony. The plan has been changed."

"On whose authority?"

Dawson shook his head. "The cover-up is over. I'll be sending out a report to every department in Washington. I can assure you that Operation Colony Torch will be called off, just as soon as I contact the president."

Colonel Garrett walked out of the room, fuming.

Dawson turned to Paul and Kendra. "I can't even imagine how this looks to you."

"You created the damn things?" Paul was aghast.

"We created a weapon."

"With no off switch!"

"This is the United States military. Damage is our first priority."

"Using living insects—screwing around with their DNA for your own destructive purpose!"

"Is it anymore horrible than biological warfare? Viruses, germs, infectious diseases, self-replicating organisms that eat away living tissue of their hosts. Smallpox, anthrax, yellow fever. It's all the same."

No one said anything.

"Look, this nation owes you a debt of gratitude. But don't try to make sense out of insect warfare. Very few people on the outside understand how the military works." Dawson rubbed the side of his face. "Sometimes I'm not sure myself."

The general was anxious to get to Russo's office and phone the president. He asked Paul and Kendra to come along.

"I'd like you both to be there for the call."

As they moved swiftly down the corridor, Dawson explained that when the twenty-five-year project was terminated, Laredo was furious. He went crazy, blowing up the entire lab, killing everyone inside, and sneaking off with a queen.

"Why *was* the project terminated?" Kendra asked,

"As you probably noticed, these ants are uncontrollable. They started eating everything in sight, doing things they weren't designed to do. There was no way to stop them, and even worse, no way to destroy them. Then we discovered that Laredo was making a deal to sell a queen to a terrorist organization. He actually did have ties to environmental groups."

"So the FBI is in on this?"

"No. Just a select group of people in the army and the CIA.

When Cameron started following our money trail, we created Earth Avenger to throw him off track. Undoubtedly, this will all come out in the hearings."

"No offense, General," Paul said, "but the military has to be off its rocker to turn ants into a weapon. Why exactly would you put all this effort into creating something so unstable?"

"Same reason the government does everything. *Money*. The United States military is stretched about as thin as at any time in history. Most of our noncombat jobs in the Middle East are outsourced to other countries and a growing number of our soldiers are paid recruits from Europe. Ever since the draft ended in 1974, the number of fighting units has decreased and with the growing unpopularity of the wars we've been fighting, the budget has been slashed to a tiny fraction over the last decade." He threw out a hand and said, "Siafu Moto were the answer to all our problems. They get no salary, no benefits and no one cares about the casualty count. There's no bureaucracy, in-fighting or pulling rank in an army of insects. They follow orders and don't make trouble. They're the perfect soldiers . . . almost."

Kendra looked at the bottled queen in her hand. "You've got to be kidding."

"These are the warriors of the future," Dawson insisted. "We can't depend on old methods anymore. There's just not enough money or support. You'll see—if it's not ants, it will be some other creature." They reached the mayor's office. Dawson led them inside and said, "And after twenty-five years we finally have a method to destroy them."

Paul and Kendra both dropped their shoulders with relief.

"Your buddy Jack Carver came through for us. He has a dozen chemists working on a metric ton of the pheromone, almost ready to take off."

Kendra closed her eyes. Consumed with fatigue, she could barely open them.

"When's the last time you two got any rest?"

"What day is it?" Kendra asked.

"Saturday."

She squinted, too tired to do the math.

Dawson grinned. "I'll call the president and get those pheromones in the air. You can both take a couple hours off. It will be at least that long before the planes are loaded."

The shower was as small as a coffin. Paul and Kendra stood entwined under a hot spray that soothed their aching muscles and washed away the filth of the streets, but not the memories. The left side of Kendra's hip glowed with an enormous bull's-eye bruise of deep purple, yellow and black that closely matched the one on Paul's backside. There were smaller bruises and scrapes, but fatigue took the greatest toll.

Kendra stared up at Paul with sleepy lids and rested her head on his shoulder, feeling the warmth of the steam. His dark hair hung long and damp, and she swept it away from his eyes, the same lovely brown as always, but she couldn't read his thoughts.

It was more than despair.

Paul turned off the shower and handed Kendra a towel. She let it drop to the floor and followed him into the shoe-box-sized room painted moss green and furnished with a simple bed and dresser, like the tiny bunks on submarines. She kicked aside the grimy Bug Out suits lying in a heap and curled up next to Paul on the cot. The narrow mattress was a tight fit so she wrapped her arms and legs around him.

He stared unblinking at the wall, his face shrouded in

grief. The weight of a little girl in his arms, the smell of blood in his lungs and the end of a natural world separate from man all spun in his mind and he struggled to keep it together. On the dresser, he could see the specimen bottle containing the queen, her body lifeless and broken. An image of Colonel Garrett, and all his boasting and warnings, played like a demented music video in his head.

"What have we done?" He sounded worn down, depleted.

"What do you mean?" Kendra's voice was raspy from shouting alarms all morning.

"*Nature.* My one solace. A world void of spite and vengeance—turned into a sadistic instrument of destruction." He shook his head. "Why?"

"Because we can," she muttered. "It's like you wrote in your book—"

"Don't remind me. How an *ant colony* can save the human race. Jesus, I'm the laughingstock of the Nobel committee."

"But you were right."

"I was wrong." Paul cringed. "What if my whole life was wrong?"

"Ah, Tolstoy." She nodded.

"It was a childish simplification, Kendra. Humans aren't ants."

"Are we so different?" She smiled at his pouting. "Your research showed that ant colonies fight for the same reason we do, variation of the species. Yet they've survived for a hundred million years. That proves diversity isn't fatal. All we have to do is accept our differences and learn to exist alongside other colonies . . . without blowing each other up."

"Yeah. That's gonna happen," Paul said. "Ants act on instinct, for the good of the whole. Man's greatest downfall has been—and always will be—individuals who think and act on their own. People like Garrett and Dawson. They don't care about getting along with the rest of the world. They just want to create a more deadly weapon."

"Which they have," Kendra replied. "And now that the world has seen the result, who knows? It may change people. That's the beauty of being human. We aren't slaves to our genetics."

"Come on, Kendra," Paul said dismissively. "This is real life, not some fairy tale. Contrary to popular belief, tragedy doesn't change people. War will continue. The madness will continue. Only now we have ants in the arsenal."

Kendra scrutinized Paul. "Why did you save that little girl last night?"

He looked away. "Because you wanted me to."

"You could have talked me out of it."

"What's your point?"

"You wanted to know she was safe, even if it meant losing precious time and our chance to save the entire city."

"It was an irrational decision."

"We *are* irrational, that's the point. I can't even imagine a world without compassion, valor, creativity and unique perspective." She forced his gaze to meet hers. "Ants have had a lot of practice being ants, and they're good at it. We're still learning how to be human."

The two lay in silence, Paul pondering her words.

"Why do you always do that?" he asked her.

"Do what?"

"Make sense of the absurd." He nodded, lost in a new direction. "Maybe you're right. Perhaps we will figure it out someday. We must be here for some greater purpose. "

Kendra seemed shocked. "You really think so?"

Paul's stare became intense. "I just look at you—and I

know." He had a fiery expression, almost angry. He rolled over and moved on top of her, his eyes darting wildly over her mouth, along the damp wisps of her hair and then into her deep blue eyes, where he saw a hunger like his own.

Kendra sighed deeply and buried her face into the nape of Paul's neck, biting lightly at his skin, still warm from the shower. The sensation of his body was maddening and every muscle tingled with a yearning she had long forgotten.

Then suddenly Paul bolted upright. Kendra protested with a groan and arched her back, wanting his warm skin against her own.

"No," he said and held her wrists to the bed. The muscles of his arms were hard and trembling. "Tell me now, Kendra, because I'm not losing you again. We might be dead tomorrow or fifty years from now, but I won't spend another day without you. It's that or nothing."

She kissed his lips. "That."

CHAPTER 40

IN THE MAYOR'S OFFICE, General Dawson pressed the phone against his ear and listened intently to the other line. He leaned back and swiveled his chair toward the wall, eyes pinched tight, and rubbed a painful spot on his temple.

"Uh-huh," he muttered.

Colonel Garrett watched him, unseen from the doorway, wondering if Dawson was speaking to the president. Garrett crossed his arms and felt the gun holstered across his chest. He hoped to hell he didn't have to use it.

It was those blasted two stars on the general's uniform that kept him from completing the most vital task the nation ever faced. Decades of research and monumental discoveries were being wasted over fears of bad publicity. Garrett and Dawson had begun their work twenty-five years earlier as part of a CIA paramilitary unit in Special Operations, and while Garrett had spent every waking moment in the laboratory with the ants, Dawson had dealt with the army brass, schmoozing and making friends with all the right people. Back then, the Siafu Moto had been seen as a viable weapon and the few who knew about the operation—only the highest-ranking officers—treated the group with a sense of awe and respect. It was Garrett and his scientists who had created the colony and Dawson rode on their backs all the way to the Pentagon. In the 1990s,

Garrett had watched helplessly as his former friend and colleague transferred management of the operation from the CIA to the army—which was deceitful enough—then rose steadily in rank above him.

Garrett drew back into the shadows as the general straightened in his chair.

"Right," Dawson said into the phone. "Tell him I'll await his call."

Perhaps I'm not too late. Garrett watched Dawson hang up the phone, count out three aspirin and swallow them dry. He stepped into the room.

"Leonard," the colonel said.

The general barely gave him a glance. "You're the last person I want to see right now."

"Have you spoken to the president?"

Dawson didn't answer.

Garrett sat down in a chair, facing the general with the utmost seriousness. "Think very carefully about this, General. Once you drop that blasted pheromone on those ants, they may be worthless."

"Say what you have to say and get out, Tom."

"The only reason the operation was terminated was lack of any way to exterminate them. Now we have the pheromones."

"It's over, Tom."

"Listen to me! We can save this weapon, start over and make it right."

"It's been nothing but problems for twenty-five years." Dawson picked up a pen and signed an authorization sheet on his desk, stuck it inside a fax machine. Garrett's heart kicked up, then calmed when the general didn't press the *Send* button. Instead, he started packing up his briefcase. It was a good sign that he was still waiting for the president's call.

Dawson held up a finger. "The president has to know about the pheromones. He has to know the facts. He's the one who decides. It's out of our hands."

"The facts are simple. We have a Siafu Moto queen. We can start the operation over again. Once you drop those pheromones, the world will know how to kill them. But if we continue with the bombing, the United States will have possession of the only living, breathing, thinking weapon on the earth."

"Use your head, Tom. If those two scientists can figure out how to destroy the ants, eventually every other country will too. The Siafu Moto are history."

"You can't destroy our work." Garrett was all but pleading. "There must be a reason we were given this second chance . . . some higher power that's made it all possible."

The general flashed a look of disgust. "You sound like Laredo."

"For what it's worth, at least he understood."

Dawson didn't say anything.

"Laredo released that queen because he believed it was his calling to save the world from itself. He knew that our ants would lead to a better, safer world."

"Is that what you believe?"

"I think we put fear in the hearts of every leader on earth. No one's gonna mess with us now."

Dawson winced. "You're as crazy as Laredo."

Garrett stood up tall. He leaned over the desk and turned up his lip. "I'll ask you again: Did you speak to the president?"

The general gave a slight motion toward the door. "Get out."

Garrett nodded but made no attempt to leave. He straightened, keeping his eyes on the American flag behind the general. "It was never the intention of the United States military to test this weapon on our own soil, but you have to concede that it has presented an opportunity. A chance to see how the colony performed and to devise a method of control. Now that the entire world has seen their devastation, the Siafu Moto are a weapon worth saving." He stared hard at the general. "Do you understand?"

Dawson gritted his teeth. "I understand perfectly."

The phone rang and Dawson reached for it.

Garrett reached inside his jacket.

Sheer exhaustion overtook Paul and Kendra. They lay entangled on the bed until the late afternoon sun began to sink over New York City and the sky turned golden over the wreckage.

A loud knock at the door startled them both awake, and they looked around, confused. Paul shook the sleep from his head and nearly fell off the cot retrieving his clothes.

"Just a minute," he said, as they dressed in haste.

Paul answered the door in a pressed blue shirt and khaki pants, fastening his wristwatch, and found Garrett looking a few shades lighter than his natural pallid tone. Sweat glistened on the colonel's forehead, but his expression was calm and cool.

"We're clearing the bunker," he said flatly.

"Now?" Paul asked.

Garrett looked past him at Kendra, straightening a white cotton sweater over her jeans, and he smiled. He needed to sound sincere, speak calmly. There was little time for discussion. "I'm sorry to inform you both. The president has rejected your pheromone solution as a way to stop the ants."

"General Dawson said—"

"The general was overruled. Operation Colony Torch is

back on schedule. There's a helicopter set to land on the roof at six. I'd advise you both to be on it."

Kendra came to Paul's side and said, "We're not going anywhere till we speak to General Dawson."

Garrett bit his lower lip, contemplating. "The general has already evacuated the building. He's instructed me to take custody of the queen."

Nobody moved.

With a sneer, Paul gritted his teeth. "What are you up to?"

Their boldness took Garrett by surprise. He didn't think they would question the orders of an army officer. It was a huge miscalculation on his part, but one he was prepared for. He watched Kendra back away toward the dresser and his gaze landed on the bottled queen.

Garrett took out his gun. "We can do this the hard way or the easy way."

"Have you gone mad?" Paul gasped.

Garrett held out his palm. "The queen."

Kendra clutched the bottle firmly, but Paul took it from her grasp and gave it to the colonel. "You got what you wanted, now leave us alone." He glanced at the Beretta on the bed and took a few steps toward it.

Garrett fired his gun with a loud bang.

Kendra cried out in fear.

"Leave the weapon right there." Garrett motioned down the hall. "Both of you—move it."

Garrett was tense, taking long strides down the corridor with his gun aimed erratically between Paul and Kendra. He was talking gibberish like a man possessed. "You're not capable of understanding the implications of these ants, how vital they are to the security of our country. What is it with you civilians? Demonizing the government, when it's our job to watch over the flock, make all the sacrifices, protect this nation from the most dangerous criminal minds. I'm not going to let the single greatest weapon in the world go to waste."

"How do you know the colony hasn't already spread?" Paul asked. "Are you prepared to bomb the whole Eastern seaboard?"

"Shut up," Garrett said.

They reached the laboratory. It was empty and Garrett motioned them inside.

At first it seemed like Garrett was going to shoot them. He pointed the gun but then scanned the room for a moment, hesitating. "Get inside the closet—both of you."

"Drop your weapon!" Agent Cameron swooped through the doorway, his Glock steady on Colonel Garrett.

Garrett froze, still holding the gun.

"I said drop it!"

"I believe I outrank you, Agent."

"Not today. I just ran into General Dawson."

Mayor Russo suddenly burst through the door behind Cameron, startling the agent.

Paul and Kendra barely ducked for cover as Garrett's gun went off like a cannon. Cameron fell to the ground, firing six loud shots and remarkably hitting no one.

Cameron lay thrashing on the floor, bleeding across the front of his white shirt, while Garrett stood frozen, the gun in one hand and the queen still in his grip. Paul lurched for the colonel, who fired off another shot, grazing Paul in the thigh. They both fell in a heap, the gun spinning beneath a counter.

Paul rolled away, moaning.

Garrett raced from the room.

Kendra was at Paul's side in an instant. The hole in his pants exposed a six-inch graze. "You're shot."

"Just a flesh wound," he said through clenched teeth.

"Over here!" Russo was tending to Agent Cameron, who was writhing in pain.

Paul got to his feet and grabbed his medical bag off the counter.

Kendra stood over Cameron, while Russo gently raised the agent's shirt.

"Shit." Cameron grimaced. "Where did he get me?"

"Just below the rib cage," Paul said, ripping open a box of gauze.

Cameron looked down at the blood pouring from a bullet hole at an alarming rate. "Flesh wound." He winced. "Just like yours."

Paul pressed the gauze against the flow of blood, but the pads were soaked in seconds.

Cameron took a wheezing breath and nodded at Paul. "Saved your ass, didn't I, O'Keefe?"

"Yes sir, you did."

The agent looked at Kendra and grinned. "No need to thank me."

She smiled bleakly. "Guess you're not so demented after all."

"Just don't tell anyone." Blood trickled from his nose and he coughed.

Paul tried to dress the wound with more gauze and bandages but it was futile. He checked Cameron's pulse and took vital signs. "You were right," he said to Cameron. "The U.S. military created the ants. They funded the entire project."

Cameron gave a weak nod. "I knew it . . . didn't want to believe it."

"Is that true?" Russo gasped.

"General Dawson . . ." Cameron's voice trailed off. "He's dead."

"What?" Kendra said softly.

Cameron closed his eyes. He tried to start himself awake, but only drifted farther away.

Paul felt the agent's pulse once more. It was weak.

He picked up Cameron's gun: empty. He tucked it into his belt anyway.

"General Dawson, dead?" Kendra was stricken, and stood up slowly. "Garrett must have killed the general before he had a chance to speak to the president about the pheromones. They're really going to bomb this city." Her eyes darted to the clock. "In half an hour."

"I don't understand." The mayor looked confused.

"Garrett told us the president is continuing with Operation Colony Torch," Kendra said.

"The last helicopter is at six," Paul said. "The bombs will drop minutes later."

Russo rubbed the sides of his face, looking worried. "We just have to get word to the president, that's all." He took a calming breath. "I'll try to reach him. Let him know the general is dead and stop this before it's too late."

They watched dolefully as the mayor headed toward his office.

Paul limped to his computer and prompted his e-mail. "Maybe we can reach Jack. Have him ready with those pheromones." He typed at the keyboard with a scowl on his face. "I can't get a line out," he said. "The Internet is down."

"Maybe the phones are down too," Kendra said in a small voice. "Even if Russo reaches the White House, will they believe him?"

Paul leaned down, and his lips brushed her forehead. "Go find Jeremy. See if you can get an outside line. Then both of you meet me on the roof by six." Paul checked his watch. "I'm going to find the colonel, get him to change the plan."

As he went for the door, Kendra stopped him. "Be careful with Garrett."

Paul pulled the gun from his belt. "I just have to be persuasive."

"Without bullets?"

"He doesn't know that."

"I'll have the helicopter crew come back for Cameron. He's in bad shape."

They looked back at the agent, slumped against the wall, eyes wide open.

He was dead.

CHAPTER 41

KENDRA REACHED THE DOORWAY of the computer room, out of breath and gasping. Jeremy was staring at a screen image, mouth gaping and eyes bulging with an icy expression of alarm. Only once had Kendra seen him in that state. A super-colony of ants had launched an all-out attack on Edwards Air Force Base, eluding all his computer programs.

When she came through the door he shuddered and said, "I have bad news."

Kendra almost laughed at the idea that things could get any worse.

"They're coming," he said.

"Who?"

"*Them.*"

A gray chunk of underground Manhattan was spinning in 3-D. The image was made up of swirling radio waves that arced around a network of pipes, cables and sewers. Anything metal or concrete was shaded in blue. Gaps and voids, such as buried subways tunnels, dried-up streams and riverbeds, were indicated in violet.

"The bunker's ground-penetrating-radar system," Kendra guessed, squinting at the image.

"Right," Jeremy answered, completely absorbed in the graphic. "It's fantastic. Far more advanced than any radar I've ever seen." The cross section of the earth was created through the transmission of low-frequency radio waves that penetrated out from the bunker walls into the ground. Whenever the signal hit an object, it would bounce back to the receiving antenna to create a picture. The high resolution and 3-D were achieved by systematically collecting multiple lines of data to form a tomogram, a very clear image of the earth surrounding the bunker. If anyone or anything tried to dig its way toward the bunker, the radar would pick it up.

Kendra had more pressing issues. "Jeremy, we need an outside line. Can you reach the Pentagon?"

"Not at the moment," he replied, still lost in the floating bedrock. "The Internet went down half an hour ago."

She closed her eyes and exhaled. "We have a problem."

Kendra summed up the events of the last half hour, including her suspicion that Colonel Garrett had killed the general and put Operation Colony Torch back into play.

"Unfortunately, that's not our biggest concern right now," Jeremy told her. "These are the last recorded images taken by the GPR." With a slide of his finger, the angle dipped farther below the earth's surface.

Kendra could clearly see the massive silhouette of the bunker in blue. Directly above was a glowing green blob, shifting and changing shape, contracting like a giant amoeba.

"Because of their rapid movement, the ants are easy to isolate. You can see the swarms moving frame by frame." Jeremy zoomed out. "The darkest green is where the ants are most dense and they disperse toward the edges." From the surface of the earth, hundreds of quivering tentacles grew and retracted, spreading downward. "They start to get fuzzy where the radar gets weak. If you follow these two subcolonies, here and here, they seem to be moving in our direction."

"The ants are headed for the bunker?"

"That's what I'm trying to tell you."

"I thought it's supposed to be ant-proof."

"Nothing in this city is ant-proof. Most of these walls are still bedrock and dirt."

Kendra looked puzzled. "So the Siafu Moto can dig three hundred feet into the ground?"

Jeremy shrugged. "Mostly they live in pipes and sewers, subways and tunnels. Their connective nests are fairly shallow."

"So how will they reach us?"

"Turtle Creek."

"*Turtle Creek?*"

Jeremy pulled up another map of underground Manhattan and placed it over the 3-D image taken by the GPR. The Viele map, created in 1874 by Colonel Egbert Viele, was the only known map of Manhattan's underground creeks and streams. It remained the bible for structural engineers, who had to reference the drawing carefully before a drop of concrete could be poured anywhere in the city.

Jeremy pointed to a long, twisted vein across the island. "New York is full of these underground riverbeds, mostly dried up and cavernous. Turtle Creek connects the East River to Turtle Bay, a subterranean river that snakes through half the city, all the way up to Riverside Park. It's located right beneath the UN, practically over our heads."

"How fast are they moving?"

"From these last images, it seems the closer they get, the faster they go."

"They couldn't possibly know we're here."

"Unless they're being drawn to a massive amount of electricity."

Kendra nodded at the bunker image. "The electrical field. It's calling them right to us . . . how long do we have?"

"It's hard to predict. Maybe an hour until they hit the ventilation system."

"That gives us time to get to the roof." She grabbed his wrist. "Let's go."

"Hold on. They might return to the surface if I shut down the power in the bunker."

"You can do that?"

Jeremy frowned, as if insulted. "I can shut down the control center, the air-conditioning, all the lights and computers." He thought a moment. "Yes, I'm sure they would head back to the surface."

She checked her watch. "We don't have time for that. The last flight out of here is in eighteen minutes."

"You're the boss." Jeremy grabbed his briefcase as she started for the door.

Kendra made it to the door and froze. Tiny hairs prickled along the back of her neck. She looked to the ceiling.

Kercha kercha kercha kercha kercha

Jeremy stopped too. "What's that?"

She stepped into the hallway. White tiles came alive in a mosaic of Siafu Moto. They rounded the bend and filled the hallway, spilled from the ceiling air vents. Kendra staggered backward in mute horror and slammed the door.

"They're here," she told Jeremy. "The hall is infested."

He looked completely bewildered. "Oh . . . I was a bit off in my timing. . . . Let's, uh, think about this."

"Think fast!"

"There might be a way," Jeremy said, pulling up a blueprint of the bunker. "I'm not sure why they built this tunnel— probably storage or some kind of vent—but it appears to be solid steel and as close to ant-proof as we'll get. It winds around the entire bunker." He highlighted the structure in red and traced it with his finger, talking fast and furious. "This is where we are, here, and if you keep going south, about five hundred feet, there's an exit right up to the roof."

"That's where the helicopter lands," she said.

Jeremy grabbed Kendra by the arm and hustled her to the back of the room. The small door was knee-high, like the closet in Paul's lab. "Get in," he said.

Kendra stooped and looked inside, wincing at the narrow space and shiny, mirror-like walls no more than eighteen inches in either direction. "Are you insane! I can't fit in there."

Jeremy eyed her head to toe and pressed both hands flat against her shoulders, as if measuring her dimensions. "Yes, I believe you can."

Kendra knelt on one knee and stuck her head inside the door. "Absolutely not."

"Hurry up." He gave her a soft push. "You're wasting time."

"But you'll never fit."

"No, I probably won't," he agreed. "But as soon as I turn off the power, the ants will go back to the surface and I'll meet you on the roof."

"I'll come with you."

"I'm not chancing it, Kendra—go!" Jeremy spoke sternly, becoming agitated.

"It's so dark." She put her head inside. "Wait, I see some small lights down there."

"Good. I'll be sure to keep them running."

Kendra paused for just a moment, regaining her nerve. She put her legs inside, then squeezed her body into the tunnel, tight as a sword in a sheath, until only her head could be seen. She lifted herself partway on her knees, but crawling would be difficult.

"This is ridiculous, Jeremy." She stuck her head out the door. "Move! I'm coming out."

Instead, Jeremy grabbed the back of her hair and kissed her hard on the lips. As they broke apart, he said, "Find Paul."

The door slammed, and Kendra was surrounded by blackness.

"Jeremy?" She listened to the outside and heard the dragging of metal. Something heavy hit the door. She struck at the seam, but it wouldn't budge. He had locked her inside.

CHAPTER 42

"JEREMY!" KENDRA BANGED A few times but knew it was useless. Jeremy was stubborn. Besides, the ants were already inside the bunker and he had only minutes to turn off the power. She would have to crawl through the death chamber alone.

Fuck, fuck, fuck. Kendra lay flat on her stomach and tried to rise on her knees but hit the ceiling. Lifting on her elbows was also difficult. She would have to squirm through the tunnel like a snake down a sewer pipe, arms bent like flippers at her side. After a few tries, it became apparent that the best way to move was by wriggling forwards on her knees and elbows in a sort of caterpillar crawl.

The walls were inches from her face and Kendra felt her heart throbbing out of her chest. The farther she moved from the computer lab, the more panic she felt. Suppose she reached the end of the tunnel and there was no exit? Maneuvering backward would be impossible, and surely a death sentence. She could feel the warning signs of sheer terror spreading over her body—sweat, trembling, heart palpitations—and she stuffed them down deep, replaced with a feeling of rage over her predicament. She could hold off the shakes for now, but it wouldn't be long until she fell into a full-blown claustrophobic attack. Her eyes yearned for even a morsel of light. Every ten feet or so were tiny blue LED panels that glowed but didn't illuminate anything else. Kendra had to squint even to notice them, but at least they guided her like a runway.

She could feel the rigidness of the steel, blunt trauma on her bruised knees, and she stopped for a moment to rest. She rolled onto her back, lifted one hand and placed it against the cold ceiling, which felt incredibly dense, like pressing against the whole planet. I'm buried alive in a tomb, she thought. Her worst nightmare had come true.

Kendra flipped over quickly and forced her body to move, taking deep breaths, and tried to remember she was a scholar, a five-time champion rower and a damn good cross-country skier. She did what came naturally: started talking to herself.

"Girl, you spent two days lost in the desert. You dropped ten pounds walking twenty-six miles in blistering ninety-degree heat, and then froze the whole freaking night. . . . Don't be such a goddamn baby." The trek became easier as she focused her thoughts and stared at nothing but each passing LED light. "What about the Congo . . . who was first to reach the study site . . . by an entire day, no less . . . like a damn monkey you took to that jungle . . . left the others in the mud, is what happened."

Before long, she had crawled about two hundred feet, and then she stopped, sniffing the air. A fetid odor wafted through the tunnel, both strange and familiar. Then the tunnel opened up wider, with a foot more head room and enough space to stretch out both her arms. Kendra clambered toward the scent and it became more distinct. She stopped short and the stench hit her face like a damp towel. Whatever the thing was, it was right in front of her. Her fingers reached out warily, as though about to touch a corpse. Instead, they brushed thin bars of cold steel and warm cedar shavings.

Rats.

Kendra poked her fingers into the cage and felt fur. Sharp teeth bit her pinky nail. She laughed a cry of relief and patted down the walls, finding what she expected: a seam in the metal. Her fingertips traced the line.

She pounded the door.

The burst of light was blinding, and she squinted at the white walls full of specimen boards, black counters strewn with paper. It was Paul's lab. Exhaling a burst of joy to be out of the tomb, Kendra squirmed from the hole. She staggered to her feet, getting her bearings, and ran for the closet, where she had seen a stack of Bug Out suits. She threw open the door with a surge of adrenaline and relief, but the feeling lasted only a moment.

Kercha kercha kercha kercha kercha

Kendra jolted. Inside the closet, Siafu Moto covered the shelves and walls. They sprinkled like rain from ceiling vents, crawled over all the equipment and the four boxes of protective suits.

Kendra slammed the closet door shut, as clusters of ants spilled into the room. They crawled overhead across fluorescent bulbs, dropping down in clumps, and scurried over every surface. She leaped onto a desk, sending a laptop crashing to the floor in a shower of papers.

The ants rushed her, stingers raised high in unison as if they were soldiers drawing swords. Heat sliced through her body and Kendra slid off the desk and spun around, slamming into a long table. She dropped to the floor and crawled beneath it on hands and knees, heading to the back of the room toward the tunnel.

The lights went out. Jeremy had cut the power.

Kendra struggled to reach the tunnel before the ants. She

felt her way to the wall and tumbled into the cramped space, shutting herself inside.

Her heart was beating like a piston and she had to stop a minute, wrapping her arms around her head. She was going to throw up.

No time for that. Keep going. She slowly started to crawl.

The LED lights brightened.

"Thanks, Jeremy," she whispered.

Jeremy Rudeau stared at the bunker main control system and switched off the last of the power. Immediately the buzzing stopped, as the electrical field disappeared. He listened to the quiet for a few moments, fairly certain the ants were headed back to the surface, preparing for their nightly raid. It seemed as if his plan had worked.

He left only one circuit running for the computer room and another one for the LED lights in the tunnel. The rest of the bunker would be dark. Jeremy crossed the room and put both hands around the heavy file cabinet. It made a piercing screech as it dragged across the floor. He opened the small door to the tunnel.

He looked inside and yelled, "Kendra!"

There was no answer. Relieved, he set off to meet her at the south end exit.

Jeremy stopped suddenly. The ant sound was low but distinct. He peered up at the ceiling, listening to the ants crawl through the vents; the sound became louder.

Not good. He rushed to the door and peeked out. Ants were everywhere. He gazed around the room, his mind racing, but it was too late to think. Jeremy scrambled to the back of the lab as hordes of ants dropped down from the ceiling like paratroopers, blazing down the walls. They blanketed the door to the tunnel, not that he would even fit inside. The sound of the ants pierced his brain as thousands of insects filled the room. Jeremy vaulted over an enormous mainframe, waist high and four feet across. He hid behind the machine, breathing like mad, his heart hammering.

Calm down, he told himself. Jeremy tried to settle his mind, think clearly. He knew the ants could sense movement. His best chance, his only chance, was to sit on the floor completely still, unmoving like a stone, until they retreated to the surface.

He breathed slowly through his nose until his lungs felt like they would explode. In his peripheral vision the colony moved under the dim light of the monitor, searching for a body to eat. A noise escaped from deep within his throat and Jeremy pinched his lips tight, focused on the robotic ants created by his computer programs.

I'm smarter than you, he thought. I know what makes you tick. I know how to fool you. Jeremy leaned back against the computer and closed his eyes. *They won't attack. Just sit tight. They won't attack. . . .*

For an instant, his mind flashed on the millions of dollars that ants had generated for his company, and he nearly laughed at the irony. In the next second, terror struck as the colony charged with a shrill cry. Eyes wide, he scrambled to his feet and sprinted over the computer, but stumbled and fell to the floor, kicking his legs and trying to stand. He gazed around the room at the explosion of life.

Jeremy knew he was going to die.

It wouldn't be long before the insects engulfed his body, paralyzed his movements with their stinging venom, and he'd be forced to live through an agony beyond his wildest imagination. Jeremy couldn't let that happen. He scanned the room for things he would need. The computer was plugged into a wall socket across the room, and just beyond that was a counter with a coffeepot. That would do.

Jeremy took a final deep breath and ran for the counter, right over the ants, leaping for the coffeepot. There was barely any liquid left, but he poured the cold java over his right hand.

Ants blanketed his pants within seconds.

All at once Jeremy was aware of the painful stings and he doubled over the counter. It was as if someone had doused half his body in gasoline and lit him on fire. They raced from his waist and arms toward his chest, and he clamped down on a scream lodged in his throat.

With trembling fingers he grabbed a pen from his shirt pocket, the silver Montblanc Kendra had given him. Jeremy winced in agony and struggled slowly down the counter to the computer cord, holding the pen firmly in his wet hand.

The weight of the ants was upon him, up to his chest and neck. They scuttled across his face, which was beginning to puff like dough.

Jeremy was blinded from swelling around his eyes. He had to keep his wits about him. His muscles were giving out, and he used all his remaining strength to reach the end of the cord. It was like wearing hot baseball gloves, but his swollen fingers managed to jerk the plug from the wall while keeping his grip on the pen, still slippery from the coffee.

Jeremy found the spot. He started to lose his faculties and hoped to make it in time, before complete paralysis set in. He jammed the pen inside the wall socket and felt the sheer force of ten thousand volts of electricity. His body jerked with spasms but he couldn't smell the burning of his own flesh.

CHAPTER 43

THE LED LIGHTS IN the tunnel flashed on and off, as if from an electrical disturbance, and Kendra paused, holding her breath.

The ants are eating the wires, she thought.

Crawling was more difficult. The earth was cold three hundred feet below the surface without any source of heat. Kendra's muscles were cramped and her hair still wet from the shower, making her teeth chatter.

"It's like a refrigerator in here," she complained, just to hear a familiar voice, and then stopped again, blowing hot breath into her cupped hands. All she wanted to do was sleep. She exhaled and lay flat on the steel floor. "Just one minute to rest."

Click.

Her elbow tripped another door. She blinked, and then busted it open. Kendra reached out a hand and felt a warm surge of air. The room was completely dark. With a breath of relief she squirmed out of the hole, overjoyed to be out of the tomb and inhaling gulps of oxygen, stretching her cramped muscles. She felt soft carpeting against her battered knees and patted her way to a piece of furniture. It was sturdy wood, perhaps a desk or table.

Then she felt a body.

Kendra scooted against a wall, panting and not moving until there appeared to be no immediate danger. She reached out to the corpse. There was a beefy arm beneath a sleeve. Her fingers ran down the stiff material. It was a man with a wedding ring. She traced the lines of the suit up to his shirt, where a cool, wet spot made her recoil a moment, before reaching back down to his shoulder and then moving slowly to his neck.

She held her watch over the body and pressed the LCD button, the closest thing she had to a flashlight.

The pale face of General Dawson was illuminated in the dark. His bulging eyes showed the fear of his impending death. Kendra saw blood on her fingers and slid the watch over the wound on his chest. A gunshot. The phone was lying by the general and Kendra grabbed the receiver. There was no signal. She pressed a few buttons, but the phone was dead.

She followed the cord to the end, where it was torn from the wall. The jagged wire spun in her fingers under the light of her watch. A cold reality hit her: the mayor had never reached the president. No one had. She sat listening to the quiet, wondering what to do next.

Kendra heard the sound of the ants. It was a low humming and she could tell they were coming from the open doorway. She turned and found her bearings along the carpet. Kendra hurried to the tunnel, heart pounding, and climbed back inside. She slammed the door three times as it repeatedly sprang open, and then finally shut with a whack. She fell back against the wall, hands pressed against her mouth and eyes clamped tight, once again safe inside the tomb. The general's white-skinned face flashed like bursts of lightning on a dark windowpane.

Kendra choked down the fear, started crawling again, slow and unbalanced. The bombs were coming and she had no clue how to stop them. "Now you're in a jam, girl. So, what are you gonna do about it?" She checked her watch once more. It was 5:50. That left ten minutes to get word to the president that the pheromones worked. Then, of course, Paul was on the roof with a lunatic. And here she was trapped underground with millions of ants ready to kill. It seemed a slim chance at best that she would ever make it out alive.

"Don't lose it now," she scolded herself. "Keep it together."

For a moment, she thought she heard the buzzing, and stopped.

"It's your imagination," she said. Still, Kendra found herself pausing as she passed each LED light, all movement and breath abated. Then she continued down the tunnel, calmed by her own voice.

"I should have been an orthodontist."

Paul crawled out of the hole onto the roof. He bent over the ladder, panting and wincing in pain from the bullet that had grazed his thigh. The gun dangled from his hand.

An ephemeral breeze had swept the smoke and ash away, and for a moment the sky was a clear Prussian blue, slowly turning to black. Paul spotted Garrett, a dark silhouette at the edge of the roof, looking out to the horizon and waving his hands wildly over his head. The Blackhawk helicopter beyond him was just a speck in the sky, but Paul glanced at his watch and knew what it was: the last train out of Dodge.

"Garrett!" he cried, and the colonel turned.

For an instant he looked confused, as if he didn't recognize Paul. He contemplated the man in front of him, struggling to breathe, blood seeping through his khaki pants, and he laughed.

Paul ventured a step and clenched his teeth in pain, raising the gun. "You're not going anywhere."

The colonel turned back toward the sky for an instant, shaking his head, then casually approached Paul with a grin.

"Stop right there." Paul raised the gun higher, his voice hoarse with desperation. "I know you shot the general. I'm going to tell those pilots everything."

He looked at Paul curiously. "What do you want, Doctor?"

"Give me the queen."

"You mean this?" Garrett took the specimen bottle from his pocket. He rolled it around in his fingers. "Anything else?"

"You have to call off the bombing."

Garrett stared back at the helicopter, shielding his eyes from the glare. It was fast approaching and he could make out the pilot. He waved his arms again, ignoring Paul.

"You won't get away with it," Paul said. "I'm not going to let you bomb this city."

The colonel smiled shrewdly, taking a few more steps closer to Paul. "But you will. And do you know why? These ants are a weapon to end all wars. They possess the power to disarm every nation. If you turn me in, the nuclear race will continue and tens of thousands of people will have died for nothing. You have the fate of the world in your hands, Doctor. Now tell me, as a human being, what should you do?"

Paul aimed the gun, but it was shaking. The Blackhawk was coming in for a landing. He could see its massive shape to his left, and hear the loud engine, feel the rush of wind from the blades that threw him off balance.

Garrett stepped closer.

"Don't move or I'll shoot."

Garrett squared his shoulders. "Go ahead. Shoot."

After a long moment, Paul dropped the gun.

The colonel nodded. "You haven't got the guts."

"I haven't got the bullets." Paul lurched forward and punched the colonel in the stomach with his fist, but it felt like granite to his knuckles.

Garrett pushed him easily aside, then swept his foot into Paul's bloodied thigh.

Paul snorted in agony and went down, throwing his arms out for balance. Anger blunted the pain and he lunged for Garrett. Paul was surprised at the strength of the older man as they grappled.

Garrett dropped the specimen jar and watched it roll across the roof. "I'm going to kill you," he hissed. The words sent Paul reeling and the two men fell to the blacktop. Garrett straddled Paul and struck several blows to his face. They seemed to come out of nowhere. Paul reached a hand to his bloodied nose but several body punches knocked the wind from his lungs and left him dizzy and coiled over. He tried to recoup and swung wildly but missed.

The helicopter was hovering overhead. The pilot yelled something from a megaphone but Paul could barely hear anything over the engine and the ringing in his ears as Garrett connected with more punches to his head: five quick jabs to the temple and cheeks, a sharp right hitting his eye.

A dazzling spotlight hit the two men. The colonel shielded his eyes with the crook of his arm and yelled something to the pilot.

Paul made his move. He grabbed the colonel's neck and shifted all his strength, rolling onto Garrett with a rage he never knew existed. He pressed down hard, squeezing his hands tight, as the colonel choked and struggled for breath, his face becoming mottled red. Paul could feel the body beneath him losing fight and slightly relaxed his grip, fearing he would kill the man, but his fingers stayed locked.

Garrett managed to turn his head and flung his arm to the

ground, touched the barrel of the Glock. He reached for it, eased it closer until his palm gripped the handle. He smashed the gun into Paul's temple.

Paul let out a grunt, clutching his forehead while Garrett crawled away, sputtering and heaving and finding himself cornered at the edge of the roof. Above their heads the helicopter was beating down on them.

Garrett sprinted toward the landing site, but Paul tackled him. Again they were rolling on the blacktop but this time at the edge, five stories above the sidewalk. Heaving every ounce of his weight, Paul forced Garrett's head over the ledge, then his shoulders, until finally half of the colonel's body was suspended in air. Now Paul could hear the pilot shouting over the thwatting blades:

"Step away from the officer! We will shoot you!"

Garrett frantically grabbed at Paul's shirt collar, wrenching himself higher until they were face-to-face. Baring his teeth, he hissed, "You're going down with me, O'Keefe. With any luck you'll break my fall."

Paul clawed at the slick blacktop, but it was futile. He was slipping, and he looked down in terror at the cement below.

A shot rang out.

Blood splattered across the roof.

CHAPTER 44

KENDRA STARED AT THE glowing face of the watch strapped to her wrist and illuminating the time: 5:55. It wasn't just despair and fatigue slowing her down. She felt woozy, with all-over body aches, as if she were coming down with the flu. The ant venom was still surging through her veins, hot and angry, while the cold temperature in the tunnel was affecting her muscles, making them stiff and slow. She struggled to fight off a feeling of hopelessness.

"Can't stop now," she said aloud. But Kendra had five minutes to make it to the roof. She thought about Paul anxiously waiting for her, holding off the soldiers in the chopper, who were most likely ready to hightail it out of the city, as the bombers came charging over the horizon. *We can't wait any longer, Dr. O'Keefe!*

Kendra swore under each breath and tears welled in her eyes; for a moment all she could do was collapse against the metal. "*Damn it, Paul. I can't do this.*"

She lifted her head and was struck by a bright red light. Just possibly, she thought, it might signal the end of the tunnel. It was enough to get her moving. The pain subsided, along with the dizziness, and in that moment she found boundless energy and scrambled for the exit.

Kendra threw herself against the last door and found herself sprawled on a dirt floor. Lying perfectly still on her back, she stared up at the caged black lightbulb in a circular room cut from the earth. The smell of damp soil hovered in the air. A metal ladder stood at one end. She had reached the south exit.

Kendra coughed and drew a wheezing breath of relief. Now all she had to do was climb three hundred feet in about a minute.

"Piece of cake," she said, and pulled herself to her feet. Her white sweater glowed violet under the black light.

Kendra grasped the first rung. "You can do this," she coaxed sternly. "You did it twice before." But that was with Paul, and now she seemed so alone, so exhausted. Kendra grabbed each rung white-knuckled, taking deep breaths.

She moved quickly at first, thinking of nothing but the next rung. Then she suddenly stopped. All at once the bottom seemed to drop out from below and taking another step became impossible. She was shaking and covered in sweat. It was as if her arms and legs were still climbing but she wasn't getting anywhere. Fear struck with pounding force and the walls of the cavern began to close in. Kendra sensed their rough exterior just inches from her face and nearly slipped off the ladder, disoriented.

She squeezed her eyes tight.

"How far to the top?" she asked in a small voice. She could feel the flutter on her wrist, light, comforting wisps. Butterfly kisses.

Kendra didn't know how long she stayed on the ladder, but her heart rate began to slow and her legs could move again.

There was nowhere else to go but up.

★ ★ ★

Paul's face was splattered with blood and he felt Garrett go limp beneath him. He backed off and let the body plunge to the sidewalk.

Mayor John Russo stood by the open hatch with a smoking gun by his side. A powerful wind from the whirling blades of the Blackhawk threw him off balance. The helicopter came in fast and low as it landed on the blacktop. Russo ducked and broke for Paul at the ledge.

"Thanks," Paul shouted over the sound of the engines. He was panting on hands and knees, overcome with relief, and wondering how many more people he'd have to thank for saving his life that day.

"You're welcome," answered Russo, looking down at the twisted body of Colonel Garrett on the pavement five stories below. "Now let's get the hell out of here!"

He helped Paul to his feet, and he started for the chopper.

"Wait." Paul took a few painful steps, then reached down and picked up the specimen jar. The queen was in three pieces and he handed the bottle to Russo. "I think we can study her, prevent this from happening again."

"Is that right?" There was a sudden twinkle in the mayor's eye.

Paul shouted, "Did you reach the president?"

Russo shook his head vigorously. "The phone line was cut. We can only hope the general got word in time—now let's haul it."

"I'm going back for Kendra."

"Get inside, Paul. Those bombs could drop in minutes."

"I'll take my chances."

Three members of a Special Forces unit spilled out of the helicopter cabin with guns drawn. One of them charged toward the two men. Paul started for the hatch but the soldier was already upon them.

"Freeze!" he yelled, the barrel pointed at Russo's head. "Drop your gun."

The mayor let his gun fall and raised his hands. "Settle down, soldier."

"You just shot Colonel Garrett." His rifle shifted between Russo and Paul as he tried to decide in his next move. Obviously, this wasn't the situation he expected. He turned to the Blackhawk, where the rest of the crew were pacing with keen eyes on him, hands ready on their weapons.

"Where's General Dawson?" the soldier asked.

"Dead," Russo told him. "Garrett shot him."

The soldier raised his rifle with an expression of renewed alarm. He looked at Paul, who nodded affirmatively.

Mayor Russo yelled at the man with urgency, "Do you know who I am?"

"Yes, sir."

"Did they call off the bombing?"

"I don't know about any bombs, sir. Now please get inside the helicopter."

"Don't you understand? They are going to drop nuclear bombs on this city! The president has no idea there's another solution. If you just—"

"My orders are to pick up the last of the civilians on this roof."

"There are people inside the bunker."

"I can't do anything about that, sir. We have direct orders to leave this site by eighteen hundred—that's now!"

A heated voice screeched from the radio receiver on the

soldier's collar, "What's happening, Sanchez? We are way be-hind schedule. Return at once!"

Paul could see it was another soldier, talking into his lapel.

In a bold move, the mayor charged Sanchez, grabbing at the receiver. "Listen to me—"

Russo was knocked to his knees by a blow from a rifle. "I'm placing you under arrest for compromising a mission of national security, and killing an officer of the United States Army. Now both of you—move!"

As the soldier pulled the mayor to his feet, Paul took off across the roof toward the hatch.

"Hey!" the soldier yelled.

"Paul!" the mayor called as he was dragged to the Black-hawk, but Paul was already out of earshot. Seconds later, the Blackhawk took off at full speed and banked toward the hori-zon, as night fell over the city.

CHAPTER 45

PAUL HAD BARELY DESCENDED twenty feet down the ladder when he heard someone struggling on the way up. He shouted, "Kendra, is that you?"

"Yes, it's me!" she cried with relief and exhaustion. "The ants invaded the bunker. Go up, Paul!"

He reached the roof and helped Kendra out of the hole, both locking into a tight embrace. She was covered in sweat, he was covered in blood.

"Thank God, you're all right," he said.

"Your face." She touched his swollen, bloody cheek.

"Yeah, well," he said faintly, "you should see the other guy." He glanced anxiously at the open hatch. "Where's Jeremy?"

Kendra shook her head. "He was supposed to meet me on the roof."

They both scanned the empty blacktop in silence. Neither wanted to think the worst, opting instead to imagine Jeremy had escaped the ants in classic superhero fashion.

Kendra forced her attention to the bright speck of helicopter steady on the horizon. Its lights blinked off and she frowned. "You should have left without me."

"No chance." He put his arms around her shoulders. "You're shaking."

Kendra grasped his arm with more bad news. "I saw General Dawson. The phone line was cut."

He nodded. "It's out of our hands. Right now the mayor's on that helicopter, hopefully convincing someone—"

There was a flash of light and a thunderous boom out toward the sea. Military planes were streaming over the horizon, headed toward lower Manhattan. The engines roared and Paul counted three in quick succession.

The first plane drew close to the UN, passing over the river, and stopped. It seemed to hover for a moment and then banked sharply to the right. Then a whirling sound echoed over the city as the plane took off like a bullet. Seconds later, a deafening explosion erupted from the ground where the plane dropped its load. Kendra closed her eyes and covered her ears from the burst.

Paul watched in horror as the lights from the Williamsburg Bridge flickered off and a huge piece of the enormous steel structure fell into the river. The sky came alive with more aircraft, and there were more eruptions and more sounds of collapse. Kendra huddled close to Paul and breathed into his neck, wanting to drown out the booms.

After a dozen massive explosions, the bridges and tunnels were gone and now they were truly an island. What would come next, they didn't want to think about.

Paul and Kendra stood alone on the roof, holding hands, as a gentle wind blew across the buildings. The smell of smoke filled the air, but the planes were gone and the city was once again deathly still. Above the smoke, the sky was transforming from a deep blue in the west to the deepest black in the east, a vast number of bright stars poking through the canvas.

Paul's voice was worried. "Do you hear them? They're coming back."

Kendra snapped out of her trance. Yes, she heard them. It wasn't the planes returning but the ants. The roof was suddenly swarming with Siafu Moto. They raced up the sides of the buildings and across the blacktop.

"Where do we go?" Kendra cried, turning in circles.

"I don't know," Paul answered.

They backed away from one side of the building, but ants were swarming from every direction. They poured from the bunker's open hatch like an erupting volcano. The entrance to the UN was blanketed by the colony, and the sea of ants began to take shape across the roof, a wide circle surrounding the scientists.

Kendra stumbled against Paul.

"Stay with me," he told her, and they clutched each other, turning with the colony, looking for a path out of this. There was none, and for the second time that day, the two scientists braced for an onslaught.

Instead, the air around them turned fuzzy gray. Kendra felt the fluttering of a thousand wings, like gnats in her face. But it wasn't gnats, it was ants.

The flight of the alates.

Kendra realized in one terrifying moment that time had run out; they would never stop the swarm. The winged virgin queens were taking off with the males in their nuptial dance.

She tried to speak but they flitted around her mouth and she wiped them from her lips. Paul was madly swatting his face.

At that moment, a sonic boom shook the building. Kendra jolted backward, searching the sky, while Paul reflexively ducked his head. Another sonic boom and the stealthy body of an F-22 Raptor cut through the heavens and hovered in the air like a snapshot.

"We've got to get out of here," Paul cried, grabbing her hand.

"Where?" she yelled back, blowing out insects and staring at the circle of ants at their feet, which were rounding faster, moving in.

"This way!"

Kendra could barely see Paul, the air was so thick with wings.

Another sonic boom cracked the sky and they lurched back, straining to see the plane directly overhead. The raptor glowed silver against the dark universe. Giant metal flaps opened like wings and the shrill whistle of a falling bomb sounded.

"Kendra, get down!"

They both hit the deck, curling up like pill bugs with Paul draped over Kendra, both of her arms crisscrossing the back of her head. They waited for the bomb that would tear them to pieces, holding their ears and bracing for impact.

A deafening explosion blew open the sky in a rumble that echoed for miles. Kendra felt the ground shudder under her knees, and the strength of Paul's body. Their ears were still ringing, when the world went silent for a moment. A soft wind blew over them.

Suddenly, Paul and Kendra were pummeled by an oily liquid.

It hit their bodies like an ocean wave and they slid across the roof, soaked and confused.

The plane was gone. They both sat up, feeling their wet limbs, making sure it wasn't blood. Ants were running in frantic circles, zigzagging in no apparent direction, searching for queens that seemed to be everywhere and nowhere at once. Paul licked his lips and tasted soybean.

"It's the pheromones," he said, excited.

Already the armies were beginning to fight. Groups of ants were attacking each other. Large soldier ants were battling small workers, and workers were slaughtering soldiers; it didn't matter. They tore each body limb from limb, unaware and unconcerned that they were colony mates committing their own form of genocide.

Dozens of aircraft were blazing over the horizon, and the sky was filled with ant-killing machines, strategically hitting their targets. The bombs would fall a hundred feet and then suddenly explode, dousing chemicals over a wide area. Behind the heavy planes were a fleet of crop dusters, blazing white under the moon and leaving contrails of pheromone that sprinkled to the earth and coated every skyscraper. Gray swarms of insects, covered in the sticky chemical, formed clusters of dark clouds all over the city, before plunging from the sky like a heavy rain. The ones that escaped flew head-on into buildings, attracted to the chemical like moths to a searing flame.

Kendra looked down at the ants breaking up into angry mobs.

"They're dying," she said.

"Yes," Paul replied, but it was with sadness as much as relief.

Kendra felt it too.

They held each other, lost in their small corner of the world. Already it seemed like a dream, or more aptly, a nightmare. She smiled at Paul, realizing it was over and he was still standing at her side.

"So where do we go from here?" she said.

"You marry me, and I marry you right back."

She liked the idea.

"Let's get you bandaged." Kendra took his arm and he leaned against her shoulder. Across the skyline, she gazed at the smoke drifting over the river. The buildings were becoming hazy. Kendra lifted a hand to her eyes but it felt heavy like lead. Sweat poured from her forehead and Paul watched helplessly as her body began to shake uncontrollably.

"Kendra?"

At first she didn't hear Paul. He called her name again, but pain struck like a hammer to her brain. Kendra fell backward, with unfocused eyes. Paul grabbed her and stared frantically into her face. His lips were moving but his voice sounded far off, his words gibberish.

Something cold trickled over her lips. It tasted thick and sweet. Even before she put her fingers to her mouth, Kendra knew it was her own blood.

CHAPTER 46

Bethesda, Maryland

THE HOSPITAL ROOM AT Walter Reed Medical Center in Maryland was overly bright and cheerful, painted in pastel blues and adorned with tall vases of fragrant white orchids, daylilies and pots of flowering cacti.

The curtains remained open all day and blinding light poured through the glass. The nurses complained it made the room hot and stuffy, but Paul insisted on sunshine every day. Kendra had thrived in the desert and she needed every ounce of strength while she was fighting for her life. He had brought her to Walter Reed because it had been transformed into the leading hospital for victims of Siafu Moto–related injuries, handling mostly patients in the armed services and medical profession, police and firefighters, as well as politicians, movies stars and the exceedingly wealthy.

The ants cut from Kendra's back had indeed released their destructive enzyme, but the medications to treat her had masked all outward signs of what was going on inside her body. None of her major organs were destroyed, but her liver and kidneys had been damaged and some systemic arteries had hemorrhaged.

Paul listened to the steady beeps of the heart monitor. It was a comforting sound that he had wanted left on all the time. In the beginning, there had been a few close calls and twice Kendra needed to be resuscitated, which sank Paul into cycles of depression. But he always managed to fight it off and never left her bedside.

That was all in the past. Today was checkout day.

Dr. Bradley Collins, a wise old man with an aversion to smiling and releasing patients, gave Kendra the thumbs-up and told Paul to take her home. Although they had no real home anymore. The East Side of New York City would be shut down until the new year, and neither of them had any desire to return to Paul's apartment on Park Avenue.

Paul had made other plans, which he hoped Kendra would find agreeable.

Wearing jeans and a red plaid shirt, he stood by her bedside, rocking slightly on the tips of his hiking boots. He kept a tight hold around Kendra's hand and watched her sleep, his eyes dreamily tracing the perfect contours of her profile from the tip of her nose, to her rosy pink lips and the point of her chin. Kendra's cheeks had filled out and she'd gained weight from four months of bed rest. She was self-conscious of the sudden plumpness on her bottom and around her middle.

In a Marilyn Monroe way, Paul had told her.

Her skin was light as porcelain. Paul frowned. Kendra seemed unusually pale, and he hoped it wasn't a relapse. Dr. Collins had been honest with them, having seen thousands of similar cases. The enzyme could lay dormant for months and without warning begin eating away at this organ or that. It was like a new form of cancer, not yet explored or understood.

Paul knew even one more day in the hospital would greatly upset his wife. *His wife.* It sounded good and he rubbed his left thumb over her ring. They had exchanged the same gold bands from their first wedding in a bedside ceremony weeks ago.

Kendra's eyes fluttered open.

Paul leaned in to kiss her cheek. "Hey, Rip Van Winkle. Third nap this morning."

"Sorry," Kendra said faintly and stretched her body like a cat. "I was dreaming of fast food." Tacos. French fries. Caffeinated soda. Chocolate. It was all just minutes away. She licked her dry lips and smiled at her husband. There were dark smears under his lids, but his creamy brown eyes still sparkled brightly. His face had been cleanly shaved for months but now he sported a sexy five-day growth.

CNN was broadcasting from a television hanging on the ceiling. The world, as it turned out, never learned of Operation Colony Torch and never knew how close it had been to being hit with nuclear bombs. General Dawson had gotten through to President Davis before his demise, and the entire affair was covered up, blamed on an imaginary ecoterrorist group called Earth Avengers.

By all accounts, it seemed Kendra's pheromone formula was a complete success.

The last round of chemicals was pumped underground into every subway, cable and sewer line, every crack and crevice, and then the entire surrounding Tri-state area was doused for good measure. The only complaint so far was that the city streets and buildings were covered with yellow goo and it was getting into the water supply. It wasn't toxic, but the drinking water tasted like soybeans.

The city was still closed for business, but had been slowly letting residents return to their homes block by block. Tourism would be shut down until New Year's Eve, when the army finished its search for ant survivors. So far they had found nothing. Jack and his team at the USDA were in charge of counting dead ants. Hundreds of thousands of winged virgin queens and billions of Siafu Moto workers had to be rounded up and counted, and some were in pieces. Jack was already seeing signs of indigenous life returning to the soil. With the help of his team, Manhattan's wildlife would be back to its former state in less than a decade.

Kendra channel-surfed and found scenes of memorials, empty city streets and disfigured victims. Her stomach felt queasy. The thought of Jeremy filled her with a remorse that she wasn't prepared to deal with yet. It would have to be some-day soon, she realized, and hoped the stories being told of his heroics would take their place in history.

Paul, too, was saddened by Jeremy's death, and thankful his former rival had selflessly saved Kendra. He was also filled with a renewed sense of hope for mankind. What Paul saw was a very different world emerging, one that was somehow . . . better. The notion that tragedy brings people together never rang so true as in the weeks following the Siafu Moto attacks. Diplomacy seemed to be sweeping the globe and the world had taken on a sort of wholesome glow. At least for now.

Kendra flipped to MSNBC and watched an interview with John Russo. He was announcing his candidacy for president of the United States. It came as no surprise. The story of Mayor Russo saving Paul's life was just one news report of many, which snowballed into tales of the mayor single-handedly de-feating the ants, and he had quickly become America's most celebrated hero, a true urban legend. Billions of dollars were pouring into Manhattan from across the globe, and Russo was shrewdly restoring America's most populous city back to its former glory.

A pretty young nurse came into the room with a farewell Cobb salad for Kendra. "A letter came for you by messenger, Dr. O'Keefe," the nurse said with a flirtatious smile. She placed the salad on a tray in front of Kendra and gave Paul the letter and a fleeting glance.

Paul opened the envelope and sighed. The logo on the stationary was for ORAN Laboratories. There was a handwritten note from John Russo. Presidential race aside, the development of the Siafu Moto had become his personal project, shrouded in secrecy. ORAN was about to open a new laboratory in the Nevada desert, to be fully operational in five years. John Russo believed that having control of the deadly ants would one day give him the greatest legacy of any American president.

Dear Paul,

I will ask you again to take the lead in this project, as operations director of the Siafu Moto colony. The data we've uncovered in the last few weeks has been revolutionary in your field and to be part of the historical precedents taking place is both a privilege and a duty. To witness this marvel is something I think you and Kendra dare not miss. Of course, I will be disappointed if you decline once again (I won't even bring up saving your life) but I am at least hopeful you will both come to Nevada as soon as Kendra is well.

Yours truly,

John Russo

Kendra picked up the letter and read it silently to the end. She felt suddenly flushed and laid her head back on the pillow.

"You okay?" Paul folded the letter and slipped it back into the envelope.

"Yeah." She shook the dizziness from her head. "I think we should go."

"All right. I'll put your things in the car."

"No, I mean to the laboratory."

"Oh," said Paul flatly. "Not if you're feeling ill. You look pale, Kendra."

"She should look pale." Dr. Collins was standing in the doorway, looking graver than usual. Kendra knew that look. He had bad news and she tensed at the thought of staying in the hospital one more day.

"Just so you know," she told him, "I am prepared to throw the rest of this salad over your head if you make me stay here another minute."

"I had one more test done," the doctor said, without a hint of a smile. "Just on a hunch."

Paul took Kendra's hand and straightened. He'd resigned long ago to be strong for her, prepared for anything. But he wasn't prepared for this.

"You're pregnant."

They both stopped breathing for a very long time.

By the time Kendra was discharged, the sun was setting in the distance over Washington, D.C. Paul wheeled her out of the hospital under a crisp October sky, and she breathed in the sweet smell of early autumn blowing in the chilly air. Leaves were already turning yellow at the tips.

Kendra couldn't stop touching her belly. Although news of her pregnancy was startling, she felt a delicious feeling of contentment. Dr. Collins, while slightly embarrassed, explained that he missed her pregnancy symptoms, as they were typical in patients taking her medication. Before she left the hospital, he had performed a quick sonogram that revealed a clear image of a baby girl, curled up tight and cozy. Kendra's heart warmed with affection for the child she'd already named Audrey, after her mother.

Paul whisked her down the long ramp to the parking lot. He wanted to surprise Kendra with something special. It had arrived weeks ago, and he was anxious to see her reaction. Abruptly, he stopped in front of a big, red bow.

Kendra looked at the roofless, cherry-red Jeep.

"Like it?" Paul asked.

She raised an eyebrow and tilted her head, as if mulling it over, and then sprinted from the wheelchair. With a burst of delight, she vaulted over the door and settled into the driver's seat with both fists hugging the steering wheel.

"Now, *this* is how a woman was meant to travel."

Paul hopped into the passenger seat and dangled the keys like fish bait. She snatched them with a grin.

"Nice, huh?"

"*Oh yeah.*" Kendra started the engine with a roar and peeled out of the parking lot, thrilled to be outside again. She eased onto the access road and revved the engine, hitting the speed limit, as the wind blew her shaggy layers of blond hair that had grown to her shoulders. She turned on the stereo and scrolled a few dozen reggae songs, settling on Bob Marley.

For a while the two sat without speaking, lost in thought. As they slowed to pass through a security gate, Kendra pressed a warm palm against her shirt and felt the beginnings of a bulge.

Paul watched with a hesitant expression.

She turned down the music. "You okay with this?"

He nodded. Paul was more than okay, he was elated at the thought of having a child with Kendra but worried about her long illness.

She saw anxiety in his face and flashed a comforting grin. "Doc says everything is fine. She's the perfect size for five months."

He smiled, nodding again.

"Where we headed?" asked Kendra, crossing the Maryland border into Washington, D.C.

"South," Paul replied. "Florida."

Kendra arched an eyebrow.

"It was supposed to be a surprise," he said. "The USDA is funding the largest IPM research institute in the world." Paul said. "The focus will be pheromone manipulation, of course. You're supposed to run the whole thing."

For a moment, Kendra was speechless. "What about your work?"

"I'm going to be your assistant."

She couldn't suppress a burst of laughter.

"What's so funny?" he asked, offended.

"There's no glory in dirt, Paul. No offense, but I think your digging days are over. Even field study won't replace your burning desire to unlock the mysteries of the Siafu Moto."

He scowled inwardly, and Kendra took his hand.

"Let's go to Nevada," she said. "To research the ants."

Paul looked away.

"Oh, come on. You'll be world famous."

"I'm already world famous."

"World famouser."

"This is *your* moment, Kendra. You earned it, and the work you do will bring about great changes to the environment. To the future of agriculture."

Kendra frowned. Somehow the future of agriculture didn't seem as important anymore. She stopped at a light and watched the pedestrians marching across the street: tourists pointing and chatting, couples holding hands, distracted teenagers texting in stride. Life had not ceased. The earth continued spinning, its inhabitants going on with the daily grind as always, barely skipping a beat after the most monumental catastrophe in the history of humankind.

We're a resilient bunch, she thought. Yet somehow, a piece of her soul had transformed and would never be the same. She wondered if it was her own evolution, or did others feel it too? She looked at the faces streaming by but couldn't tell.

The light turned green, and she turned south onto Georgia Avenue.

"You can't pass up this opportunity," she said. "There's no telling where it may lead."

"What about the institute?"

"Let Jack head the research for now. He never really wanted to retire."

Paul didn't say anything.

"I've given this a lot of thought." Kendra raised her chin, sounding defiant. "We devoted half our lives to ants. I don't want death and destruction to be their final legacy." She looked at him. "You can make sure it never happens again."

Paul wrestled with the proposal, as he'd done many times before. Living in the desert with Kendra. Studying the most dangerous creatures on earth. Raising a child in a world . . . *a child?* Suddenly, it wasn't just about him. Perhaps their research could somehow benefit future generations. "Okay, we go to the lab—but just for a look around. I'm not making any promises."

He opened a paper bag at his feet, pulled out two bottles of water and handed one to Kendra. It was warm, just the way she liked it. "To new discoveries," he said.

They tapped the neck of their bottles, and Kendra took a long drink. There was a sudden flutter in her abdomen.

"She kicked!" Kendra sucked in a gasp of air, with a hand on her belly.

Paul reached over and pressed a gentle palm. Another kick. They shared a loving glance.

"You know, we're both starved," she said.

"I think I've got you covered." From the backseat, Paul retrieved a brown cardboard case marked HERSHEY.

"No way," Kendra said, reaching into the open box and pulling out a candy bar, as Paul watched her rip open the paper, amused.

"Nevada," he said. "We should probably drive to the airport."

"I'm not flying," she replied, filling her mouth with chocolate. "I could drive all night."

"We could take a red-eye. You'd be asleep the whole—"

"I'm not flying!"

"Okay, okay." Paul knew better than to argue with a woman who had recently saved the human race.

Kendra stopped at a red light and chugged the rest of her water. "Just be ready for a lot of bathroom stops."

Paul watched her smiling profile, and he was filled with the promise of a better world, where people of every nation accepted their differences. It was naive, he knew. *Irrational.* But then hope, he realized, was the only thing that kept civilization moving forward. It was like Kendra once told him. *Ants have been around for a hundred million years. We're still learning how to be human.* Now that he saw the universe in a whole new light, anything was possible.

The light turned green against a stunning cobalt sky. In front of the jeep, the Washington Monument loomed like an arrow, pointing onward. Kendra shifted into gear with the wind in her face, and they blasted down Independence Avenue, to the last sliver of orange sun setting in the west.